"What is it you really want?"

Nick took a step closer. It wasn't a threatening move, but definitely allowed him to enter Penelope's personal space.

Penelope didn't retreat. Instead, she raised her head to look him directly in the eye.

He noticed the throb of that vein in h forehead aga̱ e to stroke it. But

He wet his li Well, now that you me to Hoagie Palace

She tilted her head. "Why?"

"It'll be fun."

"And after tonight?"

He searched her eyes to try to figure out what she was thinking, but he found himself distracted, confused...more than confused. But in a very good way.

Dear Reader,

Confession time: After graduating from Yale University with a degree in history, I had a fellowship to study in Rome, Italy. When I wasn't practicing my Italian and exploring the city, I did research on early-medieval manuscripts in the Vatican Library. Ever since then, I've wanted to incorporate the fascinating world of rare books and manuscripts into a contemporary romance. Well, now I finally get my chance.

My heroine, Penelope Bigelow, is the curator at Grantham University's Rare Book Library, and she gets to educate my hero, Nicholas Rheinhardt, on the wonders of old handwriting and the timeless beauty of historic documents. Nick is a Grantham dropout who's achieved celebrity *and* notoriety as a chef and travel-show host. He's in town to give a Class Day speech for the graduates and film an episode of his show. Can you say yin and yang? Oil and water? Total attraction?

The question is, how do you know when someone or something is the genuine article? When do the heart and the mind come together to trust that something so unique can exist in ways you never even dared to dream?

In this case, the answer's not written in the stars, but on the folios.

As always, I love to hear from my readers. Just email me at tracyk@tracykelleher.com.

Tracy Kelleher

A Rare Find
Tracy Kelleher

A RARE FIND

Harlequin®

TORONTO NEW YORK LONDON
AMSTERDAM PARIS SYDNEY HAMBURG
STOCKHOLM ATHENS TOKYO MILAN MADRID
PRAGUE WARSAW BUDAPEST AUCKLAND

Recycling programs
for this product may
not exist in your area.

ISBN-13: 978-0-373-60698-6

A RARE FIND

Copyright © 2012 by Louise Handelman

This is a work of fiction. Names, characters, places and incidents are
either the product of the author's imagination or are used fictitiously,
and any resemblance to actual persons, living or dead, business
establishments, events or locales is entirely coincidental.

This edition published by arrangement with Harlequin Books S.A.

For questions and comments about the quality of this book
please contact us at Customer_eCare@Harlequin.ca.

® and TM are trademarks of the publisher. Trademarks indicated with
® are registered in the United States Patent and Trademark Office, the
Canadian Trade Marks Office and in other countries.

www.Harlequin.com

Printed in U.S.A.

ABOUT THE AUTHOR

Tracy sold her first story to a children's magazine when she was ten years old. Writing was clearly in her blood, though fiction was put on hold while she received degrees from Yale and Cornell, traveled the world, worked in advertising, became a staff reporter and later a magazine editor. She also managed to raise a family. Is it any surprise she escapes to the world of fiction?

Books by Tracy Kelleher

HARLEQUIN SUPERROMANCE

1613—FALLING FOR THE TEACHER
1678—FAMILY BE MINE
1721—INVITATION TO ITALIAN
1762—ON COMMON GROUND*

*School Ties

Other titles by this author available in ebook format.

This book is dedicated to my great friend and
fabulous cook Inkyung Yi.

Only you could have two sets of twins and
somehow look so terrific.

CHAPTER ONE

September
A Former Country of the Soviet Union—
Far, Far Off the Grid

NICHOLAS RHEINHARDT LAY on the hard stone table, belly-side down, and hoped like hell that the moisture on the towel beneath him came from his own sweat. He gritted his teeth to stifle a groan as a seminaked and thoroughly oiled masseur squatted above him and frog-hopped down the length of his spine.

The humiliation would have verged on the comedic if the pain weren't so excruciating. He couldn't imagine anything worse, not even a root canal—two root canals—without Novocain. But he refused to whimper and beg for mercy.

After all, the cameras were rolling.

Whose idea had it been anyway to shoot several episodes of his travel-and-food show in this country so far off the beaten track?

Up until this point, the whole television thing had been a pretty good gig.

Now life had turned into a high-definition hellhole as recorded by a sardonic cameraman and a highly sensitive soundman. Was it any wonder that Frommer's, Michelin or Lonely Planet guidebooks had failed to extol the wonders of this remote village, let alone the bathhouse?

Nick felt the vertebrae cracking in his neck as the otherwise silent masseur worked his torture. And, ironically, that's when it came to him. The jackass who'd suggested they make a trek through the mysterious eastern provinces of the former Soviet Union—countries like Uzbekistan, Tajikistan and Kyrgyzstan? The same jackass who'd had this romantic notion that they'd see yaks and yurts, fiery peasants and dreadful Communist architecture?

It'd been him.

The bantamweight masseur chose that moment to slip his sinewy arms under Nick's armpits and force his elbows to lock together behind his back. A small *ugh* emitted from Nick's throat. After this workout, he seriously wondered if from now on his upper limbs would dangle uselessly at his sides. Most probably he would go through the rest of life with curious onlookers remarking, "And to think he once was able to debone a leg of lamb with the best of them."

"So, tell me. This massage you're getting. It looks pretty…ah…strenuous. Still, it's all it was cracked up to be, right?" Georgie, his jovial producer, asked from off camera.

Nick growled deep in his chest—the part that hadn't been crushed as of yet—and thought, *Just wait till I do the voice-over commentary to this bit back in New York. Because now it all comes back to me, that, between multiple vodka shots the other night, you were the sly dog who suggested this bit of local color. Yes, you, Georgie.*

The masseur slapped Nick's towel-covered rump, signaling the end of the session.

Georgie turned to the cameraman. "That's a wrap." Then he bounced jovially across the stone floor to his damaged on-air talent. "That bad, huh?"

Nick thought about raising his head off the table, but that small motion required too much energy. "Let's put it this way, I will absolutely, positively agree to do anything else rather than go through this again—preferably something that involves close proximity to a Nathan's Famous hot dog. I'm starving." Knowing no shame, Nick held out an arm. "Help your lord and master get upright, if it's at all possible."

None too gently, Georgie hoisted Nick to a sitting position. The towel, which was wrapped around Nick's waist, slipped to his hip bones, and his once-taut stomach muscles—once, as in a good ten years ago—sagged around the cotton terry cloth that had a thread count of about negative twenty.

Nick might have been thirty-seven in chronological years, and genetically blessed with a fast metabolism, but those had been hard-lived years. After turning thirty-five, even his long and lanky body could no longer bounce back from the harsh treatment due to overimbibing of fine food and not-so-fine drink.

Not that he regretted his lifestyle, mind you. Nick smiled at the memory of some of the more infamous escapades, at least those he could still remember.

His so-called adult life had taken a meandering path. After dropping out of college, he'd bummed around the world by scrounging low-paying jobs and harboring absolutely no ambition other than occasionally finding food, alcohol and the eye of a good-looking female. One winter in Paris, where he'd squatted in a tenement that lacked a shower—not to mention a toilet—he'd landed a job as a dishwasher in a traditional bistro in Montmartre. And *voila!* Nick had found his calling. Eventually he'd risen up the restaurant food chain to become a well-regarded though not quite top-tier chef.

Achieving greater fame would have required greater talent, a little more luck and, if he was going to be totally honest, a lot more dedication. Even the sudden acclaim he'd garnered for his book, a bareknuckle look at the restaurant world, had been more of an accident than a well-planned career move. After all, he'd written the damn thing in fits and spurts after shifts at various restaurants, fueled by

cigarettes and booze—more than a little, actually—
and bouts of righteous indignation.

So it was hardly surprising that as Nick looked
down at his body he felt a certain measure of disgust. And that was before he glimpsed his upper
arm. The tattoo circling his right bicep was undulating with involuntary muscle spasms. An enormous
Maori had given him that tattoo on a warm spring
day on the north island of New Zealand. *Now, that
had been a good shoot,* he recollected.

He raised an eyelid and saw Georgie silently
chuckling. "What?" he asked with a snarl.

"Is that a promise?" Georgie asked, not bothering to hide his amusement, so secure was he in his
worth as a producer. "That you'll go anywhere provided it's within sniffing distance of a New York
hot dog?"

Nick contemplated the wisdom of getting up. "As
long as it doesn't involve rubdowns."

"Last I heard, New Jersey specialized more in
rubbing *out* than rubbing down."

"New Jersey, you say?" Nick opened his jaw
slowly and experimented with trying to shut it
again. He got halfway. "You know, I was born and
raised in Jersey."

"Excuse me. Like I wouldn't know? I was responsible for hiring that underpaid intern to write your
bio for Wikipedia."

Nick grumbled. "You know there's a reason

unions were invented—to regulate the outrageous behavior of unscrupulous employers like you."

"Too bad, that's all I can say," Georgie said without any remorse. "Which is why I have decided to accept a request that came to the office last week."

"I suppose this is my cue to say, 'Could you be more specific?'"

"My pleasure. By the unfettered powers vested in me as producer, I plan to accept the offer for you to be the Class Day speaker at your old alma mater, Grantham University, this coming June," Georgie announced proudly. "Naturally we'll use it as an episode for the show—I'm not *that* generous."

"Come again?" Maybe his brain was also starting to fail.

"You know, the Commencement ceremonies for the graduating class? The day before they do the whole diploma-giving-out bit, you will speak with wit and with a soupçon of encouragement to the seniors."

"Soupçon of encouragement? Are you kidding me?"

"Well, their families will be there, as well. I think it's only right and proper," Georgie explained.

Nick stumbled to the dressing area and eased on his clothing. He didn't bother with the button or the zipper on his jeans. If his pants fell down, so be it. He couldn't be any more humiliated than he already had been.

He joined the others at the entrance to the dank, tiled bathhouse, nodding appreciatively to the manager, who had a severe lazy eye, which made eye contact difficult. The man would no doubt be dining off tales of the crazy Americans for years to come.

Georgie pushed open the heavy wooden door, and their little group instinctively huddled together. A horse-drawn cart, loaded with hay, clopped down the dirt road in front of them. Its driver paused and yelled to two men standing cross-armed in the narrow doorway of a coffee shop across the way. His loud monologue was seemingly cheerful sounding, but who could be sure?

Where is our friendly translator when we need him? Nick thought.

Then the squat and hairy horse turned its head at the sound of his master's gravelly voice, and proceeded to do his business in the middle of the street.

Nick looked over at the steaming deposit. "I think that just about sums it up." Then he creaked his neck in Georgie's direction. "You realize of course that I never graduated from Grantham, don't you? A little thing called the Junior Paper that I could never quite wrap my head around?"

"I don't think they're gonna rescind the offer, and frankly, I think they probably already know that."

"True, failure has been one of my favorite biographical topics. Still, what would be the point? I mean, I do thirty minutes of hopefully semihumor-

ous anecdotes about the world of food and travel—
minus my usual four-letter words since, as you say,
kiddies are likely to be present. And then what have
you got? An hour's TV show? I think not."

With that, the horse, the cart and its owner moved
on. The two men with grizzled beards and in severe
need of good dental work, peered suspiciously at
Nick and the rest of the crew before turning to enter
the gloom of the coffee shop.

"Think of the bigger picture, Nick." Georgie
waved his hand across the gray and unforgiving
sky. "The whole idea of graduation as the culmi-
nation of those happy college days, which, being
happy, had to have included the customary drinking and eating of large quantities of food."

"You want to check out dining-hall fare?" Nick
asked, unconvinced.

Georgie nodded. "You're missing the potential.
Think bigger, like how the whole eating experience
is the same or different from your day. What does
that say about the peculiarities, if there are any, of
the Ivy League experience?" Georgie suddenly got
more animated. "Wait a minute. Doesn't Grantham
have those Social Whatevers—their own kind of
snobby fraternities? Surely food and beer are plen-
tiful at those places for the select few."

"Social Clubs. And only a few of them were
snobby. Certainly not mine—otherwise I couldn't
have been a member," Nick clarified. Despite his

carefully honed jaded personality, he found himself becoming intrigued. "There used to be a couple of places in town that I regularly went to, too. I wonder if they're still there, especially this one greasy spoon famous for its hoagies."

"Hoagie Palace," Larry, the cameraman, piped up.

Nick slanted him a startled expression.

"Hey, I might have only gone to the University of New Hampshire, but even *I* know about Hoagie Palace." Larry wore a down coat over a down vest and a stocking cap on his head. For a supposedly rugged New Englander, he had a very low tolerance for the cold.

Georgie punched the air. "There, what did I tell you? And by way of contrast to the usual street-food shtick, we could sample some new high-end joints. You know—what the wealthier denizens of the quaint college town go for when they want a night on the town."

"As I recall, it was uninspired, nominally French food—and I mean nominal." Nick thought back to the one time the mother of one of his freshmen advisees had taken them to the finest culinary institution in town. You knew it had pretenses because it was housed in a mock, half timber Tudor building across the street from the university campus. Only minutes before meeting her Nick had learned it was a jacket-and-tie joint only, of which he'd had neither. He'd frantically scrounged something up from a guy who roomed down the hall. The waist on the jacket had been six inches too big and the sleeves three inches too short, but at least the tie hadn't had a naked lady painted on it.

"People are always curious about Ivy League colleges and picture-perfect towns. Now we'll be able to give the insider's view," Georgie continued, still selling the idea. He was a producer, after all. "Get the lowdown on whether students still go to the same places to grab something to eat when they're up all night studying. Or maybe they've developed more sophisticated palates over the years to go along with their future hedge-fund-manager lifestyles?"

Something was definitely wrong because Nick was becoming seriously interested in Georgie's idea. "I don't know if you realize it, but Grantham holds its alumni Reunions right before Commencement. So it's essentially a weeklong college-nostalgia party, where the soon-to-be graduates get to lock arms with their fellow Granthamites, thus building their sense of family and forging contacts for future employment."

Nick was acutely aware that he was talking as if he was doing voice-over commentary—in addition to regaining feeling in his outer extremities. *No wonder Larry's bundled up like a polar bear,* he suddenly realized. He shivered. A mistake, given his recent encounter with the lethal masseur.

"That's better than perfect," Georgie responded with enthusiasm. "A blend of past, present and future all rolled into one big happy, highly photogenic package." He paused. "I presume these alums are your usual crazies—all rah-rah and wearing garish school colors?"

"Oh, wait till you see their school colors," Nick said knowingly. The totally tasteless Reunions getups that the returning alums donned for the traditional parade and class functions were legendary. Then he eyed his producer. "So tell me. You think this august Ivy League institution is *really* going to allow my unique commentary on the wild and wacky world of small town, Ivy League customs?"

Clyde, the sound guy, snickered.

"Hey, just because you grew up in London and went to Cambridge, doesn't mean you can look down on Grantham," Nick shot back. "I've seen the apartment you share with three other guys in Queens. No one in your shoes can even think about looking down their nose." Speaking of shoes, he was becoming increasingly aware of just how cold he was. He also figured that once he got back to their excuse of a hotel his maimed body would be incapable of removing his own frozen shoes.

"Clyde's just being Clyde, and as to the permissions? Don't worry," Georgie interjected. "I'll have them in hand before you can say 'bourbon on the rocks.'" He seemed so gleeful that he began to skip down the frozen road.

In Nick's critical view, the producer seemed more like some demented munchkin stumbling along some nightmare version of the Yellow Brick Road. Georgie was not exactly svelte, and he barely topped five feet three.

"I love it. I love it," Georgie said to no one in particular as he continued to lead the little group down the road. Then he stopped and turned to face them. "Just think. You'll be able to answer the question that burns in the hearts of all college students." He put his hand to his chest, and if Nick didn't know better, looked truly earnest.

"What? 'Will I get laid tonight?'" Nick responded sardonically. Then he shuffled around to stare at Larry since he couldn't turn his neck. "Don't you have a bottle of schnapps back at the hotel?"

Georgie cupped his chin in his Gore-Tex-gloved hand. "I was thinking more along the lines of, 'Is it true that these are the happiest days of my life?'"

Thinking about that question suddenly made Nick feel very depressed, even worse than his usual morose state. "No, the black humor isn't covering up a mirthful soul," he once told a cub reporter for some newspaper in Peoria or Saskatchewan—or was it Lubbock? Whatever. "It's merely the surface of a very angry guy," he'd concluded before the reporter had quickly shut his notebook and hightailed it out of the hotel room.

"There's less than a third left in the bottle," Larry, the cameraman, whined, the tip of his nose having already gone from red to a worrisome ice-white.

"If you're looking for sympathy, you're looking at the wrong guy," Nick retorted. "In fact, if you're not careful, there'll be no Christmas bonus in your stocking this year."

"Hey, I've got a bottle of duty-free tequila *and* a hot-water bottle," the soundman Clyde bragged in his very plummy accent.

"You British—always ready to sacrifice yourselves for queen and country, or your boss, in this case. But, hey, I'll take whatever I can get."

Georgie exhaled through his mouth as he waited for the others to follow. His breath formed clouds in the frigid air and partially obscured his bearded face. "Just think. It'll be like old home week."

"Or something like that," Nick replied sullenly. He looked down absentmindedly, thinking of someone he could maybe call from his Grantham University days. *Was it worth contacting an old college friend after more than fifteen years?* he wondered. Then the ground came into focus. And for the first time after what seemed like hours of misery, Nick felt a smile cross his face.

Georgie, he noticed, was standing square in the steaming pile left by the horse.

CHAPTER TWO

May
Grantham, New Jersey

PENELOPE BIGELOW HELD the rare second-century
manuscript of Galen's medicinal writings between
her white-cotton-gloved hands before placing it in
the glass case for display. The Vatican Library had
a Latin translation from the Arabic version of the
ancient medicinal treatise dating from the eleventh
century, but this manuscript in the original ancient
Greek had been lost to the West after the fall of
Rome, finally resurfacing centuries later. Only
someone with a thorough knowledge of ancient
and medieval history including Byzantine history,
a background in multiple ancient languages, and the
trained eye of a paleographer would appreciate the
difference between the two versions.

Penelope had all that and more—a Ph.D in Classics *and* she had studied at the Vatican on a fellowship in Rome ten years ago. While there, she'd
also gone through the Apostolic Library's rigorous

two-year course in paleography, the study of ancient handwriting.

Holding the so-called Grantham Galen manuscript in her hands, Penelope could practically feel the power of the ancient scholar and philosopher through the gloves. Galen had been a prolific author, and in his day he was known to have hired more than twenty scribes to take down his potent words. But as she stared at the confident blocklike script, she was almost positive that this manuscript was in Galen's own handwriting. It was too swiftly written, as if it had been produced in a mad dash of insight.

She read the Greek as swiftly as if it were her mother tongue, though in her case, more her father's tongue. Stanfield Bigelow was a professor of Classics at Grantham University, and he had made it a personal crusade to homeschool his precocious older child. And it had been he, in fact, who had recovered this lost manuscript and donated it to his alma mater.

The combination of forces—the knowledge that she was holding what might be the original manuscript by the work of an ancient genius and the role that her own father had played in preserving this crucial bit of antiquity—was almost overwhelming. Excited, Penelope felt her mouth start to water.

Don't be foolish, she chided herself.

"As anyone with even a moderate IQ knows, the overproduction of saliva is attributed to specific physiological or medical conditions. And since I am not a teething infant, nor do I have a fever…" Just to make sure, she felt her forehead with the back of her wrist. "As I thought, normal. Therefore, I can eliminate mononucleosis or tonsillitis as other possible causalities," she explained to no one in particular.

This type of self-directed conversation was something she tended to do. Her brother, Justin, called it "Penelope's pontificating mode." Her father said it was yet another indication of her superior intellect and geniuslike ability to retain facts. Her mother never commented. She was too busy chasing butterflies or spying delicate wildflowers.

Penelope had her own diagnosis, which she kept to herself. Still, it didn't keep her from lecturing herself.

She lifted her chin and considered her current state further. "The only other causes of sudden drooling that I am aware of are certain medications, poisoning or a reaction to venom transmitted in a snakebite." She paused. "I wonder if a particularly virulent insect bite could also have a similar effect?"

A young man in a white lab coat on the other side of the exhibition space stopped pushing a cart. "Penelope, did you need me for something?" he asked.

She shook her head and turned to Press. "No, I was just contemplating whether a reaction to an insect bite could induce excess saliva."

"We once had a chocolate Lab who was stung by a bee and started drooling in reaction," Press answered as if it were a perfectly normal question.

"I was thinking of the reaction in humans, but I think you make a good point," Penelope said with a pleased nod.

Conrad Prescott Lodge IV, known as Press, was a senior at Grantham University. He was majoring in biology, with a concentration in paleontology, and while his dream student job would have been to work in a natural history museum, Grantham, alas, lacked such a facility. Given his respect for the fragility, not to mention the importance, of old objects, Penelope had immediately chosen him out of all the applicants for the job of part-time assistant at the university's Rare Book Library. She had recognized a soul mate when she had asked him about his interest in paleontology and he had launched into a passionate discourse. He eventually stopped when, embarrassed, he realized he'd gone on for almost twenty minutes.

"I'm so sorry," he had apologized. "I guess I got carried away."

"No need to be sorry. To be sorry is to express regret for doing something that has upset someone. On the contrary, I found your intense interest illuminating. You may set your mind at ease. The job is yours," Penelope had announced, followed by the news that she intended to raise his hourly salary by two dollars.

"But I haven't done anything yet," Press had protested.

"Oh, but you will. Many things. And by paying you more I just want to ensure that very fact."

The way he had responded to her query about insect bites just now reaffirmed her initial faith in him.

"I brought over some additional manuscripts for the show," he said, pointing to the protective boxes lying flat on the shelves of the metal cart. "The illuminated manuscript from the Burgundy, Captain Cooke's logbook from his voyages in the Pacific and Woodrow Wilson's love letters to his wife."

Penelope smiled. The show she was putting together for Grantham University's main library was comprised of manuscripts held in the university's Rare Book Library. The show was to run during Reunions and Commencement and, therefore, she had chosen only manuscripts that had been donated by Grantham alumni.

"Thank you, Press. Yes, they're the 'warhorses' of the show, though I must admit…" She gazed at the manuscript in her hands.

Press walked over and stood next to her. Penelope also wore a white lab coat over her clothes, and her strawberry-blond loose curls were twisted to the back of her head. A No. 2 pencil held the unruly mass in place.

"The Grantham Galen?" he asked, on noting what she held. "Now I get why you were asking about bites and stuff."

Penelope made a face. "Clearly we have been working together too long, and it's time for you to graduate."

"Amen," Press agreed with a praying motion.

Penelope eyed him. "Are you teasing me?"

Press held up his hands. "Would I do that?" He shrugged. "Well, probably. Anyway, you know, you should really give a talk to the alumni about the show, especially the Grantham Galen, what with your book contract and everything," Press suggested.

"That may be so, but I think it's better that I don't. Interaction with people has never been my strong suit." Penelope was sure that Press knew all about her being terminated as an assistant professor at the University of Chicago when she didn't get tenure. That career low point had eventually led to her current position as the curator of Grantham's Rare Book Library.

Penelope laid the priceless manuscript in the display case, locking it and her memories away. Then she glanced at her watch. "Goodness, it's practically six o'clock. You should get going, or you'll miss dinner at your Club."

Press shrugged. "Somehow, I think Lion Inn will go on without my presence for one night." The Social Clubs at Grantham were the bulwark of the college students' social life, providing dining facilities besides a continual round of parties and sports leagues. "There's still a lot of work to be done, and I don't want you to have to do it all."

"Nonsense. I'm sure you want to spend your remaining time with your friends. Pretty soon you will graduate, and you will all be going your separate ways."

Press shrugged. "I guess I'll miss some people, and I'm sure I'll enjoy the graduation activities. You remember them, right?"

Actually Penelope couldn't recall any festivities when she graduated from Grantham, but that was because she hadn't attended any.

Press carried on without waiting for an answer. "To tell you the truth, though, a part of me is so ready to get out of here. Four years is a long time to be in one place. On top of which, I grew up in Grantham anyway. So even though I've lived in the dorms the whole time, it's really kind of like I never left home. All I want to do now is to get out of here—far, far away."

At one point, that had been Penelope's ambition. After all, she, too, had grown up in Grantham. But here she was, back again, doing a job that her family never would have thought was in her future. Not that she didn't find fulfillment in her current position. But life, as she had found out, didn't always proceed as planned.

She was about to impart this pearl of wisdom to Press when he blurted out, "I can't wait to take off for Mongolia. It'll be amazing, don't you think? Especially going out into the countryside."

Penelope smiled and answered, "I think it will be a fascinating venture, especially the sites of recent paleontology discoveries. You must contact the relevant academics in the field. Perhaps I can help? I know a bit of Mongolian, as it turns out." She recognized what appeared to be astonishment on his face. "What?" she asked. She was never quite sure if she was gauging body language correctly.

"You know Mongolian?" Press asked.

"Just a smattering. I was interested in languages written in the Cyrillic alphabet at one point. Standard Khlakha Mongolian, the dialect spoken in Mongolia proper, as opposed to the autonomous Inner Mongolian region of China..." Penelope stopped, noticing a certain fog settle over Press's expression.

She waved her hand dismissively. "There I go, off in my own little world. I told you I was no good with social interactions. Now, as for staying—there's absolutely no need. I'll be working on the installation for several days. Furthermore, I am very keen for you to go to Lion Inn tonight because, if memory serves me correctly, it is Beer Pong night. You must promise to give me a full rendition of the competition. I am very much interested in the sociological aspects of the game, with the idea of establishing an anthropological link to Roman drinking games."

Actually she had almost no interest in Beer Pong. But perhaps in telling this little white lie she was exhibiting a certain sensitivity to social interactions. At least she was trying.

CHAPTER THREE

June
Grantham

NICK RAISED HIS GLASS of red wine. "To old college ties," he toasted. "With an emphasis on the *old*." He took a large sip of the Australian shiraz.

"Speak for yourself," his host, Justin Bigelow, replied. Justin and his wife, Lilah Evans, who was also a Grantham University classmate, lived in a modest one-bedroom apartment in the center of Grantham. They called it home when they were in the States, but spent much of their time in Africa on behalf of Lilah's nonprofit organization. Back in her senior year at Grantham, Lilah had founded Sisters for Sisters to help women and children in the central African country of Congo. Now, eleven years later, it was going strong, providing health-and-educational services in rural settlements.

"Lilah and I are as youthful as ever," Justin chided him.

"Speak for *yourself*," Lilah piped up.

"Hey, there's nothing wrong with getting older. I earned my gray hairs," Nick announced grandly.

"If you're going to claim they're a mark of hard-earned maturity and wisdom, don't even try. No one with even a smattering of fully functioning brain cells would have submitted to that crazy massage." Justin chuckled. "I loved that episode."

"Glad to oblige." Nick took another sip. He had lived to regret that episode in more ways than one. Not only was his neck perpetually out of whack, but people who met him for the first time inevitably brought up the massage debacle. The price of being semifamous, he told himself.

"Even back in college when you were my Residential Advisor, you were not exactly a role model. Not that I didn't enjoy myself, of course. I still remember you orchestrating all us freshmen advisees in stealing the clapper from Grantham Hall."

It was a well-known tradition for students to try to steal the clapper from the bell tower atop the administration building in the center of campus. This centuries-old battle between the students and the administration had led to some epic adventures and even more epic tales.

"Excuse me. I did a good job. Did you guys get caught? Hell, no. Not on my watch," Nick boasted, and took another gulp. He really should slow down, but then, hey, he wasn't driving. He barely needed to roll down a gentle hill to get back to his hotel.

Then there was the irritating fact that despite the easy manner with which Justin had invited him to dinner on his first night back to Grantham, he wasn't feeling all that relaxed. There was something about returning to the scene of his first big screwup—not finishing college—that had a disquieting effect. All those parental dreams that he had squashed without a second thought.

Lilah, seated across the wooden table, shook her head. "I like that. Your definition of morality is that it's all right as long as you don't get caught."

"I bet you never considered stealing the clapper, did you? I have vague memories of you being always on the forefront of whatever good cause was going around, and from the looks of things, you've made that your life's work." Nick poured himself another glass of wine and held the bottle out to Lilah. "Drink?"

Lilah laughed. "No wine for me, thanks. I'm three months pregnant."

Nick eyed Justin. "As I recall, you always were a fast worker." Then he turned to Lilah. "And I guess congratulations are in order. If anyone could reform a party boy, it's you." He picked up a fork and dug into the pasta that Lilah had just served. It followed an absolutely superb appetizer of marinated grilled eggplant.

"Yum. This is good." Nick nodded after a large forkful. "Actually, speaking of great food, my producer's been laying the groundwork around town for this show I'm filming, but frankly, I've got my number-one priority—Hoagie Palace."

Justin passed the freshly grated Parmesan. "Oh, yeah, you gotta go to The Palace." He used the student slang for the beloved greasy spoon in town.

"And I was hoping you'd both accompany me on my pilgrimage," Nick said. "You know, some nice on-camera interplay of how the food conjures up certain episodes of our wild college youth."

"Speak for yourself. The Palace for me was strictly late-night fare when writing papers," Lilah said.

"For me it was *the* place to go after practice," Justin remarked. He'd been captain of the lightweight crew.

"You know, comments like that are perfect," Nick agreed. He took another bite. The pasta was good. More than good.

"I'm not sure I'd be the best person for your show, though," Lilah admitted sadly. "The way my stomach is now, just the thought of all that grease is enough to make me queasy."

"Bummer, I was viewing it as a family moment," Justin teased her. Then he patted her arm. "Not to worry. I've got a great idea for somebody else. Press Lodge," Justin announced.

"Is this someone I should know?" Nick asked.

"Remember Mimi Lodge, who was a classmate?" Justin asked. "She's now a foreign correspondent."

"You mean, have-war-will-travel Mimi Lodge?"

"That's the one. Well, she has a half brother, Press, who's a graduating senior."

"And he's practically been adopted by the owners," Lilah added. "Not surprising, given his family situation." Then she covered her mouth. "I shouldn't be gossiping."

"Don't worry. Other shows deal with family strife. I'm after the food scene, and the idea of having a true insider in artery-clogging food is better than perfect. You think he'll do it?" Nick asked.

Justin shrugged. "I don't see why not, especially if it means publicity for Hoagie Palace."

"I know Mimi came in today for Reunions. I'll call her, and she's sure to twist Press's arm."

"Ask her if she'll come, too. The more the merrier." Nick rested his fork on the edge of his plate. The pasta had been so delicious he had gobbled it down in record time.

Justin reached for more bread from the wicker basket by his elbow, then held it up. "Anyone else?"

Nick shook his head. "No, thanks, but I gotta tell you. This pasta is truly to die for. What's in it? I mean, I can see there's sausage—though it's like no other sausage I've ever had. But what're the greens?"

Lilah furrowed her brow in thought. "I can't remember." She looked to Justin. "What did Penelope say she put in it?"

"Wild fennel. She said something about foraging it somewhere near the Delaware Water Gap," Justin explained.

Nick tipped his chair on the back two legs and craned his neck from side to side. "So where are you hiding this Penelope? This place doesn't seem big enough to accommodate a golden retriever, let alone another person."

It was true. The quaint apartment had lots of Victorian charm, including the bay window with a window seat and the original molding, but square footage was at a definite premium.

"It's more like Penelope hides herself. She doesn't exactly socialize," Justin explained.

Lila touched her chin. "Penelope is definitely her own person."

Justin looked at Nick. "Penelope's a little weird. As her younger brother, I should know."

"So she's your sister." Nick narrowed his eyes. "Wait a minute, didn't she go to Grantham, too? Like a year behind me? I have this fuzzy recollection of her always going around campus with her face buried in a book."

"That would be Penelope." Justin chuckled. "She was born almost legally blind. Even with glasses, she had to read with the book an inch from her nose.

The miracle is that she's had laser surgery, and now she doesn't need to wear glasses anymore."

Nick held his bloated stomach. "As far as I'm concerned, anyone who makes pasta this good can be blind as a bat. The woman's a genius in the kitchen, that's for sure."

"Well, she actually happens to be a genius," Lilah said. "And please, have some more." She indicated the large ceramic bowl.

"I know this is the wrong thing to do, but since when have I ever turned down an opportunity to eat myself silly?" Nick reached across the table and grabbed the serving utensils. "So your sister's become a chef?"

"No, it's more a…a…" Justin searched for the correct word. "I wouldn't exactly call it a hobby, but a…a…"

"It's more a passion," Lilah finished his sentence. "When Penelope takes an interest in something, it's total immersion."

"She's into southern Italy. You know, Calabria?" Nick started on his second portion. "Not personally, but I know the region you're referring to."

"Anyway, somebody left her a house there, in this dot-on-the-map town called Capo Vaticano. It's all a bit of a mystery, especially for someone on her salary. Though I guess she rents the place out."

Lilah rested her chin on her hands. "Well, I for one am not complaining. She let us stay there for our honeymoon. The house is in the private garden on a cliff overlooking the Mediterranean."

"And don't forget the infinity pool." Justin's eyes clouded over. "When I die and go to heaven, I hope it looks like that infinity pool."

Nick set his fork down—for him, a real concession. "From what you're all saying, Penelope's passions have led to some pretty good things—the house, this food..." He pointed it out. "That type of passion I can deal with. In my experience, indifference is a lot harder to cope with, believe me."

He didn't elaborate, nor did they ask. If they had, Nick supposed he could have made some snide remark about his ex-wife. Heaven knows, for years after their divorce he hadn't had any problems commenting on her faults. Now, those faults had become dimmer with time, and mostly what he felt was moderate disdain or worse, nothing, when he thought about her. Which, granted, he tried to do as little as possible.

He quickly forked down another mouthful and gulped. There was definitely something about the pasta that was incredible. "So why is your sister doing whatever she's doing instead of cooking professionally?" He looked up. "It's gotta be another passion, right?"

"I hope so." Justin ripped his hunk of bread into smaller pieces. "Penelope had been groomed by our father to be another Classics professor, and...well...

that didn't quite work out." He munched thoughtfully. "For the past year, she's been a rare-book librarian."

"Here at the university," Lilah added. "Which means we get lucky sometimes and get some of her cooking."

"Well, if this pasta's any indication of her culinary prowess, all I can say is wow." Nick pointed at his empty plate. "Take the sausage she used. Only someone truly into cooking would take the pains to track down something that good."

"Actually she makes it herself," Lilah said. "But if you liked this, you should taste this other spreadable kind she makes. I can't remember the name exactly, but it's smoky and hot."

"I think it's called *N*-something," Justin said. "It's some unpronounceable word in a Calabrian dialect."

"You don't mean 'nduja?" Nick pronounced it instead like "endooya." "My accent sucks, but you get the drift."

Justin nodded. "That's it!"

"That stuff's legendary in southern Italy, you know. Supposedly the Calabrians concocted it in the eighteenth century while the French kings were ruling over that part of Italy. It's essentially their version of the French *andouille*—you know, smoked pork sausage?"

"I learn something new every day. I guess it pays to invite a food expert to your place," Lilah remarked. "In all sincerity, I'm glad you could come over tonight. Having said all that, can I get you to sign a copy of your book? I've got it right here." She pointed to the wall of shelves and rose to get it. "And I want you to know I paid full price—no discounts." She walked in her bare feet to the front of the room, all of five paces.

"I'd be happy to. This is what an author lives for—that, and the royalty checks." Nick opened to the title page and began writing. "So, tell me, if I want to get in contact with your sister, Justin, what do I need to do? I presume she lives nearby."

"Right here in Grantham," Justin answered.

"So you think she'd be interested?" Nick handed the signed book to Lilah. "I mean, I've never heard of anyone being able to get 'nduja in the States, let alone make it."

"Interested in what?" Lilah smiled as she read the message written in her book.

"You mean you want to meet her?" Justin asked. He pushed back his chair and beckoned his wife over.

"Well, that—"

"You mean for your show, don't you?" Lilah said. She sat on Justin's lap, squirming to get comfortable.

"Of course."

Justin shook his head. "I'm not sure that would work. Penelope isn't exactly a people person. Listen,

I'm no professional, but from my experience teaching kindergarten, she seems to show a lot of the symptoms of Asperger's—the mild form of autism. Not that she's ever been diagnosed."

Nick leaned on his elbows and opened his palms to the air. "I may not know your sister, but anyone who spends this kind of time and effort cooking a masterpiece like this—" he waved at his empty dish "—and then gives it to you no questions asked? You want my view?" He didn't wait for a reply. "That person is definitely interacting with you on a fundamental basis. So she likes to be by herself. Hey, I've met a lot of people, and frankly, I can understand that. And that she doesn't make chitchat in the normal superficial ways that, say, you or I do? In my case, that's probably a good thing."

He rose. "I tell you what. Why don't you both think more about how I can get her to meet with me, and in the meantime I'll clear and wash up. I may not be trusted to cook in a fine restaurant anymore, but I can still be counted on for my busboy and dishwasher abilities."

Justin watched as Nick expertly lined multiple plates along the length of his arm without stacking. "Are you trying to show up my KP skills?"

"You're just jealous," Nick spoke over his shoulder as he turned toward the kitchen.

His cell phone started to chime in the back pocket

of his jeans. He looked down. "Damn." He juggled the dishes.

"Here, let me," Lilah volunteered, hopping off Justin's lap. "It's not every day I get to come into close contact with a celebrity."

Nick crooked his hip to offer up his back pocket. Lilah slipped her fingers in gently.

"*Now* I'm jealous," Justin kidded.

"Nothing wrong with a little jealousy." Lilah slid the bar across the screen to activate the phone.

He cocked his head sideways against the screen. "Hello," he answered the call, still juggling the plates.

"Daddy? I'm ba-ack!"

CHAPTER FOUR

IT WAS A SMALL MIRACLE that Nick hadn't dropped the plates. Maybe it would have been better if he had.

Then he'd have an excuse to disconnect the phone and regroup before responding to the caller. Instead he looked up. "I better take this call." He eased the plates into the sink and stepped out of the kitchen into the hallway. He figured he needed as much privacy as possible where his seventeen-year-old daughter was concerned.

"What's up, Amara? I got your email about your graduation, but unfortunately I'm shooting an episode right now, so there's a possibility that I won't be able to make it." He glanced out the arched window over the landing to the traffic below. Across the street the Grantham Public Library was ablaze with light. *Maybe there still were people who read books,* Nick mused.

"Well, it's not like I really expected you to come. Since when have you made it to any of the important moments in my entire existence?" a sarcastic, high-pitched voice complained. "Anyway, Mom was the one who told me to tell you."

Well, I was there at the moment of your conception, Nick could have said. But he wisely kept that remark to himself.

"Anyway, there's no need for you to interrupt your busy schedule on my account," Amara went on.

"I really want to," Nick insisted ingenuously. Hanging out at the snotty prep school Amara attended in upstate New York—and where his well-mannered, maturely sensible ex-wife happened to work in the development office—was not high on his list of favorite activities.

"Don't even pretend, Daddy." She made the word sound ugly. "Besides, it's not like I'm going to be there anyway." The last remark was almost a throwaway.

Nick was immediately suspicious. "Are you trying to tell me that you're not graduating? I thought you were supposed to be some hotshot student?"

"Have you ever seen a single one of my report cards?" she snapped back.

"No, but, somehow I remember you or maybe your mother…"

"Forget Mother."

Gladly, thought Nick.

"She's out of the picture, on her honeymoon in Tahiti with Glenn."

"Honeymoon? Tahiti? And wait a minute. Glenn?"

Nick heard a sigh of exasperation on the other end of the line.

"God, you're so lame. Don't the two of you ever talk? I don't know why I even bother to ask. Anyway, I blamed it all on defective genes, inherited from you."

Now Nick was really suspicious. "Back up there, Tonto. Blame what on me?"

"My getting kicked out. I figure I'm just keeping up the family tradition."

So this is what fatherhood was all about? Not that he would really know, given his rare contact with his daughter. "Listen, Amara," he responded, not bothering to hide the annoyance in his voice. "As amusing as you may find it to pick on your old man—" he heard snickers, which didn't improve his mood one bit "—it's quite another to get kicked out of high school right before graduating. If nothing else, just think of how your mother will take this." That sounded like something his father would have said about him growing up, Nick thought.

A loud *whooshing* noise on the phone drowned out whatever Amara was saying. That's when he went beyond being suspicious to downright panicked. "Where are you? Did you run away?"

"Hardly. I'm at the Grantham Junction train station. I called your production-company office and the receptionist told me where you were. The school wouldn't let me leave except into the custody of a parent. And since Mom is now doing the dirty with Glenn…"

Nick cringed at the thought. Whatever affection he had had for Amara's mother, Jeannine, had long since vanished. Still, he couldn't deny a sense of irritation that his ex had managed to get on with her life while he was still floundering through random relationships.

The least he could do was put on his big-boy pants and do the right thing. "So I guess this means you're planning on staying with me, right?" he asked.

"It looks that way." Amara was not giving an inch. "So are you going to pick me up at the station, or do you plan on sending one of your lackeys? I always thought your cameraman was kind of cute."

Now Nick was really scared. "I'll be there. It'll be a few minutes. My car's in the garage, and I'm at a dinner party right now."

Lilah approached him with a look of concern. "Problems?" she asked.

"Are you sure that party's just dinner?" Amara asked sarcastically over the phone.

Nick narrowed his eyes. "The voice you heard was my friend and *married* host for dinner, thank you very much. Listen, I'll be right over. Whatever you do, don't move. And don't talk to any strangers," he barked before hanging up.

He thrust his phone into his pocket and rolled his eyes. "That was my teenage daughter. She's unexpectedly descended on me." He didn't feel the need to elaborate. "I'm just going to pick her up at the train station, and somehow I'm gonna find her a place to stay, which, given that Reunions and Commencement are just about to start, is going to be quite a feat." He rubbed his mouth. "I don't think she's up for the close, personal experience of sharing a room with me."

"Surely there's another option." Lilah frowned in thought, and Nick could practically hear the machinery of her altruistic fervor grind into action.

Lilah snapped her fingers. "I've got it. I was going to call Mimi about Press and Hoagie Palace. Why don't I ask her if your daughter can stay at her family's place on the western side of town? The house is enormous."

"It could easily provide shelter for a whole village," Justin said.

"Well, it's probably going to take a whole village to keep my teenage daughter in line."

"It can't be that bad," Lilah said with a shake of her head. "Listen, wait a minute. I'll call Mimi now before you leave and that way you'll know."

Nick watched her leave and turned to Justin. "Is she always this determined?"

"Why do you think she's so good at what she does?"

"You've got a point." Then he waved to the sink. "Move over, and let a pro take charge."

After a few minutes, Lilah returned, phone in hand. Nick was wet up to his elbows with soapy water as he washed the dishes before passing them to Justin to dry.

"Mimi says it's no problem. The pool house is vacant, so she can have privacy."

Nick turned as he sponged off the silverware. "If she's sure? I wouldn't want to impose."

Lilah repeated his words into the phone, then looked up. "She says it's no problem." Then she listened to the phone again, nodding, before hanging up. "So, it's all settled then. Mimi even said that if your daughter—"

"Amara," Nick supplied.

"Amara, nice." Lilah smiled. "Anyway, if Amara wants to help out, she can probably provide some free babysitting for Mimi's little half sister, Brigid. She's adorable. Seven going on forty. Here, I think I even have a photo of her on my phone from last year's Reunions." She quickly pressed the screen on her cell phone, scrolling through her photos. "Here she is. Doesn't she look cute with the ribbons in her hair? I think she even insisted that Mimi put them in." She held out her arm so that he could look.

Nick passed the forks to Justin. "Cute," he said, barely glancing at the photo. That seemed to be the thing one said in these circumstances.

"She looks a little like Mimi, but really, I see a lot of Noreen in her. Noreen's her mother, and she works with me at the nonprofit." She began flipping through more photos. "Wait, here's another." Lilah thrust out her hand again. "You've got to see this one."

Nick stopped washing the large serving bowl and squinted. He saw a little girl laughing as she sat on the shoulders of a young guy. She seemed to have lost one of her ribbons, not that it bothered her. But it was the guy that really got Nick's attention. His mussed-up blond hair looked sun bleached from high-class stuff like sailing or polo. He wore an orange polo shirt that hugged his slim body. Could you say negative body fat? His large hands gripped the girl's small ankles. A row of perfect white teeth seemed to shine as his smile pierced his cheeks, the sunburned skin showing nary a blemish. The gods would not allow it.

Nick's nose started to itch and he rubbed it with the back of a soapy hand. "And he's?" Nick asked, pointing but careful not to drench the phone.

"Oh, Mimi's half brother, Press. The one we talked about earlier? He graduates from Grantham in another week."

Nick's felt a sense of dread well in the base of his throat. "But he lives in the dorms, right?" *Please, pretty please,* a little voice inside begged.

"Sure, just like we all did." Lilah kept her eyes on

the phone's screen as she went through some more pictures, a smile curving her lips. "Though maybe with exams and everything over, he's moved back home."

CHAPTER FIVE

PENELOPE GLANCED DOWN at the watch on her wrist.
The appointment had been for eight o'clock. It was
now eight-oh-six. Exactly. Penelope knew it was
correct since every morning she set her watch to
official U.S. Time, using the government website.

Justin had called her around seven in the morning, knowing she was an early riser, to let her know
that the celebrity chef and author Nicholas Rheinhardt was in Grantham to speak at Class Day ceremonies and also to shoot an episode about local
cuisine. Penelope remembered him from her college
days, not that he would remember her. He had been
Justin's Residential Advisor, and as far as she could
tell, he spent most of his time avoiding anything re-
sembling advising, let alone remaining in residence.
He had appeared to be more interested in taking the
train to New York City to hear grunge bands, only
to return to campus toting several Peking ducks,
heads and all.

And now it seemed that he had mentioned to
Justin an interest in filming some scenes in the Rare

Book Library. Something to go along with a more scholarly approach to food and society.

Penelope found this odd. Not that someone would be interested in the library. Grantham University, after all, had one of the finest collections in the country, if not the world. Research scholars, museums, other libraries, and film and television people asked to use specific works, or to borrow manuscripts for all kinds of scholarly and commercial endeavors. The process for approval varied from object to object, with the standard legal, financial and insurance hoops to jump through.

Mr. Rheinhardt apparently preferred not to do any jumping.

So, she had reluctantly agreed to meet him, assuming nothing would come of it in the end. "All right, Justin, you may tell him that I'll be here. I'll go in early and pull a few texts relevant to his particular field. But this meeting is strictly preliminary. No cameras." She'd cringed at the idea of cameras.

"Of course, of course," Justin had agreed in his usual easygoing fashion. Somewhere in his prenatal development he had acquired a mutant "no worries" gene that was not a normal part of the family mix. "I'll let Nick know. He'll be very happy."

Unconvinced, Penelope had hung up. But like the conscientious person that she was, she had arrived at the library forty-five minutes early to search for manuscripts pertaining to food and its preparation—not that she didn't know the entire extent of the holdings already, but one could never be too careful. Then she'd pulled the material and put it on display in a locked conference room off to the side of the main reading room. The whole procedure had taken twenty-six minutes.

That had still left nineteen minutes to check her email, make a cup of coffee and do some deep-breathing exercises.

Now as she stood sentry at the front double doors to the modern building, she looked at her watch again. If she had known Mr. Rheinhardt would be late, she would have used the extra time to watch one of his old episodes online, to perhaps gain some insight into his character since his college days.

And then what? They'd discuss the street food of Penang Pen? She thought not.

But then she remembered an episode she'd accidentally caught while flipping channels. Yes, much to her father's dismay, Penelope owned a flat-screen television—a small one, mind you. "The nature shows on public television are quite fascinating," she had argued, appealing to her mother's interests. Her father had coughed dismissively.

Nature shows weren't the only things fascinating, Penelope thought as she cooled her heels. Nicholas Rheinhardt had definitely aged in the seventeen years since she'd last seen him in college. But at least on-screen, those years appeared to have provided real-life knowledge—as opposed to the book-learning variety—and a sense of mocking self-deprecation that only someone truly confident in his skin possesses. Not that she personally had ever experienced such a sensation.

Penelope pursed her lips. Perhaps she should just watch an episode after all?

"WHERE THE HELL IS SHE, and why doesn't she answer her phone?" Nick threw his cell phone on the dashboard of the rental car.

Georgie, who was driving, glanced over. "Hey, watch it. That's genuine plastic. And besides, what are you getting all worked up about? It's only eight in the morning. Amara's probably fast asleep with her phone turned off. My kids at that age used to sleep past noon when they didn't have school."

"That's the whole point, isn't it? She should have been *in* school," Nick replied.

The traffic inched forward on Main Street only to grind to a halt when the light turned red. "So why'd she get kicked out?" Georgie asked. He tapped his fingertips on the steering wheel.

Nick stared at him. "You know, I didn't even ask. What kind of a father doesn't even ask his kid the reason for being thrown out of school?"

"I don't know. A total screwup?"

"Thanks for the vote of confidence." Nick glanced past Georgie at a small movie theater on the corner.

The marquee displayed the title of some esoteric foreign flick. "Maybe Amara would want to take in a film? She seems like the artsy-fartsy type."

The light changed and the traffic sputtered forward. Georgie eased his foot on the gas pedal. Three cars advanced. Then a car wanting to turn left held up everybody behind it. Naturally the light turned red again.

Georgie shook his head. "If I had known traffic would have been this bad in this two-bit town, I would have suggested walking. I hate being late. Maybe we should give this Penelope lady a call?"

Nick reached for his phone on the dashboard and checked the time. "Nah, we still have five minutes."

Georgie looked unconvinced. "You're really sure this is worth it? I mean, we've already got that Hoagie joint set up for tonight."

Nick held up his hand. "Which reminds me. I've got to text Mimi Lodge—"

"The war correspondent?"

"Yeah, that one."

"Definitely get her to come. She'd be fantastic for ratings. Plus, I've never known any other woman to do quite so much for a *kuffiyeh*—you know, those Palestinian scarves all the correspondents wear?"

Nick tapped away as he texted. "Glad to know you're such a fashion maven. Anyway, she promised to have her kid brother there, too. A nice…ah…sort of quasi-multigenerational thing."

Georgie nodded.

The light changed. "Finally we have action." Georgie gunned the engine so they didn't waste any more time. "According to the GPS we're within spitting distance. Hey, isn't that *the* Hoagie Palace?" He pointed to the left. The building's trim was painted a combination of orange and black, Grantham University's colors, so it was virtually impossible to miss.

Nick sighed. "My heart is already going pitter-patter." He fluttered his hand on his chest. In deference to meeting a librarian type, he'd traded in his usual frayed souvenir T-shirt for an open-neck oxford-cloth shirt and a blue blazer. Only the quest for the Holy Grail—homemade 'nduja—could bring out this sartorial condescension. "Trust me, this library gig will be worth it. We'll go through the whole food-manuscript charade, and then get down to the real meat and potatoes, so to speak."

"Okay, supposedly just a right at the next light, and we're practically there," Georgie said.

The next light changed to red.

Nick laughed. "That'll teach you to be optimistic."

Georgie nodded in agreement. "Why do I even try?" he joked. Then his face turned more serious. "You know, Nick, I wouldn't beat yourself up about your relationship with Amara."

"You mean my lack of relationship—totally my fault, by all stretches of the imagination."

"Yeah, well, it's not like I really had anything to do with bringing up our kids—not with the constant travel. It was all Marjorie, really." He bit down on his bottom lip.

Georgie's wife, Marjorie, had died two years ago of an aneurism. Nick knew that the suddenness had rocked him, but through it all, Georgie had insisted on working. "It's my therapy," he had said at the time in an unthreatening voice that was so not Georgie.

"She was a great lady," Nick answered now.

"She was," Georgie agreed. "But you know, even she had her moments with the kids, especially Sallie, our second, when she was Amara's age. Kids are kids. They talk tough and give you all sorts of grief. But deep down you can't imagine life without them."

"You promise?" Nick asked.

AMARA LAY IN THE QUEEN-SIZE BED in the pool house staring at prints of America's Cup sailboats artfully arranged on the walls. On the nightstand, the glass eye of a sculpted seagull stared back at her. She blinked, grateful that she hadn't noticed it last night before she'd fallen asleep.

It was about the only thing she had to be grateful about. Mostly she was scared stiff that by getting kicked out before graduation she'd blown her acceptance to Grantham University.

The headmistress had informed her that her guidance counselor would be letting Grantham know about her changed status. "In light of that news, do you have anything further you'd like to say about the incident?" she'd asked, her half-glasses sliding down her nose. Photographs of the woman shaking hands with an Academy Award-winning actress and a prominent female senator, both graduates of the Edwina Worth School for Girls, had been prominently displayed.

Amara had silently shaken her head. She wasn't about to rat out anyone else. She was already something of an outsider. Not only was she a day student among mostly boarders, her mother also worked in the development office. A double strike against her.

True, having a father who had a TV show counted in her favor. But the positives of being Nicholas Rheinhardt's daughter stopped there, as far as she was concerned. He was a nonentity who, when she was younger, didn't always send monthly checks. In more recent years, though, he was far more generous where the money was concerned.

As for any personal interaction? Did one week a year in Manhattan count as father-daughter bonding time? When she mostly ended up going to museums by herself or sitting in his production offices reading? Sure, he seemed cool and all—some of her classmates said that, for an old guy, he looked sexy.

But to Amara he remained someone she was supposed to love, who she wanted to love but who had hardly shown any interest in her love.

So screw him.

Yet, here she was. With him.

Her so-called father might have noticed the black fingernail polish and the purple streak in her dark hair. And if he had—a big if, in Amara's opinion—he might have assumed that they were signs of subversive behavior. Truth be told, these affectations were more an indication of boredom. After all, there wasn't a lot to do at an all-girls private school in what had to be the dreariest town in upstate New York.

And as she mulled her sorry state, Amara heard a splash in the pool outside. She got out of bed and peeked through the white sailcloth curtains. It was a guy. A couple of years older than she. The cutest guy ever, swimming laps. He was strong, fit. And he had shoulders, actual shoulders, and real abdominal muscles just like in the ads.

She pulled open the door a few inches and took a tentative step into the sunlight.

He reached her end of the pool and slapped his fingertips on the wall before standing up in the shallow water. He whipped back his head. Water sprayed. He casually ran his hand through his wet hair, pushing it off his forehead. Then he placed his hands on his hips where the waistband of his low-slung trunks hung. "I thought I spotted someone looking out the window," he said with a smile.

Amara blinked as she watched a droplet wander down the pale line of blond hair that trailed toward his waistband.

"My name's Press," he announced.

Embarrassed, her head shot up. "I'm Amara," she squeaked. "This woman, Mimi, said it was okay for me to stay here for a few days while my father has work in Grantham."

Press laughed. "That's just like my half sister—to invite someone when it's not really her house."

"If it's any problem…"

"Don't be ridiculous. Of course you can stay." Then he studied her. "So how come you're here? Shouldn't you be in school?"

She pulled in the sides of her cheeks. "I got kicked out of private school right before graduation."

"That sucks." He ran his hand through his hair again. "Can't your parents just bribe the school administration with some fat donation? Happens all the time."

"My father barely knows the name of my school, so I don't think that's going to work."

"What about your mom?"

Amara pressed her lips together, then sighed.

"She doesn't know I was suspended. She's on her honeymoon on some Polynesian island, and her phone doesn't seem to be working."

"Well, won't she be surprised when she shows up at your graduation and you're not there?"

Amara swallowed. "I hadn't gotten that far in my thinking. The whole thing just blew up yesterday."

Press picked up a beach towel from a chaise and started to dry himself off. Amara turned her head away, taking a sudden interest in the climbing roses on a trellis. Out of the corner of her eye she could see the way he moved the towel across his back. This time her throat was too dry to swallow.

He tossed the towel over one shoulder and slipped his feet into a pair of well-worn flip-flops. "So what are you planning on doing? Hang around the pool all day?"

Amara nervously slipped a lock of hair behind her ear. "No, I think from what my father and your sister Mimi said, I'm supposed to be babysitting. You have a little sister?"

"Half sister. Brigid. She's cool. For a seven-year-old. But she's in school until three, so you still have most of the day to yourself."

"I guess I'll just wait around here. I've got a book I could read."

"That sounds pretty boring. Why don't you just hang out with me?"

"Shouldn't I let your other sister know?"

"You mean Mimi?" Press shook his head. "Trust me, Mimi will eventually wake up later, a little fuzzy about the fact that she invited you to stay here." He used the tip of the towel to get water out of his ear. "I mean, you can say no. Or if you think your father wouldn't like it?"

Amara shook her head. "I'm sure he wouldn't mind since he's really tied up with work. My being here suddenly has only complicated his life." She didn't feel like filling him in on the details of who her father was. The conversation would then inevitably turn to questions about what Nicholas Rheinhardt was really like, was he really as cool as he seemed on TV. The thing of it was, she really didn't have the foggiest idea how to answer.

"Well, in that case, why don't I meet you back here in about fifteen minutes? I need to take a shower." Press pointed over his shoulder to the house. It was a stately brick Georgian manor complete with towering columns and shiny black shutters. "And then we can go to the club to get some breakfast. Normally I live in a dorm on campus and eat there. But since I'm graduating from Grantham next week, and classes and exams are done, I decided to crash at home for a change." Unconsciously he rubbed his tanned washboard stomach.

Amara's mouth dropped open.

"You haven't eaten yet, right?"

She snapped her jaw shut. "Ah, no." She hadn't even had dinner last night.

"They have scrambled eggs and bacon and stuff like that at the club. You're not a vegetarian, are you? A lot of girls are vegetarians. I just don't get that. There's no way I could live without bacon."

Amara hadn't had a bite of meat in more than three years. It was a philosophical thing—she couldn't bear the thought of hurting animals—not a weight thing, the way it was for some of her friends.

She was torn. She believed in standing up for her principles, but there was no way she was going to piss off this amazing guy....

Her stomach growled loudly. She looked down, horrified.

Press laughed. "I guess bacon it is. After that I'll take you to meet Penelope."

She glanced up, doubly stricken. "Is she your girl-friend?"

Press laughed, this time louder.

CHAPTER SIX

PENELOPE WAS JUST FINISHING the episode that took place in some remote corner of the former Soviet Union, which seemed solely notable for its frigid temperatures, temperamental plumbing and thin potato soup. When she leaned back in her ergonomically designed desk chair and glanced out her office window, she caught sight of two men coming up the walkway.

One was short and squat, his legs doing a twostep for every long stride of the man to his right—or her left.

Technically she ceased observing Man Number One after less than a millisecond. There was nothing technical about the way Penelope bit the inside of her cheek and gazed openly at Nicholas Rheinhardt—in the flesh as opposed to on screen.

Oh, my. No amount of cyberknowledge had prepared her for the accelerated heart rate and tightness of breath that she was currently experiencing. Her agitated state made her recall the conversation she'd had with herself when she'd held the Grantham Galen several weeks earlier. Now, mentally, she did a checklist once more of the causes of these physiological effects. There was only one explanation.

Clearly Nicholas Rheinhardt was poison.

And she had no idea of the antidote.

Still, ever stalwart, she rose and walked softly on the wall-to-wall carpeting of the reading room to the front of the building. She pushed open the central glass door and waited.

It seemed like a good idea to take the offensive. Penelope gulped. Whatever she did, she refused to muss with her hair in classic female flirtatious behavior.

"Our apologies for being late," the shorter man said. He stuck out his hand.

Penelope looked down. She noticed the man bit his nails, but they were otherwise clean. She extended her hand to shake his. "I'm Penelope Bigelow. My brother, Justin, mentioned over the phone that Nicholas Rheinhardt wanted to visit the Rare Book Library." She raised an eyebrow.

"Yes, well, I'm Georgie De Meglio, Nicholas's producer. Think of me as Nick's alter ego." He smiled wide.

A seemingly genuinely pleasant man, Penelope thought. Then she focused on the man rocking on his heels. "And you must be the ego, then?"

For a moment—several moments actually—he stared intently. Even Georgie appeared to notice because he jabbed him in the ribs. "Nick isn't his best in the morning, are you?"

"Mr. Rheinhardt, I presume," she said.

"Nick, please," he responded, his eyes locked on hers. He held out his hand.

They made contact. This time Penelope's heart stopped beating, her jaw became slack and breathing was all but forgotten. *Poison, definitely.*

"I'm sorry we're late," he said, his hand still holding hers. He didn't appear to be as disturbed as she felt, but Penelope could have sworn she saw his pupils dilate. He wasn't as unaffected as he appeared to be.

"The traffic. It was murder. But then, you probably know all about that seeing as you live here." He gave her his famous camera-ready smile.

Penelope blinked. "I usually bike."

"Oh." The smile dipped in wattage. He dropped his hand.

"Shall we go inside, gentlemen," she said, recovering. Penelope held out her hand in the direction of the conference room. "From what my brother mentioned, you're interested in seeing some of our food-related manuscripts." She walked briskly in front of them. She was aware of the sound of her ballet flats clipping along the stone floor of the entrance hall.

She opened the second set of glass doors to the well-lit reading room and its long tables. A hushed silence enveloped the space. She continued to the conference room on the right and opened the door. "I tried to intuit what you had in mind."

"I've never been intuited before," Nick quipped.

Penelope was taken aback. Then she saw him purse his lips. *Aha.* "I'm sorry. I didn't realize you were making a joke."

"He does that frequently. Is that a problem?" Georgie acted the mediator.

Penelope gave it some thought. "No, I don't think so. The more you do it, the more I should be able to read your verbal and facial cues to know when you are attempting to be humorous."

Nick raised his dark eyebrows. "Talk about being put in my place."

Penelope saw he still had a smile. "That was another joke?"

"No, that was serious," he said.

"Trust me, he could use being put in his place," Georgie reassured her. He walked over to the conference table to get a better look at the works she'd chosen. "Hey, don't tell me that the marginal notations in this are by that famous chef? You know, the one who basically introduced French cooking to America?"

Penelope joined him. "You have a good eye. This is the proof copy of her work, and those are her comments—not entirely happy, as you can tell. The head of the publishing house at the time was a Grantham alum and kindly donated the book."

"Hey, Nick, get a look. It's pretty interesting. I suppose we *could* do a short bit giving a kind of academic feel to the episode—that cuisine and scholarship go hand in hand in these hallowed halls."

"As opposed to what's served in the residential college dining halls?" she asked.

"Is that a joke?" Nick asked. He stood close on Penelope's other side.

She immediately felt disconcerted. She slanted her head and eyed him askance. "I suppose so. It's not a skill that comes naturally to me." She quickly avoided more of his searing gaze by concentrating on material that was far more in her comfort zone— the books and manuscripts that lay displayed before them. "If you want to emphasize the richness of Grantham's holdings, you might also be interested in an exhibition that I put together over at the main library. It showcases rare manuscripts donated by alumni."

"That's another way to go." Georgie nodded as he peered more closely at a handwritten list. "What's this? I can't read all the writing, but it looks likes a shopping list of some sort."

Penelope sidestepped to keep up with him—and move farther away from Nick. "It's a list of provisions needed for the Continental Congress when it met here in Grantham."

"So now we know what John Adams and Thomas Jefferson ate for breakfast," Nick remarked. He scratched the side of his face as he leaned over to read the items.

Penelope caught a whiff of unadulterated bar soap and strong coffee. The smells of morning. Somehow she automatically thought of sex.

He seemed to be pointing at something and saying something that might have been directed at her, but Penelope wasn't sure. She supposed she would have to think of something quick, something informative about the nutritional preferences of eighteenth-century gentlemen or how the penmanship reflected a certain educational stature of the writer, but at the moment she was having a hard time remembering her own nutritional preferences.

The door to the conference room cracked open behind her.

Penelope felt a rush of hope. Saved by the proverbial bell. She swiveled around.

Except the action caused her to brush up against Nick's outstretched arm, the one he'd been pointing with. And it wasn't just her shoulder that did the brushing. Her breasts also made contact as she rotated counterclockwise, which was decidedly odd since Penelope was sure she normally turned in clockwise fashion.

Tell that to my tingling nipples, she thought—crudely. Her father would no doubt have chastised her language, although it was not as if she would ever, *ever* have had this particular conversation with him. Luckily the white lab coat she wore over her scoop-neck top prevented any embarrassment.

So, trying to compose herself, Penelope swallowed and applied a stiff smile to her face as she turned to face the interloper.

"Hey, Penelope, I hope it's okay that I brought a visitor to take around the place?" Press gave her a salute. He stood at the door to the conference room, looking fresh and full of life, his hair wet from a shower, his wrinkled madras shorts hanging loosely from his narrow hips. A white T-shirt stretched across his taut chest.

Next to him was a young woman, a girl really, with shocking-pink highlights in her long black hair. She wore an oversize work shirt with black leggings. Penelope had never seen Press with a girl.

"Oh, wow." Press stopped dead in his tracks. "I didn't realize you had Nick Rheinhardt as a visitor. I mean, I knew you're going to be our Class Day speaker, and I can't tell you how excited we all are. The episode where you got that killer massage? Amazing. It went viral on YouTube."

"It's my pleasure to be speaking at your graduation ceremony," Nick replied formally.

Penelope looked over at Nick, who for some unknown reason looked somewhat perturbed. "I suppose introductions are in order?" She nodded toward Press. "This is my student assistant in the Rare Book Library…"

"Press Lodge." Press stepped forward with his hand outstretched. "It's a pleasure." He politely introduced himself to Georgie, as well. Then he turned around. "And this is a guest at my house, Amara."

The girl clenched her jaw.

Strange, thought Penelope.

Then she heard Nick Rheinhardt inhale dramatically.

Even stranger.

"Hello, Amara," he said after a beat, his voice tight.

"Hello, Daddy," she replied without any warmth.

"Daddy?" Press asked. "You didn't tell me you were Nick Rheinhardt's daughter this morning."

"And you—" Nick stared at Amara "—didn't tell me that he was the reason you didn't answer the phone when I called earlier."

CHAPTER SEVEN

NICK RECOGNIZED AMARA'S obvious displeasure. Clearly, she'd been hoping to avoid her wayward father. Not to mention the other whammy of having to watch her new little buddy—this college kid flaunting his preppy testosterone and gee-whiz smile—fawn all over said dad. And having Georgie practically hopping on his toes, no doubt hoping to work unexpected encounters like this into the episode, only added to the sense that a crisis was looming. Not to forget the librarian.

Yes, let's not forget the librarian, Nick thought. *Penelope.*

He closed his eyes, feeling all over again the brush of her breasts across his arm. And the thing of it was, he was simply not one of those guys who ever harbored a librarian fantasy.

Not that she looked like anybody's idea of a librarian. That shapeless lab coat couldn't hide her whippetlike frame that somehow had all the requisite curves. And then there were her legs…*oh, boy, those legs.* He'd never been a fan of skinny jeans—until now. And the way they ended just above her delicate anklebones, leaving a stretch of tantalizing bare flesh before her little slip-on flats. And not just any flats—ones with what looked like pages of an Italian newspaper covered in photos of Brigitte Bardot. A librarian wearing a sex goddess—could he ever have imagined?

Her ankles weren't the only irresistible features. Her heart-shaped face with its pale skin, the delicately arched brows and a nose so narrow it was like something out of a painting by Vermeer. Still, the determined set of her jaw spoke of fire and passion—totally Rubens. Then there was her hair—that fairylike mass of ringlets that haloed about her head. Was it gold or russet? And then there was something else about her face that had him searching—for words, for insight.

But it wasn't just her face. It was the way her mind worked—so orderly, so precise. Posed with a problem—such as finding manuscripts ASAP for some demanding TV host—she had analyzed the situation and come up with an imaginative yet totally logical solution. So different from the chaos that seemed to consume his own life. So refreshing. So calming… So soothing…

Perhaps he was having librarian fantasies after all….

He shook his head. And narrowed his eyes when he focused on his daughter's defiant face. "I tried to reach you this morning to set up a time to get together."

"I must have been out by the pool when you called," she shot back.

The guy—he was definitely part of the equation. Nick had no doubt. Which is why he was about to suggest—no, order—that from today onward, while Amara was under his watch, she'd be sleeping on a cot in his hotel room. But before he could do so, Georgie spoke up. *Good ol' Georgie. Ever ready to make things go smoothly.*

"Well, you both found each other anyway. So no harm in the end," Georgie chimed in. He held out his arms and approached Amara. "C'mon, you're not too old to give your uncle George a big hug." Troll-like, he enveloped her in his expansive arms, and Amara leaned into him naturally.

Nick felt a pang of jealousy. The two of them had barely exchanged a peck on the cheek.

When Georgie and Amara broke their hug, his librarian—yes, he was already beginning to think of her as his—spoke up.

"As long as you're here, why don't you come over and see what I've put out for your father and Mr. De Meglio to see." She stepped to the side and indicated the conference table behind her. "I know that Press is accustomed to my little impromptu lectures on various holdings, and he has always kindly demonstrated an interest, genuine or otherwise."

"Excuse me, when have I ever not thought something was really interesting?" Press asked, holding his hand up.

"The collected dry-cleaning bills from the last five years of Henry Ford's life?"

"Okay, that was just weird. But that was the exception." He motioned Amara over to the table. "So what have we got here?"

"These are all food related, as you might have guessed, given the circumstances. We've just finished looking at the work by a celebrity American chef and a provisions list from the Revolutionary War period, and now we're on to something a little older and quite unique."

Nick stepped aside and let the two younger people shoulder their way front and center.

Amara stared intently at one of the folios on display. "Hey, cool. Look at this." She motioned to Press.

"The Grantham Galen. You brought it over from the exhibit?" Press asked.

"Just for this meeting. It goes right back," Penelope answered.

"So what's a Grantham Ga-something?" Georgie asked.

"It seems to be an old Greek manual that talks about using all these cooking herbs like cinnamon and ginger and laurel." Amara pointed toward the text. "I'm not quite sure what this one is." She looked to Penelope. "Am I right about it being an herbal treatise?"

"Our little Amara reads ancient Greek, and you never told me?" Georgie looked to Nick.

Nick opened his eyes wide and held up his hands. "Hey, whatever she's learned she didn't get it from me. And as far as languages are concerned, my accomplishments beyond mangling the mother tongue extend only to restaurant French, which is heavy on the swear words."

"And possibly very useful in certain contexts," Penelope observed. Then she immediately turned her attention to Amara. "Yes, it does talk about herbs, which nowadays are used in cooking, but in ancient times were the mainstays of medicine. And the word you were unsure of is *cardamom*," she noted.

Amara lowered her head and studied the folio some more. "Is it? Wait a minute. If this is one of Galen's writings, like Press said, wouldn't it be his Theriac electuary?" She was addressing Penelope.

"A Ther-i-what?" Georgie asked, coming forward to take a better look.

"It sounds like a kind of enema," Nick suggested, feeling more and more peripheral to the discussion.

Penelope appeared to take no notice of his comment. "A Theriac electuary, also known as a Venice treacle, is a mixture of sixty-four drugs—including what today we think of as herbs and spices, such things as cinnamon, cloves, mustard seed—"

"And cardamom," Amara interjected.

Penelope nodded before continuing. "Including cardamom, which was formed by pulverizing the mixture with the addition of honey as a binder. It was supposed to be an antidote to poison. The recipe here is one attributed to Galen."

"Galen who?" Nick asked. He could be as academic-y as the next person, he told himself.

Georgie leaned to Nick. "That would have been my next question, too."

Amara raised her hand. "He's Aelius Galenus. Also known as Claudius Galenus and Galen of Pergamon. He was of Greek ancestry, but lived in Rome, and was an important philosopher, and physician, and, really, one of the most famous medical scientists in the classical period. Unfortunately, with the fall of the Roman Empire, his works were lost to the West until the Renaissance, when he was rediscovered and his works were translated from the Arabic versions into Latin. In fact, since the original texts were mostly lost to the West, sometimes these translations were actually translated back into Greek. But this one…" Her voice trailed off.

"Is an original from the second century A.D.," Penelope confirmed.

Amara cupped her hands over her open mouth.

Even Nick was too stunned to speak. Sure it was

mind-boggling that they were looking at something written that long ago. But what was more startling was the bald demonstration of his daughter's intellect and education. Not to mention Penelope's complete command of arcane information and the assumption that everyone wanted to know about it.

Which, come to think of it, he did. Nick shook his head. He wasn't a total ignoramus, and he respected people with genuine intellectual curiosity. It's just that he had never equated himself with the latter.

And that's when he found himself becoming mesmerized by that throbbing blue vein on the side of her forehead.

"His contributions to anatomy and pharmacology are obvious—"

"To some of us." Press interrupted Penelope with a smile.

Penelope frowned. "Press, are you making fun of me?"

"Never...well...okay, but no more than normal."

Penelope smiled in an understated way. She was satisfied with his answer. Indeed, she was rather pleased that the two of them had this convivial relationship. It was...almost normal. "Yes...well...but in addition, in light of this manuscript, one can see that he made enormous contributions to pharmacology."

"Don't forget his philosophical work," Amara noted.

"Of course, you're right. His studies of logic are very important." Penelope crossed her arms. "That's very impressive for someone of your age."

"Or any age," Georgie added.

Penelope acknowledged his comment before addressing Amara again. "So you're interested in the ancient languages and thought?"

Nick found himself leaning forward, curious about the answer.

Amara shrugged, appearing awkward as the center of attention. "I just took a bunch of courses in ancient Greek and Latin in school. But it's not like it was a big deal. I mean, I'm one of those people who seem to have a thing for languages. Like some people can throw a curve ball, or be good with map directions, I'm good with languages."

"Amara, honey, that's fantastic," Georgie congratulated her. "There's no need for modesty. And you speak other languages, too?"

"Yeah, Spanish and French and Italian. But once you know one Romance language, it's pretty easy to pick up another."

"You must learn German," Penelope instructed. "I'm sure you'd find its logical construction fascinating, and then you'll be able to enjoy all those great writers like Goethe and Thomas Mann."

"Oh, *Death in Venice*," Amara practically cooed.

"I loved that. I even cried. But of course, I only read it in translation. Hey, maybe I could take a German course this summer, although…"

"Wow, I'm impressed. I thought I was doing well when I passed the language requirement for Grantham, and that was only French," Press said.

Penelope shifted her gaze to Nick. "You must be very proud of your daughter. Very few young people these days have an appreciation for the past, let alone such expertise."

"Proud? Stunned is more like it," he admitted. "Makes me embarrassed that I didn't know anything about this before now."

Penelope raised a critical eyebrow as she digested this information. Then she turned to Press. "As long as Amara appears to be interested in manuscripts, perhaps you'd like to show her around the library before you take over at the information desk."

"Sure, if you want," Press agreed.

Amara nodded eagerly and she inched closer to him as he headed for the door.

"Where's a camera and a cameraman when we could use one?" Georgie said to Nick. "They look very cute together, don't you think?"

"Way too cute," Nick muttered.

NICK LIFTED HIS HEAD and spoke up, "It will have to be a quick tour, Amara, because you're coming with me when we're finished here."

"Maybe I should just go back to the pool house, then." Amara looked as though she was about to pout.

"I know, I know, not the most exciting option, but it'll give us a chance to catch up," he offered. He held up his hand to get Press's attention as he started to turn. "And, Press, did Mimi mention to you that we'll be filming at Hoagie Palace this evening? I understand that you're a real insider, and it would be great if you could join us."

Press bobbed a nod. "Yeah, I heard from Mimi. It will be great. Angie and Sal—they're the owners—are amazing. I'm happy to do anything that'll help them." Press looked at Amara. "If you've never had hoagies from The Palace, you haven't lived."

"On the other hand, perhaps you'll live longer if you haven't tried the saturated fat and cholesterol content," Penelope observed.

"Yeah, but you only live once," Press replied.

"Spoken like someone whose doctor has not mentioned that fateful word—Lipitor," Nick added.

"You gotta come," Press urged Amara, seemingly oblivious to Nick's caustic humor.

Amara seemed torn. Nick could tell she wanted to hang out with lover-boy here. Yet the thought of spending any more time than necessary with her father was a complete downer.

"You must go," Penelope intervened, stepping between the two young people. "I believe someone

with your intellectual interests would be a good influence on Press." She leaned closer to Amara and
whispered loudly, "He's what I like to think of as a
diamond in the rough."

Press rolled his eyes.

"You see? He's suitably embarrassed, so you have
no choice but to go."

"Okay," Amara conceded.

"Good, now that's settled." She shooed them out
the door. Then she looked back at Nick and Georgie.
"I'll be right with you. I want to make sure Press
gives Amara a glimpse of the maps of the Holy
Land and ancient Rome. They are sure to be of interest."

As soon as she left, Nick turned to Georgie and
smiled. "The camera's going to love her," he murmured with a shake of his head.

"You could be right," Georgie replied. He worked
his mouth.

Nick knew that face. "What is it? What's bugging
you?"

Georgie snapped his mouth shut and heaved a
sigh. "Tell me, what is it you actually want with her?
Penelope?"

"To taste her 'nduja."

"Is that what they call it now?" Georgie looked
dubious.

Nick shook his head. "This is strictly aboveboard.
When you get a load of this stuff, you'll know why

I want to get it on film. It'll be like tasting ambrosia. And who knows? This other stuff?" He waved his hand at the manuscripts on the table. "We should include it, too. I mean, it wasn't what I had in mind going into this project. But, hey, as you are always telling me—adaptation is key."

"Sometimes I wish you wouldn't listen to me." Georgie frowned. "She's a nice lady, Nick. I saw the way you reacted. I get what's going on with you."

Nick held up his hands defensively. "Then you get more than I do."

Georgie gazed over his bushy eyebrows. "She doesn't need any trouble."

Penelope came striding back into the room. She looked squarely at Nick. "Before I show you any more items from the collection, I have a question."

Nick raised his eyebrows.

"What are you really doing here?" Penelope asked. "I've been at this job long enough and dealt with other production companies. Usually, when someone wants to use our collection, they contact us months in advance."

Nick glanced at Georgie. "Maybe that's why we're still on basic-cable television?" He turned back to Penelope and attempted his aw-shucks smile.

Penelope crossed her arms.

Georgie covered his mouth and coughed.

Nick rubbed his nose. "Okay, you caught me. The manuscripts you showed us are great. It'll provide some kind of academic context for the show. After all, this is Grantham, an Ivy League school. And dunce that I am, I really didn't put all that together until I was talking with Justin last night, and he happened to mention your position here."

Penelope tapped her foot.

Nick looked down. The photos of Brigitte Bardot on her shoe jiggled up and down provocatively.

"Maybe I'll just wait outside?" Georgie suggested. "I have a few phone calls to make." He slipped out.

"I would hardly call someone who has written a bestseller, hosts and writes his own award-winning travel-food show and has a degree from Grantham University—"

"Full disclosure," Nick interrupted. "I never got my degree."

She waved off his comment. "I repeat again, what is it you really want?"

He took a step closer. It wasn't a threatening move, but definitely allowed him to enter her personal space.

She didn't retreat, but instead raised her head to look him directly in the eye.

He noticed the throb of that vein in her forehead again and felt an irresistible urge to stroke it. But he didn't.

Instead he wet his lips and said in a low voice, "Well, now that you mention it, I want you to come to Hoagie Palace with us tonight."

She tilted her head. "Why?"

"It'll be fun."

"Fun?"

"Yes, not to mention a free meal."

"And after tonight?" She toyed with the collar of her lab coat.

Never had a uniform been so alluring. "After tonight?" he repeated her words. He searched her eyes to ascertain what she was thinking, but he found himself distracted, confused...more than confused. And then it dawned on him—what he hadn't been able to figure out before. The reason he felt so off balance around her? "Why, to find out what a woman with eyes each a different color does for excitement."

TRACY KELLEHER

She tilted her head. "Why?"
"It'll be fun."
"Fun?"
"Yes, not to mention a free meal."
And after ... with the collar of
her lab coat.
Never had a uniform been so alluring. "After to-
able to figure out be

CHAPTER EIGHT

"THIS IS JUST THE KIND of place that makes me very, very happy," Nick announced on camera. "I'm here with a student from Grantham University who is such an aficionado of Hoagie Palace, he even has a sandwich named after him."

"Not just named after me. I came up with the combination," Press clarified. He waited expectantly as Nick thrust himself wholeheartedly into eating his enormous hoagie. The long split roll barely contained a full chicken cutlet, half-a-dozen mozzarella sticks and a bunch of French fries—all covered in hot sauce.

Nick chewed and swallowed. "That's some kinda wonderful. Who said the youth of America had nothing to offer these days? Press, this is inspirational." Nick took another bite.

Actually the hoagie was delicious, which meant Nick was currently thinking good thoughts about Mimi's half brother, instead of wanting to cut off essential male parts because he seemed to be the object of his daughter's constantly adoring gaze.

Nick swallowed and turned to Angie, the co-owner of the establishment. The mass of them were jammed into the tiny greasy spoon located on Main Street. Nick and his crew. Justin and Lilah—in the end, she had decided to risk it. Along with them was the überfamous network correspondent Mimi Lodge, wearing a Hoagie Palace T-shirt and an attitude, as well as Press, Amara and, yes, Penelope. Not that the presence of the film crew had stopped the hordes from piling in, too.

Nothing, it seemed, could stop the locals, especially the high school and college students, from lining up for the kind of appetite-satisfying food that required a loose waistband and possibly a roll of Tums afterward. Not only did the line snake around the inside of the small store, but it made its way out onto the sidewalk, where eager customers joked under the shade of a flowering pear tree and stared soulfully at the lucky few munching away nearby at several benches.

Fortunately it was a happy crowd content to wait and shoot the breeze.

Things were heating up on this balmy late-spring day. While the humidity outside was still at a tolerable level, inside the shop the deep-fat fryers and grills were going full blast. The three short-order cooks, all wearing Hoagie Palace T-Shirts in the ubiquitous orange-and-black, turned out the food in rapid, coordinated fashion. Normally Angie manned the cash register. Tonight, it was Sal's job so Angie could be front and center.

"Angie, I gotta tell you, I remember Hoagie Palace from my college days at Grantham. But this is better than all my memories combined," Nick announced. He stooped down to better converse with the middle-aged owner.

"We just try to keep going what my husband's uncle started in the seventies. We still use our special 'saltpeppaketchup,' and we still get our extralarge rolls from the same bakery in Trenton."

Nick looked directly at the camera. "See, supersizing has a long and distinguished tradition."

Angie smiled. For a purveyor of high-caloric food, she was remarkably trim except for a thickening at the waist. Business was obviously good—or Sal was clearly a good husband—because she sported a tasteful gold-and-diamond bracelet. "But we are constantly looking to meet the tastes of our customers," she continued earnestly.

"Tell me you are not going healthy?" Nick pleaded.

"We do offer tasty Greek and chef salads, but truthfully, they're not our biggest sellers." She heaved her shoulders and cupped her hand in front of her in the familiar New Jersey gesture. "Still, we like to add special combo hoagies to the menu that some of our favorite customers have devised." She pointed to Nick's mammoth selection. "The Big Press being one of the most popular."

Nick could tell she wanted to pinch Press's cheek. "Hats off to you, kid. The combination of all the flavors, the inspiration of putting the fries *in* the hoagie instead of having them on the side—pure genius."

Press looked abashed. "Maybe I should put it on my résumé when it's time to get a job. What do you think?"

Nick waved his hand. "You've got my letter of recommendation, no problem."

Angie smiled and tried to look serious. "Press doesn't need a sandwich on his résumé. He's graduating next week with honors. Then he'll take a year to travel and get his master's degree before enrolling in graduate school for a Ph.D in paleontology. We're so proud of him. He's grown up so beautifully. We think of him as our own." Finally she couldn't resist and gave an embarrassed Press a squeeze. Then she looked over her shoulder toward the cash register. "Right, Sal?"

Sal, who was efficiently handling payments, looked up at the sound of Angie's voice. "You bet, Ang," he called out with a smile on his face and a twenty in his hand. "Just like a son."

"Clearly you treat your sons right," Nick said. It was kind of humbling to realize that Angie knew more about Press's plans than he knew about his own daughter's. "So, can I be your son, too? Hey, I've been a short-order cook, maybe not very accomplished, but passable."

Angie eyed him suspiciously. "I don't know. You don't strike me as being such a nice boy."

Nick did a mock gag. "She knows me too well. Which is probably why she knows how to please her customers. Let's see how the other Grantham alums think you stack up compared to their college memories." He turned to the huddle. "So? How is it?"

Out of the side of his eye, he spotted Penelope, who had managed to separate herself from the hordes and was gazing serenely at the array of photos of Hoagie Palace patrons wearing their signature T-shirts in far-flung places.

She would have to wait. Instead he angled closer to his buddy Justin. "As good? Better than you remembered?"

Justin swallowed and wiped the corner of his mouth with the back of his hand. "The chicken parm is amazing—as always. Truthfully I should have ordered a half hoagie, but I couldn't control myself."

Nick scanned the others.

Lilah was being a real trooper and chowing down on an egg-salad sandwich. "I need to eat lighter now that I'm expecting." She apologized for not holding up her end. "But it's still great."

"Ha, I'm certainly not eating lighter. It's a sausage hoagie for me—first, last and always," Mimi chimed in, smiling confidently toward the camera. But then, cameras were a part of her daily existence. And she sure knew how to capture a story in a sound bite. "I don't know what it is about The Palace. It makes coming back to Grantham all the more worthwhile," Mimi said.

Nick was delighted to have her star power, but he didn't want her dominating the show. Besides, this was his chance to finally do something for his daughter. He wasn't beneath currying favor. "And my own daughter has made the pilgrimage to this temple of goodness. Amara, you're not a Grantham alum, but we'll let you into the club." He winked.

Amara, partially blocked by Mimi, was busily chomping on a huge side of French fries slathered with ketchup. She waved when the camera pointed in her direction. "But I'll be coming in the fall as a freshman," she said in a high, nervous voice. "So I get a head start on the tradition."

Georgie was standing next to Larry, the cameraman, and he gave her a thumbs-up.

Which left Penelope. She couldn't hide forever. Nick sidestepped the refrigerated case of soft drinks and honed in on her. "We have another Grantham alum here, too. Not only was she valedictorian of her class—" he'd had Georgie do some homework "—but now she's curator of the university's Rare Book Library. So what's your take on Hoagie Palace, Penelope?" he asked, not sure what she'd say.

She blinked nervously for a moment, then with

great deliberation, launched into her observations. "Hoagie Palace is a Grantham institution. That goes without saying. My favorite part is that it's kept the same sign all these years. Other things might change in town—more stockbrokers, coffee shops and yogurt stores—but The Palace remains a comforting presence no matter what. It's comfort on a roll." She turned toward the cash register. "About the roll, Sal, I have to compliment you on how fresh it is, and just the right combination of crustiness and chewiness. Not a newfangled artisanal loaf by any stretch of the imagination. Just a pure, Italo-New Jersey roll. Now, that's real local." She held it up and punched the air.

Sal blushed—though never stopped making change.

Nick stood stunned. Not only had she spoken the copy that he would have written, she…she… Was it possible to say that someone could radiate? Practically levitate with serenity and sexiness at the same time? He wanted to tell everyone else to go home—tell the world to go home—so he could find out more, much more about this mysterious and totally mesmerizing woman.

Nicholas Rheinhardt, Mr. I'm So Jaded I Yawn At The Sight Of Presidents And Popes, felt giddy. Beyond giddy. Corny as it sounded, cupid's arrow had struck suddenly, and defying all of his previously held beliefs, Nick found himself in love at second sight—their first library meeting having set the stage for simple infatuation—not that he was an expert on the difference. But Nick was sure there had to be one.

And like a dope, he just stood there with the camera rolling.

And Penelope? She appeared to be either fixated on him or the Hoagie Palace souvenirs hanging on the wall.

Should he take heart or feel slighted? And he would have asked her which reaction was appropriate—at least, he told himself he would have returned to earth and rekindled his ability to form words and place them one after the other—except that Georgie got in the way.

The producer, from his position off camera, shouted, "Rheinhardt, you fool! Let's make like we're working here."

Which, of course, broke the whole starry-eyed phenomenon. "Georgie," he whispered under his breath. When in doubt, Nick's motto was always to blame it on the producer.

"Nick, Nick. Psst." Georgie became more insistent. "Turn to the counter. Ten o'clock." He immediately shifted in that direction as though someone had just lassoed him.

Nick narrowed his eyes at Penelope, who didn't shy from his gaze, before he reluctantly noticed what all the fuss was about. "Oh, an honest-to-goodness celebrity mover and shaker." Nick peered into the camera. "Viewer, I kid you not. This was totally unplanned." He held out his hand for Larry, the cameraman, to follow, bringing into the viewfinder an extremely tall woman in a pearl-gray business suit and high heels. Her back was turned toward Nick and her head was bent over the end of a paper bag. "Vivian Pierpoint, former CEO of the largest online auction house and current candidate for governor of Connecticut. What brings you to our fair shores?"

Vivian turned, a gob of pink sauce dripping from a corner of her mouth. "Excuse me?" Then she saw the cameraman and plastered a smile on her face. "Hello. And you're...you're...you look very familiar, but I don't think we've met."

"Nicholas Rheinhardt from the Voyage Channel."

"Of course. I loved the episode where you had this painful massage in some remote locale. I can't remember the name, but it looked very cold."

Nick cringed. "Thank you for reminding me of a moment I'd rather forget. But before you go on and remind the viewers of any more of my embarrassing moments, I should tell you that you have some sauce on your cheek." He pointed to his own to indicate the location. "I don't want to be accused of biasing the election by not telling you. That's how nice a guy I am." He looked over his shoulder to Angie for approval.

She frowned, indicating she wasn't totally convinced.

"So you're a Palace aficionado?" Nick inquired.

"Always when I return for Reunions to Grantham, it's my first stop," Vivian supplied. "I'm also on the Board of Trustees at the university, so I have an excuse to visit The Palace on multiple occasions during a year—much to my physician's chagrin." She smiled a politician's smile and lifted her hoagie, still wrapped in the bag. "Now, you tell me, who can resist The Palace's turkey-extreme hoagie with extra Russian dressing? Not that Grantham doesn't offer many other fine dining experiences, which I presume you're going to sample, as well." She turned an inquiring eye to Nick.

Since Vivian was level with him in her heels, the glare was powerful. "Do you have any suggestions?" Nick asked dutifully. The woman scared him silly.

"You must eat at Bégart. It's new, very elegant, Grantham's answer to molecular gastronomy. We like to think it's our own French Laundry," she said, referring to Thomas Keller's famous restaurant in the Napa Valley.

"The tasting menu is to die for," Vivian continued with the politician's eager delight in having the spotlight. "If you don't have a reservation, perhaps I could use my influence?" She winked in a way that could never be confused as flirtatious.

Nick smiled awkwardly. Talk about losing control of the conversation. He was ready to bring the interlude to a finish when Vivian reached out with the darting motion of a giant squid. He would have seriously become concerned for his health, if her arm hadn't stretched past him as she shouted out, "Lilah, of all people."

Vivian pushed past Nick with a polite "If you'll excuse me. It's been very nice, but I see an old friend." She immediately clasped Lilah to her chest.

Nick's first thought was to wonder where her hoagie was in all this embracing.

Vivian released Lilah, and miraculously the hoagie appeared unscathed. She turned and grabbed Nick, dragging him close. "Now, if you want to interview someone, it should be Lilah here. She's done more to address the plight of Congolese women and their children through her organization Sisters for Sisters than most NGOs and governments combined."

Lilah smiled weakly. "Thanks, Vivian, but to tell you the truth, I'm not feeling totally well at the moment."

It was true. Nick noticed she had a bilious green cast to her skin and perspiration dotted her forehead.

"Lilah?" Justin rushed to his wife's side. "What's wrong?"

She shook her head. "I think it's just the heat

in here and probably the smells. They've suddenly gotten to me." She lowered her head.

"First trimester sensitivities to smells," Penelope suddenly announced, materializing from her perch by the wall. "Justin, take her outside into the fresh air." She riffled through her purse, producing a small bottle and a snow-white handkerchief. "When she's outside, put some of this on the cloth and let her breathe it. It's rose water. It will diffuse the smells."

"Make way, make way." Angie parted the crowd. "We have a pregnant woman here who needs help."

"Please, I just need a little air. No one has to fuss," Lilah protested. "Once I get outside I'll be fine."

"If we want to make a fuss, we'll make a fuss," Justin said protectively.

Vivian rested a hand on Lilah's shoulder. "My husband, Pierre, is just like Justin—always ready to defend me. It's a primal need of males to protect their mate."

Lilah turned to Justin and clutched his hand. "I'm not quite sure what Vivian is talking about. But I do know that I think I may throw up."

Penelope slid her hoagie out of its long paper bag. "Here, take this. Think of it as an airsickness bag." She thrust it at Lilah as Justin led her to the door.

Then Justin, his arms around Lilah, stormed the

door with Press and Amara acting as blockers and Penelope bringing up the rear.

"You don't think it's my fault, do you, I mean, hugging her like that?" Vivian asked no one in particular. She glanced around the crowd, taking in the reactions. Then she seemed to perk up. "Mimi, I didn't see you there," she called. She made a wedge in the crowd to reach the journalist. "What do you think?"

Mimi chewed thoughtfully on her sausage hoagie. "I don't think it will have a big negative impact on your campaign numbers, but if you want to do damage control, perhaps you could suggest she name the baby after you." She trooped outside.

Vivian stood there in silence before pulling out her BlackBerry.

Nick turned to Georgie. "So you think she's calling her campaign manager?"

Georgie shrugged. "Either way, it's great television."

"The cameras are still running?"

"When are they not?" Georgie chuckled.

Nick craned his neck this way and that, looking for Penelope. He leaned back to Clyde, the soundman, who was wielding his boom and barely managing to avoid contact with the crowd. "So have you seen the librarian?" he asked oh-so-casually.

"You mean the Botticelli Venus? The one who

walks in beauty, like the night. Of cloudless climes and starry skies—"

Nick found himself more than mildly annoyed. "Quit with the Keats."

"Byron, you illiterate Yank," Clyde complained.

"Who pays you on a regular basis?"

"Like I said, Keats, Lord Byron? What's the diff?"

"The lady?" Nick prompted again.

"Outside with the damsel in distress."

"Then *vamanos,* my willing followers." Nick pushed through the crowd, with Clyde and Larry in tow. Georgie skipped along behind, stopping only to give his card to Vivian, who was still talking on the phone.

Once out the door, Nick spotted Lilah sitting on the wooden bench, holding a handkerchief to her nostrils.

"I feel positively Victorian," she complained.

"But it's working, right?" Justin was on his knees in front of her.

She nodded and took another long and loud sniff from the handkerchief.

Press turned to Amara. "See, I told you Penelope knew everything. That's why I like hanging out with her."

"I think you like hanging out with her because she says things like, 'You are a diamond in the rough.'" Amara knocked him down a peg or two.

Nick watched as she casually gathered up her long hair and flipped it over her shoulder. *That kid Press is toast,* he thought, not really sure if that was good or bad. Probably bad.

Press grinned at her sheepishly. "Ya think? So, maybe you're just the person to polish my edges?"

Amara pursed her lips. "Maybe? You never know."

Nick grimaced. Amara might think she knew her own mind, but she was still his daughter, and he didn't want her looking for trouble on his watch. She was definitely moving out of Mimi's family's house ASAP.

But then his attention was drawn to a much more pleasant image. Penelope. Ah, the lovely Penelope. He moved to where she was sitting on the bench next to Lilah. "Could we talk?" he asked.

She looked skeptical. "You need to talk to me?"

"I do." He took hold of her hand. He felt as if a spotlight was focusing on them alone. Well, maybe it was Larry, the cameraman. *Never mind.* "I have something to confess."

Her one green eye and one blue eye gazed into his brown ones, inscrutable. "I'm waiting," she prompted him.

"You asked me what I want? I want to taste your 'nduja."

She blinked. "Is that all?"

"No."

"I didn't think so."

"I want to do it on camera."

Penelope's eyes widened. "Frankly I wasn't expecting that."

"And that's a wrap!" Georgie called out.

CHAPTER NINE

"DAD, I DON'T LIKE PANCAKES," Amara complained
the next morning.

"I don't care. We're shooting at Pancake Heaven,
and I want you where I can keep an eye on you,
since you don't have to babysit today." Nick marched
briskly along Main Street, not bothering to slow
down so that she could match his long stride. He
could have really done with a cigarette right now,
which was a bummer since he'd given up smoking
about nine months ago. If ever there was a time to
relapse, this was it.

After magnanimously giving up his queen-size
bed in his hotel room for Amara, he'd suffered
through a night of misery on the pullout sleeper
sofa. Every spring felt as if it had embedded itself
into his spinal column. He was getting too old for
this job.

He was certainly too old—or too something—to
be a father.

"I still can't believe you made me leave the pool
house. I can't stand sharing that room with you. I
mean, I don't have any privacy," she complained.

She started to pull at a strand of her long hair as she tried to keep up with him. The thick soles of her Doc Martens *kerplunked* on the sidewalk.

"Like I have any privacy?" Nick slanted her a glance. For someone who'd prided himself on disrespecting authority, he found it irritating that his daughter was decked out in full Goth attire on this bright and sunny day. "Look at it this way, at least Press has his privacy back, right?"

She snorted. "So that's what this is all about? Jeez, Dad, he's older than me."

"Not that much older." It was more like she wasn't that much younger.

"You just don't trust me," she shot back.

"After getting kicked out of school, you think I should trust you?" he snapped. Even Nick recognized that he was sounding immature, but somehow he seemed incapable of raising the level of this conversation.

How typical, he was sure his ex-wife would say. When would he ever grow up?

"Do you even want to know why I was kicked out?" she asked, purposely looking away as she talked.

"Do you want to tell me?" he asked.

"Not really."

They stopped along with everyone else for the light to change at the corner of Main Street and Whalen Avenue. A bank asserted its formal financial exterior on one side, and a jewelry store show-cased expensive rings and watches on the other. On the other side of Main Street, wrought-iron gates separated the university campus from the real world, or as much as Grantham was the real world.

The light changed, and Nick stepped off the curb. "If you don't want to talk about it, I won't ask, then." Though he supposed the discussion would have to come sooner rather than later. Speaking of later, was he supposed to do something about it? he wondered. He would have to talk to his ex when she got back from her honeymoon. Whatever the outcome, he was sure it would cost him.

Didn't it always?

The rest of the short walk passed in silence as they cut a determined path. Rather than look at his daughter, he took in the blur of stores—the ubiquitous Starbucks, a yogurt shop and another jewelry store. *How upscale did a town have to be to afford two jewelry stores in one block?* Nick wondered. He kept moving past the university bookstore, a stock-brokerage, a brewpub and a photocopy store. What more did a college student need?

Up ahead, he spotted Georgie, Larry and Clyde hanging out in front of Pancake Heaven. The exterior was imitation brick. Black shutters and striped awnings framed the windows—a decor that looked like fake Colonial meets Jersey Shore.

The Grantham Historical Society next door must be having kittens, Nick figured.

But when they reached the middle of the block, Nick put out his arm to stop Amara. He glanced at the shop—a shoe store. Orange-and-black banners hailed alumni around a collection of men's dress shoes and women's high heels.

He turned to Amara. "Hold on."

She halted and glanced disdainfully at the shoes. "Having a footwear moment?"

Nick bit his tongue and tried to channel Georgie's words of wisdom about dealing with kids. He couldn't remember a single one, which meant he'd just have to wing it.

He crossed his arms, but then uncrossed them. *More approachable,* he told himself. He smiled.

Amara winced.

Okay, so maybe no smile. "Listen, we might as well get this over with. Why were you kicked out? Just tell me. I'm your dad. No matter what, I'll support you."

"Are you just saying that, or do you mean it?"

"To be honest, probably a little bit of both."

Amara shrugged her shoulders like a downtrodden old man. "Yeah, it's not like I would have believed some sudden outburst of parental concern anyway." She glanced up and down the street. "I was staying on campus when Mom left for her honeymoon—"

Nick nodded. "And?"

"And I used her car. To go to Planned Parenthood." She gulped noticeably and gave him a belligerent stare.

Whatever he thought she was going to say, it wasn't that. "You're pregnant?" It was the first thing that came to him.

She shook her head and looked away. "I knew this was useless."

"No, no, whatever you've done, we can handle it together." A sudden flashback materialized: running into Jeannine on Fifth Avenue in New York right after he'd just quit Grantham University. She'd been pushing a stroller with a sleeping toddler while wearing a rumpled yellow dress. He could still see that outfit—it'd had daisies and he'd hated it on sight. And the kid? He found out then and there she was his.

"Berlin? The rock concert where we met and proceeded to act like rabbits in heat, after which you took off at dawn without even a simple goodbye?" Jeannine had reminded him bitterly on that putridly hot and humid day. It seemed that during the two-year gap between high school and college, when he'd traveled Europe with a Church youth group— unbelievable in hindsight—he'd promoted more than just world peace. A one-night stand had led to increasing the population by one infant girl—Amara. When she'd found out she was pregnant, Jeannine had gone back to live with her parents in Mineola, having lost complete contact with Nick until that very moment. It didn't help that she didn't know his full name.

Nick, to give him credit, had immediately offered to marry her, convinced by too many lunchtime beers and not enough sleep, that the fates had declared it. He was meant to drop out of college after all, he told himself. They'd spent the next six months living in a walk-up one-bedroom apartment in the Lower East Side—*before* it became gentrified. Needles littered the sidewalks. And their bathtub sat in the middle of the tiny kitchen.

Two months later, Nick skipped out. Jeannine had claimed she was glad to see him go. Aside from Amara, they'd had nothing in common. Jeannine thought her job was to be a perfect mother—reveling in staying at home and taking care of Amara. His was to provide. In reality, he hopscotched from one dead-end job to the next while managing to become a regular at the bars in the neighborhood.

He supposed, in retrospect, that they'd both gone into the marriage blind. Still, it was not one of his finest hours by a long shot.

Amara's voice brought him back to the here and now. "You can breathe easier. I'm not pregnant. I didn't even go for myself."

"Then I don't understand."

"I took a friend to a gynecology clinic because she had an STD."

"She had motor oil?" he asked, referring to the name of a well-known brand name.

"Oh, brother," Amara scoffed. "She had a sexually transmitted disease—vaginal warts, if you really want to know."

It was Nick's turn to wince. "Perhaps that's too much detail."

"Anyway, she was afraid to tell anyone but me, and she clearly needed treatment."

"And the school infirmary couldn't handle it?"

"They would have told her parents, duh."

Even Nick could sympathize with that. "So where was the boyfriend in all this?" Nick asked.

"Nowhere to be found—like most guys," Amara said with disgust.

Nick couldn't help feeling that he'd made a lousy role model.

"So, I told her that a boyfriend who didn't use a condom wasn't a boyfriend—just a moron, and she didn't want him around anyway. She was lucky that it was only an STD."

Amara rubbed her shoe back and forth on the sidewalk. "Anyway, I said I'd take her. But because we didn't want anyone to know, we didn't sign out for leaving campus, and I kind of took the keys that Mom had left in her desk."

"Took?"

"Okay, I stole them. But I put them back. Which turned out to be the big mistake, since her secretary spotted me. There was no way I could deny I'd taken her car."

"And your friend. What did she say?"

"Nothing. Just like I told her to. She didn't need any more grief. Besides, she's a scholarship student—only a junior. If they found out, she could lose her scholarship, maybe get kicked out."

"So you took all the blame?"

Amara held up her hand and dropped it. "Yeah... well...to tell you the truth, I didn't really think I'd get kicked out. It was Mom's car after all, not somebody else's."

Nick looked at her, his mouth open.

She sniffed. "Okay, okay. I get the message. I guess I didn't know what I was thinking." She crossed her arms over her chest. "So? Now you know. Not only did I get kicked out, but the headmistress told me they're going to tell Grantham University. They'll probably rescind my acceptance."

The belligerence was still etched on her face, but when her mouth twitched, he also detected fear and uncertainty. Underneath the whole I So Don't Care What The Establishment Thinks getup was a frightened teenage girl.

"So?" she asked again. "I suppose you think I was stupid to get involved."

"Do you have unprotected sex, too?" From the

sour look on Amara's face, that was so not the right thing to say.

"I should have known. You just don't get it, do you?" She stormed down the sidewalk.

Nick put his hand out to stop her. "I'm sorry. That was a stupid thing to say. It just blurted out because I panicked. I may be a lousy father, but that doesn't mean that I'm not concerned. Listen, I get it. Your sex life is not the topic of conversation right now." Nick paused. "And I'm not sure I can handle that anyway."

Amara looked down at herself, then at him "Dad, do I look like the kind of girl that boys are running after?"

Beneath the somber, shapeless clothing and dyed hair, Nick could see that a slender, attractive young woman was hiding. *Jeez, don't blow it again.*

He wet his lips and wet them again. Then he really tried to say the right thing. "If they're not looking at you, they're stupid. But listen. Truthfully—" he raised both hands "—as a father, I prefer to think of you as strictly off-limits. Because, like you said, most boys *are* morons, and I speak from personal experience." He rubbed his mouth. "But as to the other thing."

"'Other thing' meaning my getting kicked out?"

"Yeah, that 'other thing.' What you did taking the car keys was wrong, but I think we'll be able to make them give you some slack."

"Why? Because you're my dad? Some celebrity who can buy them off? Press told me about how rich parents do that all the time."

"I bet the little pri..." Nick stopped himself. He didn't want to set the guy up as his adversary. It might just encourage Amara's infatuation even more. He knew the way immature minds worked. Instead he nodded. "The kid's got a point. But that's not what I was driving at. Maybe if we explained your reasons for using the car."

"Dad, I'm not going to rat on my friend."

"I'm not asking you to name names." Out of the corner of his eye, he saw Georgie checking his watch nervously. "Hon, I've got to shoot this scene now. Look—" he pointed "—your uncle Georgie is ready to have a shi—" once more he censored himself, something that was totally out of character "—a fit. We'll have to talk about this later."

"It can't be much later because my graduation is supposed to be the end of next week."

Nick looked to the sky. And noticed it was overcast. "Great. Okay. In the meantime, what does your mother say?"

"Earth to Dad. Don't you remember that she's on some remote island for her honeymoon? No phone, no email. She's not due back until two days before graduation."

"I can't believe her new husband, the lawyer,

would go someplace where he couldn't stay in touch with his office 24/7."

"Glenn is nice. He wouldn't do that to Mom on her honeymoon."

"Meaning he's old and rich and doesn't need to." When he saw her sour look he held up his hands. "Okay, I won't say anything mean about your mom's new husband. God knows that after me she deserves a break."

"That's what she says, too." For the first time, there was a smile on her face.

If it took a collective agreement that he was a schmuck to make Amara happy, so be it, Nick thought. He placed his arm around his daughter's narrow shoulders and gave her a squeeze.

She angled her head and looked up at him. "You're not suffering from some delusion that this is a rosy father-daughter moment, are you?" She looked critically at his hand on her shoulder.

He dropped it right away. "Heavens, no. No one would ever accuse us of sharing one of those, would they?"

But the ironic thing was, both father and daughter had a smile—true, more a smirk—but, nevertheless, a smile on their lips.

CHAPTER TEN

NICK SAT IN THE FRONT BOOTH of Pancake Heaven next
to Mel, the owner. "I gotta tell you, Mel. I'm not
usually a big fan of sweet things. On the other hand,
I completely get the need for a major hit of carbs
to get over a hangover. Given that this is a college
town and that Pancake Heaven appears to be thriv-
ing—" he gestured around the packed establishment
"—I think we can all see where I'm going."

On weekends, a line of people at Pancake Heaven
wended their way out the door and down the sidewalk as far as the movie theater. Unlike Hoagie
Palace, Pancake Heaven tended to attract families
and the older crowd.

Nick felt a lump forming in his stomach. He'd
done his best to tackle the large mound of gelati-
nous bacon and an overly sweet chocolate milkshake. He had smiled politely for the camera. But
he was reaching his limit.

Out of desperation, he glanced out the window.
Through the kitschy stained glass, he watched the
traffic inch forward—much like the doleful progress of the milkshake as it made its way south of his

esophagus. Only by chance did he spot a female bi-cyclist whizzing by.

Despite the black helmet obscuring her face, Nick was sure he recognized the ponytail trailing out the back and the long legs, encased in a pair of skinny jeans, pumping madly.

He craned his neck in order to follow the cy-clist as she headed through the intersection. And he caught a glimpse of the back of her blue-and-white-striped shirt. Until now, he never knew he had a thing for women in French sailor's shirts.

He turned reluctantly back to the scene inside. "You know, Mel, I'd love to stay and chat some more, but we've got another appointment in town." He reached across to shake hands with the owner, Mel.

Nick stood impatiently.

"Are you sure I can't tempt you with another cup of coffee?" Mel asked. Close to retirement age, his spreading stomach stretched the white buttons of his blue oxford-cloth shirt.

Nick patted his chest. "I'll have to pass. If I get too jacked up in the morning, I tend to crash later in the day."

Behind Mel's back, Georgie was gagging.

"But your cappuccino, hey, what can I say—unique," Nick offered. It had come topped with a whipped cream that no amount of DNA testing could ever attribute to a cow or a cowlike species.

Georgie rallied the troops, including Amara, who had been sitting visibly bored at the counter during the filming. About the only thing she had touched the whole time was bottled water. *Probably a wise move,* Nick thought in hindsight.

He waited outside along with Georgie and Amara while Larry and Clyde packed up their equipment. Nick could tell that Georgie was confused. "What's the matter?" he asked.

"I don't get it," Georgie answered. "What's up with cutting the session short? We've still got almost an hour before we have to be at the Rare Book Library. There really wasn't any hurry. Even if we have to roll on our stomachs the whole way, we'll still be early."

"You know me. Mr. Punctuality."

"Oh, please, who was ten minutes late this morning?" Georgie replied.

"I was busy talking with my daughter," Nick explained.

"Then that's all right." Georgie gave him a fist pump. "We always have time for Amara. I'm proud of you, Nick. You're a slow learner, but you're not without hope."

"Please, I don't think I'm in the running for the father of the year award, as Amara here will probably agree." Nick was secretly hoping that she'd back him up, saying he wasn't so bad after all.

Instead she was engrossed with texting on her iPhone.

Nick looked to Georgie and shrugged.

Georgie made a "take it easy" gesture with his hand, and held the door open wide so that Larry and Clyde could slip past the people waiting in line. Then he focused on Nick again. "What I don't get is the lack of snarkiness back there in Pancake Hell." Before the filming, Georgie had ordered a large stack of buttermilk pancakes. He'd even poured on the maple syrup with great gusto. But after a few bites, he'd put his fork down and pushed the plate away. Nick hadn't seen Georgie refuse food since... since... Wait a minute. He'd never seen him refuse food.

"I didn't think it was all that bad," Clyde interrupted. He had gleefully finished Georgie's pancakes.

"What would you know about food? You're English," Georgie replied.

"Whoa! Look who's snarky now. Of course I have no opinion of the food since no one thought to offer me any," Larry moaned.

"Don't be such a baby." Clyde removed the keys to the rental van from his jeans pocket and opened up the back doors. Parking was at a premium on Main Street, and the crew had obtained permission from the borough to hood a meter for their use.

After loading up, Larry slammed the doors shut and looked around. "This sudden bout of niceness wouldn't have anything to do with your librarian, would it, Nick? What do you think, Amara?"

Nick snarled.

A car horn beeped.

Amara, oblivious to the conversation around her, turned her head. A BMW was blocking traffic in the intersection. She waved.

Nick didn't need three guesses to know it was Press.

Amara whipped around to face her father. "That's Press. I forgot to tell you that he invited me to hang out with him while he's working for Reunions."

"Yes, you did forget to tell me. And don't Reunions start on Friday? Last I checked it's still Wednesday," Nick replied. He was working really hard not to raise his voice.

"Yeah, but apparently there's a lot of preparation to do up front like cleaning rooms and moving beer kegs and stuff."

"Since when have you ever cleaned your room?" Nick asked.

Georgie elbowed Nick. "Give the kid a break."

Amara's phone jingled with an incoming text. She looked down. "That's Press. He doesn't want to get a ticket. The Grantham cops are supposed to be notorious. Listen, I sat through one shoot, how many more can I sit through in one day? And Noreen, Press's stepmom, doesn't need me to babysit later today. She's taking Brigid to the hair salon."

"C'mon, Nick. She didn't complain at all through the shoot, which had to have been pretty boring," Georgie defended her.

Nick caved. "All right. But whatever you do, don't touch a single beer keg. If the cops are as notorious as you say, I don't want to hear that you've been charged with underage possession of an alcoholic beverage. You're in enough trouble as it is already." Nick bit his tongue. That hadn't come out quite right.

"Gee, like I needed any reminders." Amara took off without even saying goodbye.

"Call me every hour," Nick shouted out after her.

Clyde opened the driver's door to the van. "You really think that's going to happen?"

"No, but I can pretend," Nick lamented.

Georgie shook his head. "Relax. She seems pretty savvy about boys."

Nick watched Amara scamper through traffic and slide into the passenger seat. "I hope you're right."

"Hey, is there any food at this next shoot?" Larry whined, hanging on to the door.

The BMW pulled away, its engine gunning as the light changed from yellow to red.

Georgie gave Larry a look. "Is that all you think about?"

Nick gazed heavenward. "Please, please, just give me the strength to survive the next few days."

CHAPTER ELEVEN

MIMI'S CELL PHONE SPRANG to life, ringing loudly from the nightstand. She rolled over. The sunlight stabbed her eyes. After quickly covering her face with her arm, she felt around for the phone and found it just as it started to vibrate onto the carpet.

"Still got the old reflexes," she mumbled to herself. Mimi had been captain of the Women's Water Polo team when she was a senior at Grantham.

She moved her wrist and ventured to open one eye so she could read the screen on her phone. The number was not one on her extensive contact list. She considered rolling back over on her stomach and letting the damn thing go to voice mail, but her inner newshound got the better of her.

She pressed the screen and answered gruffly, "This had better not be a solicitation for the Policemen's Benevolent Association."

"Mimi, is that you? It's Vivian, Vivian Pierpoint. Noreen gave me your phone number. I hope I haven't disturbed you?"

Mimi shut her eyes. Nothing like being woken the first thing in the morning by your second stepmother's close friend. Okay, the bedside clock said eleven, but that was splitting hairs.

For a long time Mimi had hated Noreen, almost as much as she had hated her first stepmother, Adele, who was Press's mother. Adele had originally been *her* nanny, until she'd supplanted Mimi's own late mother. Adele was beyond the pale. Everyone agreed. The woman cheated at tennis, was addicted to plastic surgery and actually cared about things like backgammon tournaments.

But beginning last year Mimi had begrudgingly begun to accept Noreen. And while she found it a little hard to cope with Noreen's sunny disposition and glamorous good looks, she realized that she actually liked her—a little. After all, Noreen was the CFO in Lilah's nonprofit and by all accounts, didn't shirk from hard work. The woman had brains, too.

That still didn't mean she wanted Noreen's friends calling her at all hours.

"Mimi? Are you still there?" It was Vivian again.

Mimi opened her eyes and stared at her bedroom ceiling. "Yes, Vivian, I'm here." She tried to sound tolerant.

"Oh, good." Vivian cleared her throat. Then she cleared it again.

Even semicomatose, Mimi found the hesitation uncharacteristic for the normally overly confident businesswoman, university trustee and political candidate.

"I was wondering if you'd heard anything more from Lilah?" Vivian finally asked.

"Lilah? No, why should I?"

"After her weakened physical state yesterday, I was a bit concerned that perhaps I had, had, you know… I was concerned."

Mimi ran her hand through her hair. She'd recently cut it to chin length to make life easier in the field, and she wasn't yet used to it. "I haven't heard anything, and if something were really wrong, I presume Justin would have called. We're planning on getting together later, so if anything was wrong, I'm sure I would have heard by now." Now that returning to Reunions had become their annual ritual, she and Lilah always got together.

"Well, that's good to know." There was another pause. "Actually there was another reason for my call."

The real reason. Mimi parsed Vivian's words. This time she waited, letting silence fill the air. It was an old trick she'd learned as a cub reporter on her days back on the *Daily Grantham,* the student newspaper. Invariably the subject felt obliged to fill the vacuum, sometimes revealing the most telling information.

"I thought that maybe you'd like an exclusive interview," Vivian finally announced.

Mimi was intrigued but wary. Just because they were both Grantham alums didn't mean that Vivian could mine Mimi's press connections for some free publicity. "That's very kind of you to think of me, Vivian. But to tell you the truth, I'm here on vacation—to go to Reunions, catch up with friends and spend time with Brigid. That kind of thing." Her little half sister was definitely the only member of the family that truly mattered. No, that wasn't true. Press had his redeeming qualities, but since he was no longer seven years old, he didn't look at her with adoring eyes and a heart full of unqualified love.

"And, you know, state politics is not my regular beat. I wouldn't want to infringe on anyone's turf. Reporters are pretty touchy about things like that. But if you want, I can get you in touch with the right people at the Network? They'd be only too happy, I'm sure…" She gracefully tried to decline while leaving the possibility open.

"Of course, of course," Vivian replied. "I understand the importance of family. The love and the trust." She hiccupped.

Mimi decided to amp up the empathy factor. "Vivian, is there something wrong? Something… something personal I can help you with? Completely off-the-record, of course?" Nothing was off-the-record.

Mimi could hear Vivian inhale deeply.

"Thank you. It's silly, really. I'm sure it's happened to other people. I just never expected it to happen to me," Vivian confided.

The lack of detail was practically killing Mimi. She sat up in bed and clutched the phone. She could hear Vivian blow her nose. "Vivian?" she prompted. "Are you all right?"

Vivian continued to blow her nose. Long and loud. "To tell you the truth, no, not really. My husband, Pierre Renard?"

"Yes, of course." Pierre Renard was Belgium's former ambassador to Great Britain, a successful businessman with a vast media empire, and the owner of the most successful soccer team in his home country. He was known as The Fox, not just because it was the English translation of his last name, but also because his business ventures had had remarkable success.

"Is he in town, too?" Mimi asked. Getting an exclusive interview with one of the most powerful men in Europe would be more up her alley.

"No, he's at our place in Connecticut—or was supposed to be." Vivian sniffed.

Mimi had seen the photos of the "place"—an understated eighteenth-century farmhouse with miles of picturesque stone walls, a formal perennial garden framed by boxwood hedges and a four-car garage that held a Ferrari, Land Rover and two Mercedes limousines—his and hers—not to mention the chauffeur and his wife who lived above.

"I thought he would probably be bored coming down to Grantham, what with the trustees meetings and all. Besides, all the folderol of Reunions isn't really a European's fancy, if you know what I mean." There was a catch in her voice, then a moment of silence.

The next thing Mimi heard was the sound of something hitting something else with a thud.

"Mimi? Are you still there?" Mimi switched the phone to her other ear.

"Sorry, that was just the Kleenex box. I threw it against the wall," Vivian announced, her voice suddenly forceful. "I feel much better now, much better."

"I'm glad." *Though confused,* Mimi thought.

"I think I've shed enough tears, don't you?"

Mimi figured it was a rhetorical question and didn't answer.

"Now where was I?" Vivian went on. "Oh, yes, I was saying that I thought he'd be bored. Bored my ass. It seems since my departure to Grantham, the lying toad has decided to run off to France with the nanny."

Whoa! Mimi hadn't seen that one coming. She frowned. "The nanny?" This sounded remarkably like the scenario in her family. Then she really was confused. "Wait a minute. You don't have any children."

"That's true. It was the dog's nanny. Daphne."

"Daphne's the nanny?"

"No, Daphne's the dog—a bichon frise. Florence is the nanny. She came highly recommended. All the right schools, her mother a member of the DAR."

"Those Daughters of the Revolution, they're not to be trusted," Mimi commented.

"I don't blame the girl, though."

"Girl?"

"Yes, Florence is only seventeen. She just finished her junior year at Miss Porter's. This was a summer job."

Holy mother of... Mimi thought. "Abduction of a minor *and* fleeing the country. And you found all this out how?" She needed solid confirmation if she was going to break the story.

"He sent me a note this morning. As far as I know, they're on the evening flight to Paris."

Terrific! was Mimi's first thought. Written confirmation. Later on, she told herself, she would feel sympathy.

"I just got a call from Florence's mother because their daughter had missed her appointment at the dermatologist and hadn't returned any of their calls. Little did they know that acne was the least of their worries as far as Florence is concerned. I told them what I'd heard, and, needless to say, they've contacted the police. When I think back now, I realize I should have anticipated something. Yesterday evening, when I spoke to him on the phone from Hoagie Palace, he wouldn't put Daphne on the phone for me to say hello. That's something I like to do when I'm traveling—just to let the dog know that I haven't forgotten her."

Vivian was a little crazy, that's all Mimi could think. Though in voters' eyes, she supposed, a little crazy was preferable to running off with an under-age nanny.

Speaking of the dog. "So how's Daphne holding up?"

"Traumatized, I'm sure, but you'd never know it. You see, Pierre had the dog couriered to me over-night. She arrived this morning with the breakup note attached to the crate."

Mimi got up out of bed to find a notepad and a pen. She had to get this down. "Tell me, in light of all that's happened, do you plan to drop out of the race?" She imagined the headlines with Vivian cast as yet another wronged wife, the victim of a power-ful husband. Would she stand stoically next to him if he were ever forced to return to face charges of corrupting a minor and abduction?

"Drop out! Absolutely not!" Vivian responded ve-hemently. "But right now, the race isn't my focus. Right now my main concern is for Florence, that she's safe. Once I can verify that, then I intend to crucify him. As for the governorship? Eventually, when it's time to address that, we'll have to see. Whatever the outcome, I must say I feel energized. This could be a blessing in disguise, especially now that I know Daphne is safe with me. The one thing I want to make sure of is that I'm the first to tell the story. That's why I thought of you. I don't want it to leak out from Pierre's end, or be covered up somehow."

Mimi didn't want to think about Pierre's end in any form. But she was totally on Vivian's side when it came to taking down a no-good, vile, conniving husband. "In which case, I'll need a camera crew. I can put in a call to New York."

"Actually I have another idea," Vivian suggested.

CHAPTER TWELVE

PENELOPE DIDN'T NORMALLY have problems with being patient or keeping focused on a task. And being surrounded by books—the things she most loved—should have made her toes curl with delight—not that Penelope believed in the literal interpretation of the metaphor, of course.

But as she leaned over the cookbook on French cuisine and explained for the third time—in front of a camera, no less—about the history of ownership of the work, she couldn't help but feel…well… distracted.

"Yes, the author returned the annotated proof copy to her editor, who sent it out to a copy editor, who then returned it to the senior editor. She then passed it to the publisher, who, since he was a Grantham alum, decided to bequeath it to…" She found herself gazing into Nick's deep chocolaty-brown eyes. Naturally, since they were discussing a cookbook, her thoughts turned to food. Or had they?

"Cut," yelled Georgie. Ace producer that he was, Georgie had managed to obtain in record time all the necessary permissions to film. "Nick, buddy, you're supposed to be helping Ms. Bigelow here, not leaving her hanging out to dry. My feeling is we might as well call it a day. We've got enough in the can anyway."

Nick threw up his hands. "I know, I know, and I'm sorry. It's just that I'm distracted."

Distracted? thought Penelope. *Could it be me?*

"It's Amara," Nick said with a shake of his head. "I texted her earlier. I even left messages on her voice mail, but she still hasn't gotten back to me."

The answer is no, apparently, Penelope told herself. Then, like the supremely logical person she was, Penelope slipped her own phone from her back jeans pocket and scrolled her contacts. She placed a call.

"You think you'll have better luck?" Nick asked.

Penelope held up a finger for silence. "Hello, Press," she said, when the call went through. "I'm sorry to bother you. I know you must be busy preparing for Reunions….What?…Learning to roll the kegs on their rims, you say? It sounds as if your coursework in physics is coming in handy….Why did I call? It's regarding another matter. Amara Rheinhardt? Have you seen her?…Oh, good…. That's okay. I'll tell him."

Penelope ended the call. "Press said that she's sitting in the shade while he's working setting up the drinks tent for the Fifth Reunion site. He's—and I quote—'kinda swamped.' So I said I would relay the information."

"I can't believe you knew how to get through that way. You must be an expert on the teenage mind."

Penelope shook her head. "I know nothing about teenagers—male or female. I was homeschooled and never really interacted with children of any age group. Frankly I find teenagers rather intimidating—especially boys en masse. On the other hand, I do know something about being a daughter."

"Well, my daughter is hanging around beer kegs with this...this guy."

"Technically she's sitting in the shade," Penelope corrected. "And I don't know why you're so critical of Press."

"He's young. He's good-looking. And he has a penis." He counted off the points on his fingers. "Need I say more?"

"Press is a very bright and determined young man. He's working Reunions to make money for his trip to Mongolia this summer to look at various significant paleontology sites. Then he's going to Australia to work under a noted scientist who has developed the latest three-dimensional scanning techniques for evaluating fossils. And, as I distinctly remember Angie from Hoagie Palace telling you, he then plans to come back to the United States to pursue a Ph.D." Penelope waited. "All that information should set your mind at ease."

"Only the part about him being far, far away." He studied Penelope. "But I have one question."

"About Press's trip to Mongolia?"

"No, I've been there and it's fantastic—you just have to get used to a diet of animal fat and *airag,* which is fermented mare's milk."

"Hmm, interesting. I suppose that's necessary, given the prolonged frozen temperatures."

"Yes, I suppose. But that's not what puzzles me."

Penelope crossed her arms and waited.

"Why would anyone who's born a Lodge need to work at Reunions? I've seen their house. Even if generations managed to fritter away much of the family millions, his dad is a well-known mover and shaker on Wall Street. When the economy was tanking for the rest of the country, I'm pretty sure he took a healthy bonus. He's got to be as rich as Croesus."

Penelope considered his statement. "Contrary to popular opinion, I believe it was Croesus's use of gold coinage as the standard of purity that led to the legend of his own personal fortune."

Nick closed one eye and just looked at her. "You know, Penelope, I find myself strangely fascinated by your breadth of knowledge. But that's still not my point."

Penelope nodded with great seriousness. "I realize that. Sometimes I can't help myself. I apologize."

"Don't apologize. You would be a very good companion to have on a long trip."

"I've never thought of myself as a good companion. You're very kind."

"No, I'm not."

"I think you like to think you're not." And before Nick could protest, she continued, "As to why Press needs to work, I believe that his father, whom he commonly refers to as The Bastard, has Press's money in trust until he reaches thirty. Something about building backbone, which is anatomically impossible since bones tend to lose density with age." She saw him raise an eyebrow. "Yes, I know, it's a metaphor, but as I said…"

Nick put aside her explanation. "So the kid isn't some rich layabout?" he admitted begrudgingly. "Still, I don't like the idea of Amara glomming on to him. She's very vulnerable right now. How can I say this? There've been some issues with her boarding school."

"I don't understand. Clearly she's a bright and accomplished student."

"A bright and accomplished student who just got kicked out of school before graduation."

"That's terrible. Have you contacted the school?"

"I only found out the reason earlier this morning. I more or less had to pry it out of her. You see, it's not like she tends to confide in me," Nick responded sheepishly and explained what little he knew. "I'm more a Write The Checks And See You Once A Year kind of parent."

"Oh." Penelope's voice dropped off.

"You can say that again."

And she did. "Oh. And her mother? I presume she is of the I Take Care Of Everything Else On A Daily Basis kind of parent?"

"I've always assumed that was the case. But as to her knowing what's happened, at the moment she's out of communication on her honeymoon, and she won't be back until Amara's graduation—or what was supposed to be her graduation."

"Imagine her surprise?" Penelope paused and repeated his words more thoroughly. "You said 'assumed'? You assumed her mother handled crisis situations?"

"I confess. It's not like I've kept close tabs—or any tabs for that matter. What can I say? I'm a lousy father. Something Amara'd agree with, especially now that I've made her vacate the pool house at the Lodge's house and had her move into my room at the Grantham Inn. I've never heard so many complaints about the accommodations."

"I've heard they *are* small rooms."

"Very small," Nick concurred.

"Overly close proximity doesn't necessarily improve already strained relations."

"How could you say that?" he retorted.

Penelope frowned. "I presume that was sarcasm."

She took a step toward him. "You may be a delinquent father, but that doesn't mean you can't be the grown-up in this situation."

"You intend to reform me?"

"No, I'm thinking of your daughter. You, as far as I can fathom, may be beyond reform."

"I'm sorry to be a disappointment." He hung his head.

Penelope shook hers. "You misunderstand. Unfortunately that is also part of your charm."

CHAPTER THIRTEEN

GEORGIE LISTENED TO THE back-and-forth between Nick and Penelope with amusement. There was clearly something going on between them. What, he couldn't quite put his finger on.

The librarian lady confused him, to say the least. On the one hand, she seemed to be the absent-minded professor type—out of touch with reality and immersed in a world of arcane facts. But the way she'd given Amara a boatload of respect yesterday and the polite dressing-down she was giving Nick right now warmed the cockles of his heart.

Georgie loved Nick. He really did. Deep down, Georgie was convinced that Nick cared. Even if the guy could be a selfish bastard.

When things in the end had been bad with Marjorie, Nick had told him to take as much time as he needed, at full salary no less. No questions asked. And when insurance had only paid so much, Nick had made sure the difference was covered. He'd claimed that the cable-channel accountants had negotiated with Georgie's secondary insurance, but later Georgie had found out that Nick had covered the lot out of his own pocket. When Georgie had tried to thank him, Nick had brushed him off, putting his generosity down to a moment of weakness after an amazing and highly alcoholic meal at Per Se in Hell's Kitchen.

That was *so* Nick—reluctant to admit he had a good heart, embarrassed when somebody discovered the truth. The problem was, he just needed to accept that good heart himself. And who knew, maybe the librarian?

Georgie shuffled away from their conversation so as not to appear to be eavesdropping. "Clyde. Watch the boom," he said to the English soundman as he leaned against the table. "Scratch one of these babies, and who knows how much insurance will cover."

"Bloody hell, as if I've ever had any accidents over the years," Clyde argued.

"Well, there was that time at the dim-sum place in Chinese Taipei," Georgie reminded him.

Larry laughed. "All those shelves. All those dishes."

Clyde gave him a rueful stare. "Thanks for reminding me."

Georgie chuckled. Then he felt his BlackBerry vibrate in his pants pocket. He fished it out and answered. "De Meglio here."

"Georgie, it's Mimi, Mimi Lodge. We met yesterday at Hoagie Palace?"

As if he didn't know who Mimi Lodge was. That was like saying he'd never heard of CNN or *60 Minutes*. "Mimi, what's up? You looking for Nick? We're almost done here."

"Actually it's you I was looking for." She ran through the situation with Vivian and the need for discretion.

Georgie nodded along with her story. One thing about Mimi, you could tell she was a pro. She certainly didn't bury the lead. The news about Pierre Renard was certain to go viral.

"So you need a crew?" he asked.

"No, they have one of those satellite studios at the university. You know, the kind they use to interview experts on Public Television?"

"Yeah, I know what you mean. It's got a fake skyline of Grantham in the background or scholarly looking tomes on walnut shelves."

"Exactly."

"So why do you need me?"

"I need an experienced producer. We're doing this live."

"When?"

"Around six o'clock. On tonight's evening news." He mentally ran through their shooting schedule.

"Are you in or are you out?" she prompted.

"You need to ask? I'll just need to slip away from things here, which shouldn't be a big problem. We have a local organic farm to do at noon.

That should run until fourish—no way beyond that.
Nick can only look at lettuce and peas for so long,
though. I think there may be animals. Whatever,
the usual slop. And then we don't film again until
lunch tomorrow—some swank new restaurant that
Vivian mentioned yesterday. So it must be all right."

"Then we're set. Great to have you onboard. Just
to confirm—you're staying at the Grantham Inn,
right?"

"Yup."

"Then why don't I pick you up at five. One thing,
Georgie. About this—tell no one. And I mean no
one."

"Boy Scouts oath, and by the way, that's genuine.
I actually was an Eagle Scout."

"Which is why I knew who to call. Be prepared."

CHAPTER FOURTEEN

"THE BEST SOLUTION IS FOR you to come to my house," Penelope suggested after considerable thought. They were still standing next to each other in the conference room of the Rare Book Library. Georgie was engrossed in a phone call while Clyde and Larry were packing up. The shaded windows, muted carpeting and temperature-controlled environment provided a hermetically sealed cocoon from the outside world.

"Your house?" Nick repeated. His eyes lit up. Any thoughts of waiting for Amara to call back vanished. All his attention was drawn to Penelope's pouty lips and swanlike neck, her skin exposed to the wide neckline of the striped shirt beneath her lab coat. He practically sighed. Last night he'd found himself fantasizing about that lab coat....

But then reality hit.

He glanced down at his watch just to confirm what he already knew. "Only problem is we still have another shoot after this—at some organic farm. Apparently they have the happiest pigs in the county."

"I didn't mean now." Penelope looked aghast. "Naturally I have to work the rest of the day. And besides, your daughter isn't even here."

"My daughter?" Had he completely jumped to the wrong conclusions?

"I was talking about dinner—with you and your daughter, of course."

"Of course." *Dummy,* he chastised himself.

"And then I'll make up the foldout bed in the study."

"The foldout bed?" He didn't quite follow.

"Naturally I don't propose that we sleep together."

"Naturally." Had he just received a put-down?

"I mean, your daughter needs her space."

The lightbulb suddenly went off. "Of course. Amara clearly needs her space."

"If she sleeps in the study downstairs, she'll also have her own bathroom. Privacy in the bathroom is very important at that age for a girl."

"I believe you."

"And this won't be a problem for your crew or Mr. De Meglio—Georgie—if you're occupied elsewhere?" She pointed to the others.

"Georgie?" Nick called out.

The producer pocketed his phone and trotted over. "You rang?"

"You and Larry and Clyde are capable of finding your own way for dinner tonight, right?"

"Actually I was just about to tell you that I have other plans, too."

Nick lifted his eyebrows. *"Que pasa, kimosabe?"*

"I'm meeting Mimi Lodge."

Nick whistled. "Mimi Lodge?"

Georgie shook his head. "It's not what you're thinking—whatever you're thinking. All I can say is, watch the nightly news broadcast this evening."

"A new war has broken out in Grantham that she needs to cover?" Nick asked only in jest.

"You're surprisingly close. But my lips are sealed," Georgie answered.

"Okay, so go. Go chase the Pulitzer. Meanwhile, the dynamic duo here." He turned to Larry and Clyde.

"Don't worry about us, boss," Larry said with a shake of his head. He pulled a baseball cap out of his jeans pocket and set it on his head. In brazen defiance to Nick's loyalties to the Yankees, it had a Boston Red Sox logo.

Clyde sidled over. "We heard mention of beer kegs earlier in your conversation." He waggled his eyebrows at Penelope.

Nick wasn't sure which one he should fire first.

"You were eavesdropping?" Penelope asked incredulously.

"Guilty as charged. Take me away, fair lady, I implore you." Clyde held out his wrists to Penelope as if waiting for her to handcuff him.

Penelope covered her mouth.

Nick growled, "Listen, you two losers, just don't let your imbibing get in the way of work tomorrow."

"Like you've never functioned on a hangover?" Larry asked. He adjusted his cap. He was clearly feeling feisty.

"All right, all right," he conceded. "As long as we stick to tomorrow's schedule." Nick was feeling generous. After all, she might not have invited him into her bed, but she had invited him into her house—for dinner. Almost as good.

Nick turned back to Penelope. "So it looks as if I'll be able to accept your gracious invitation after all. If the meal is anything like the food I had the other night at Justin and Lilah's, I will be more than content."

"Uh, yes. That's very kind, if I understand the metaphor correctly."

"Speaking of pigs—this time not metaphorically—is it true you make your own 'nduja? Justin and Lilah told me when I was at their place. Ever since then I've had a craving for it."

"Really?" She opened her eyes wide.

"I've been known to like things spicy."

She looked at him askance. "So I gathered." She paused. "Tell me, the 'nduja? Is that all you've been craving?"

Out of the corner of his eye, Nick saw the others leave the room. He smiled. "Actually, no." He wet his lips. "I have been craving you. Let me ask you. Do you believe in love at first sight? Instant infatuation?"

"I believe that when two people meet there's a possibility for an immediate chemical reaction characterized by elevated levels of dopamine, causing the symptoms of a racing heart and sweaty palms," she answered. "Norepinephrine can also produce intense energy and elation."

"So, I gather that's a kind of yes. You agree there can be this euphoria, a sense of excitement?"

"Mr. Rheinhardt, I may not relate socially to most people, but that doesn't mean I don't have normal biological urges."

"Toward me?"

"Most definitely."

"In which case, call me Nick. I think we've definitely advanced to a first-name basis. So that's settled."

"Not quite."

"Not quite?" He felt heartbroken. Forget his elevated cholesterol levels. *These* sudden mood swings were going to be the death of him.

"I agree that there appears to be a definite chemical-biological reaction going on between us. Nevertheless, from an ethical standpoint, I have a problem."

"I'm not married, if that's what concerns you."

"Through research into your background, I already know the details of your personal life—or as much as is available on the web. Besides, if someone had asked me to form an opinion from our limited contact to date, I would have hazarded the opinion that you do not appear to be a person who engages in long-term monogamous relations."

"I agree that I haven't been the most mature person in my relationships, but in my defense…"

Penelope cut him off. "I'm not concerned about your inabilities to commit."

"You're not?" Back came a sense of elation, followed inexplicably by a bruised ego. "You're not?"

"No, not at all. I'm not sure I believe in the possibility of a long-term relationship myself—biologically speaking. No, my concerns are far more immediate. Your daughter."

"My daughter? Yes, privacy could be an issue with her around, but I'm sure we could figure something out."

"The logistics are not what concern me. It's your relationship, or rather lack thereof."

"I've already confessed to being a lousy father. Though, I don't think that failure inhibits my performance in bed. At least, I hope not."

She smiled. "I like your sense of humor. I understand it—most of the time. No, I'm not talking about your abilities to please a partner in bed."

"That's a relief."

"It's more complicated than that. I find myself drawn to you but reluctant to go any further—"

Nick closed and opened his eyes as if he'd just tasted something extremely tart.

"Because," Penelope continued, "I am troubled by your lack of trust in your daughter."

"You want me to trust someone who's just been kicked out of school?" Nick pressed his hand to his T-shirt.

"Absolutely. It seems to me that she needs that more than anything. From your brief account of what happened, she acted out of friendship and honor. Those are traits to be commended. And yet you seem to spend most of your time expecting her to go astray. It appears to me that you don't give her enough credit. True, she acted rashly, but she is seventeen. You, on the other hand, have no excuse. You are thirty-seven, at least according to your website."

"Unless my mother and father lied to me, I believe that to be true." He was feeling highly defensive.

"I'm sorry. I don't mean to upset you. I can see that I've done that, which on the positive side indicates how well I seem to relate to you. And in my defense, I only mention all this because I actually have a very high opinion of your sense of forbearance."

He looked up. "You do?"

"No one who is not extremely kind and patient

would put up with me. Excuse the double negative, but I know that for a fact. I just wanted to point out the potential problems between you and Amara because I don't want to see either of you hurt. It's so fragile, you see—that relation between a father and daughter."

"You mean your reluctance to go to bed with me is because you want to help Amara and me?"

"I suppose that's one way of putting it. So I guess it's up to you, isn't it?" She pulled a pair of white gloves out of the pocket of her lab coat and pulled them on with a snap. Then she turned and carefully gathered up the books and manuscripts she had laid out for the shoot, and placed them carefully on a cart. Then she looked up. "By the way, say hello to Mike."

"Mike?" *Who the hell is Mike?*

"The pig farmer you're visiting? He supplied me with the pork for my 'nduja."

Nick rolled his eyes. "You're killing me with this talk of your 'nduja."

She smiled mysteriously.

Nick stepped forward.

She whirled around. Her shoulder brushed against his chest. She took a sharp intake of breath.

Nick stared at those two different-colored eyes of hers—one blue and innocent, the other green and sultry—and knew he was a goner.

"Just to clarify, tonight?"

"Tonight?" He felt his heart rate skitter around like a pinball.

"We won't be having 'nduja."

He hesitated. "Are you speaking metaphorically or literally now?"

"Literally. My parents are not inclined to spicy foods."

Nick waited for the shoe to drop.

"And they'll be joining us."

That's when the other shoe dropped—metaphorically speaking.

His phone rang.

CHAPTER FIFTEEN

AMARA HUNG UP THE PHONE and sighed.

Press ambled over to where she sat on the grass under a large hemlock. He'd taken off his T-shirt and was wiping the sweat off his chest. "Problems?" he asked, standing over her.

Amara gazed upward and gulped. Then she shook her head quickly. "Just the usual. My father said that after they finish up filming at some pig farm, I'm having dinner with him and Penelope and her parents. Then apparently I'm going to sleep at her place instead of bunking with my father." She shrugged. "I'd rather hang out with you."

It wasn't normal for her to be so obvious.

But then there was nothing normal about Press Lodge, as far as she could tell.

Other girls at her school might not have found single-sex education a detriment to their sex life. But it had sure slowed down hers. So at a couple of the dances, Amara had kissed some guys. Mostly it seemed pretty sloppy—too much saliva. And she wasn't quite sure what to do with her teeth. She'd only gotten her braces off two years ago.

Besides which, when your mother worked at the same school and sometimes chaperoned the dances, it was almost impossible to get past first base, no matter how hard you tried.

Only when she was at sleepaway camp last summer had she made it to second—petting on top, that is. There'd been this boy camper from Montreal. His name was Etienne and he was pretty cool. He had a lip ring and wore leather braided bracelets. She had liked him, even if he did quote Sartre in French. The French part wasn't the problem for Amara. She understood it perfectly well, even when Etienne felt obliged to translate.

No, as she listened, the problem was she never quite got Sartre's whole existentialist philosophy— that everyone is all alone, living in a world with no larger moral system. Amara was all for independence and not having to rely on other people. But at the same time, she yearned for a sense of cohesion, a comforting moral compass to help her navigate. Most of the time, she felt she was drifting, and she wanted some reassurance that she was doing okay.

But Etienne had said she just didn't understand Sartre. Amara quickly figured out that *he* didn't understand Sartre. Which is why she only let him get to second base.

It's not that she thought that losing her virginity was so big a deal. She just couldn't see sharing something so intimate with someone who seemed intellectually pretentious, and, well…maybe not as bright as she was. Even if he did have a cool lip ring.

But Press was different. Press was smart. And he didn't try to show off about it. When he talked about paleontology and what he wanted to study, it was because he was passionate about it—something she hoped she'd be one day. And Press was kind. He let her tag along and didn't make her feel as though she was younger or not worth talking to just because she hadn't gone to college yet. And Press was…well… Press was also incredibly hot.

He was going to be the one, she decided. Her first. Because he looked as though he knew what to do with his teeth, and probably other parts of his body. He was worth it.

She watched while he finished wiping the sweat off his chest and tucking the shirt in the back waistband of his shorts.

"Why would you rather hang out with me? Penelope's great. And besides, she's an amazing cook," he replied to her announcement. He seemed totally clueless to her thoughts. "Anyway, I couldn't make it tonight."

"What? You've got exciting plans or something? With your classmates, right? I suppose you want to spend as much time together before you all take off." She tried not to sound hurt.

"It's just that later tonight I'll be hanging out with some of the guys from my Social Club. And before that I gotta have dinner with my family." He ran his hand through his damp hair. "And believe me, you'd much rather be with Penelope and your father. I know I would."

"Penelope seems cool, but you don't know my father," Amara argued.

"Please, let's not get into a discussion of lousy fathers because, trust me, I'd win hands down. Like I said, you're better off on your own tonight."

Amara craned her neck up to get a better view of Press's expression. "You're not saying that because it's annoying to hang out with me, are you? 'Cause I can take a hint, you know."

Press squatted down next to her. "No, it's not that—not that at all. I mean, sure, I like you a lot. You're a nice kid." He placed his hand on her knee.

She looked down at it. "I'm not just a kid." She brought her gaze back to his. "I'll be eighteen in August."

Press gingerly removed his hand. "Listen, Amara, you may be mature for your age, but for now, you're still seventeen. There are some rules that can be bent. And then there are others engraved in stone. This is one of the stone kind. I like hanging out and all, but I don't want you to read too much into the time we're spending together."

"No problem. I get what you're saying." That didn't mean she was willing to give up. "But when you're cold and hungry in some remote Mongolian steppe…"

"Probably more like dying of the heat—it'll be summer," he corrected.

"Okay, dying of the heat," she repeated dramatically. "Whatever. Maybe then you'll take a moment to think of me, sitting around the pool at my new stepfather's house, wearing an itty-bitty bikini, oiling up to get a great tan." Amara only had a racing suit, but she wanted to conjure up a certain image.

She noticed Press wet his lips, so maybe it had worked.

But then he sprang to a standing position. "That sounds like fun. It'll be nice to know that you'll be relaxing. Maybe hanging out with your girlfriends, too. It's just what I'd want a little sister to do."

Ya think?

CHAPTER SIXTEEN

AS USUAL, PENELOPE'S parents arrived early.

Why was she not surprised?

Her father, Stanfield Bigelow—member of the Grantham University class of '68 and the Vivian Pierpoint Distinguished Professor of Classics at Grantham—liked to have his wife, Beatrice, make his martini at six. At six-thirty they dined on a meal consisting of clear soup, followed by a chop or roast chicken and overcooked green beans or, more recently, steamed kale. Everyone in her family always sat in the same chairs around the table in the small, formal dining room—her father at the head and her mother at the bottom. Her younger brother, Justin, used to slouch in the chair to her father's left. More often than not, he would gaze out the window. Penelope had sat opposite him, her posture erect, her back to the window. This position afforded a view of an eighteenth-century map of Asia Minor that her father had picked up as a graduate student while traveling in Italy. "A steal from a small bookshop in Naples, of all places," he would explain if a dinner guest made inquiries.

Penelope had always found this regularity comforting. But somehow when she was preparing dinner tonight she couldn't help wondering if Nicholas Rheinhardt always sat in the same chair night after night. She doubted it. He didn't seem the type to sit in the same dining room, let alone the same chair. That thought had made her smile. And it had also led her to act impetuously and drag her IKEA table outdoors.

Her small, whitewashed brick house was part of a faculty neighborhood close to Lake Vanderbilt. With the table moved to the terrace outside the French doors of her living room, they would be able to sit and survey the rolling lawn down to the lake. Watch the geese and canoeists and a sleek racing scull or two ply the otherwise tranquil waters.

Or rather, that had been the plan until her father and mother had shown up in their ancient Volvo station wagon. Even her brother Justin's miraculous way with cars would be hard-pressed to do anything about the layers of rust that edged the panels. Her father knocked loudly, accompanied by a cough.

Penelope opened the door. Stanfield took one look through the French doors at the table outside and announced, "But I always have my martini in the living room."

"Tonight we are dining outside, Father," Penelope replied cheerfully. "But you are welcome to have your martini in the living room if you wish."

She glided barefoot to the kitchen to take a chilled glass from the refrigerator. She already had the cocktail stirrer on the counter along with her father's favorite gin and vermouth. She could hear him harrumph behind her, but she told herself not to take any notice. Tonight would be different. And she smiled as she used the larger jigger to mix her father's drink.

She spied her mother through the kitchen window. Beatrice had tiptoed outside in her Birkenstock sandals to look at the table setting. An avid butterfly watcher on her husband's sabbatical stays to Greece and Italy, her mother floated silently, much like her favorite insect. She wore two barrettes on either side of her face to keep her graying hair out of her eyes. With each dipping step, the locks fanned out like wings.

"How positively charming," her mother cooed. "It will be like dining alfresco at Piazza Armerina in Sicily." She pointed with her finger as she counted the place settings. "Are your brother and Lilah joining us for dinner?" she asked, raising her voice.

Penelope returned to the living room with her father's martini in one hand and a glass of white wine for her mother in the other. "No, they are tied up with entertaining before Reunions this weekend. I've invited people I don't think you know—a former Grantham student, one year ahead of me, and his daughter."

Beatrice positively levitated through the open French doors in the direction of her drink.

"One year ahead? I wasn't aware you were friendly with any students ahead of you, let alone your own classmates." Her father took a sip of his drink. "No olive?"

Penelope tried not to feel hurt on both counts. "I thought lemon peel might be more appropriate for our picnic atmosphere. And, you are quite right, I don't keep up with people I went to school with, but I've recently been interacting with this person at the Rare Book Library."

"A professor?"

"No, a chef and travel critic. Perhaps you've read his books or seen his travel show? Nicholas Rheinhardt?" She turned to head back to the kitchen. "I'll just get the hors d'oeuvres."

"I don't read what passes for popular books these days and, as you know, we don't own a television."

"Didn't I see somewhere that he is the Class Day speaker, dear?" her mother asked in more mollifying tones.

"That's correct," Penelope said upon returning with a tray of antipasto—a colorful array of brine-cured olives, roasted red pepper and eggplant, scamorza and mozzarella cheeses and wafer-thin slices of mortadella and dried salami. "Mother, if you'd take the bowl of unsalted peanuts. I may not have Dad's usual cocktail olives, but I did remember the Planter's."

"Well, I can't imagine what someone like he wants with the Rare Book Library," her father said. He munched on the nuts.

"You'd be surprised, Father." The amused smile on her face grew larger.

"I'm sure you'll be able to share your experiences traveling in the classical world, Stanfield. And a daughter, you say?" her mother asked, turning to Penelope.

Penelope stood there holding the tray. "Yes, she's graduating from a very fine girl's prep school and will be matriculating to Grantham in the fall." No need to elaborate on any of Amara's current problems. "She's already quite a scholar of ancient Greek and Latin, Father. You shall have to talk to her about your courses."

Her father was comfortably ensconced in the armchair by the fireplace. "It will be my pleasure." Stanfield was at his happiest talking about his teaching and research, both of which had garnered wide recognition. "Speaking of teaching, I understand from a colleague at Berkeley that they will be advertising a position in the Classics Department next academic year. They're looking for a Latinist, midcareer, with a proven teaching and publication record. Naturally I thought of you."

"I'm quite happy where I am, Father," Penelope

said. "Being a curator is ideal for me. I now realize that my determination to get a master's degree in library science while I was in Chicago was actually quite fortuitous."

"On the contrary. It was time you could have better spent writing articles and attending conferences," her father reprimanded her.

Penelope looked around for someplace to put the tray that was out of striking distance of her father. Stanfield maintained a trim frame, but he had an amazing way of devouring food.

"Can I help you with anything?" Her mother rested her glass on a coaster on the coffee table. "We bought you these at Alinari in Florence, didn't we?" She pointed to the coasters.

"Yes, and I love them." It was a conversation they had every time her mother spotted them. "If you'd like to help, you could bring this tray to the table outside while I do some last-minute fussing in the kitchen."

"Nonsense." Stanfield continued taking no notice of the interchange between his daughter and wife. "Working in the library is all well and good, but for someone of your talents and intellect, we all know that a professorial position is far more appropriate."

Penelope walked to the kitchen to check on the swordfish pies cooking in the oven. She lowered the oven door and peeked at the crusts. They needed a few more minutes to turn properly golden.

Her father called out, "I didn't tutor you all those years so that you'd become a glorified cataloger."

Penelope closed the oven door and turned to wash the radicchio and baby greens. She had already made the vinaigrette dressing. As she opened a bottom cabinet in the tiny kitchen to get the salad spinner, she heard footsteps.

"Penelope, are you willfully trying to disappoint your mother?" It was her father. He was standing at the open door to the kitchen.

Penelope glanced over at her father and saw the empty glass in his hand. "Why don't I make you another martini?" She reached for the tumbler. "And, you know, Mother doesn't give any evidence of manifesting anxiety about my current employment."

The doorbell rang.

"Shall I get that?" her mother offered.

"Please." Penelope was busy mixing her father's drink. She heard voices coming from the front door. Her mother had always been an enthusiastic hostess for her father's students and colleagues.

"I believe Penelope is just busy in the kitchen," she could be heard announcing after clucking over Nick and especially Amara.

Penelope, her heart rate beating faster than normal, looked up as she handed her father his martini.

Nick, all six-foot-three of him, leaned past her father and gave her a kiss on the cheek.

Penelope's molars tingled. "You clearly found your way without any trouble," she managed to say, betraying only a little nervousness.

"Not only did I find my way, I come bearing gifts." He handed over a package wrapped in white paper. "Pork chops from Mike—who says hello, by the way." Then he stepped to the side, nodding in acknowledgement to Stanfield. "And here is one teenage daughter with backpack."

"Amara, I'm so glad you could join us. I'm very excited about the prospect of you staying with me. I can put your backpack in your room if you'd like."

"I'm sure Amara can do that herself. If you just point her in the right direction?" Nick then thrust out his hand. "You must be Penelope's father. Nicholas Rheinhardt. I actually took your survey Latin comedy course way back in the dark ages."

Stanfield gave him the once-over. "I don't remember you."

"You wouldn't. Your class met at nine in the morning, and I usually rolled out of bed at around noon, which, believe me, was not a commentary on the quality of your lectures. I was indiscriminate in my poor attendance record, I'm ashamed to say."

"I believe you," Stanfield said. He jiggled the ice cubes in his drink.

Penelope touched Amara lightly on her shoulder. "Why don't I show you the way? I think it might be easier."

"We can't all be scholars," she heard her father go on.

Nick laughed. "Probably a good thing for the academic job market, too."

No, she didn't need to worry. He could hold his own against her father.

She left Amara to unpack in the study, then returned to the living room. "I'd thought we'd eat outside. It's such a sublime evening."

Nick rubbed his hands together. "What a great idea. But first, let me help make some drinks. I see Professor and Mrs. Bigelow are already served. At least allow me to do my part for the chef and Amara. And, Mrs. Bigelow, be sure to save me a seat next to you. I want to hear all about raising Penelope."

"Please, call me Beatrice," she said.

Penelope swore she heard her mother giggle. She shook her head and headed for the kitchen. Time to remove the swordfish pies.

She was bent over, derriere in the air.

"The view out back may be lovely, but this is far superior."

Penelope turned her head. Nick was lounging against the doorjamb. She stood up, holding one of the pies between oven mitts, and carefully placed it on a nearby trivet. She repeated the motion for the second, rather enjoying his attention.

He stepped toward the countertop to inspect her handiwork.

"You're quite large and this kitchen is quite small," she commented as the side of his body brushed up against hers.

He turned. "Professional chefs are used to working in tight quarters. People are usually surprised to see the limited space that five-star chefs have to work with."

"I'm not a chef, five-star or otherwise."

Nick looked at her openly. "No, you're much more appealing. Mainly because you're not swearing like a drunken sailor, and let me tell you, no chef I know has legs like yours. And I say that not in a sexist way but as an appreciative gentleman."

Penelope was wearing a pale, floral sundress, and she'd pulled the top of her hair back in a small braid that hung down the back of her floaty locks. Her toenails were painted shell-pink.

"My descriptive capabilities seem to have abandoned me for the moment, so…so…I'll just say that you look lovely." He leaned in closer to her neck.

She thought he planned to kiss it. Penelope tilted her chin to make the move easier.

Then Amara barged into the kitchen unannounced. "Wow, Penelope, I can't believe the number of books you have."

Penelope and Nick jumped apart.

"Your father was just helping me take the dinner

out of the oven," Penelope said. And as if to show the evidence, she pointed with an oven mitt at one of the swordfish pies.

Nick bent dutifully. "It looks and smells delicious."

"I thought you said you were going to make the drinks?" Amara asked suspiciously.

"So I did. Thank you for reminding me." Nick rubbed his hands together. "What can I get you ladies?"

"There's a bottle of Prosecco in the refrigerator and champagne glasses on a tray on the counter." Penelope shifted the oven mitts to one hand and moved to turn the oven off.

"Definitely what the doctor ordered." Nick opened the refrigerator. "Right, Amara? After all, we need to celebrate your graduation."

"I wouldn't count on it." She wore a hangdog expression.

"Never fear. Nicholas Rheinhardt is here. I put in a call to your headmistress this afternoon, and while her schedule was full today, I have an appointment to speak with her Friday—that's tomorrow."

Pleased, Penelope smiled. Her eyes met Nick's.

"You called? I can't believe it." Amara seemed amazed.

Nick wet his upturned lips, then turned to his daughter. "I haven't worked my magic yet, but at least I'm not a total do-nothing dad. Who knows, maybe this summer we can even spend more time together?"

Amara was visibly excited. "That would be great. I mean, I'm going to spend time with Mom and Glenn and maybe take a language course later in the summer. But that still leaves some time for us to take a trip together, maybe to someplace exotic?"

Nick popped the cork on the Prosecco, the Italian version of champagne. It spewed out the top of the long-necked bottle, but he deftly caught the bubbly foam with the tip of a champagne flute. "We'll see about that, kiddo."

Penelope noticed he deflected answering Amara's question as expertly as he poured the drinks. "Amara, why don't you invite my parents to the table outside so we can begin with the antipasto? You can have a little Prosecco, too. This is a celebration after all." She handed the girl a glass.

She watched Amara hold her drink aloft, looking very pleased at being treated like a grown-up. Penelope also noticed that she had abandoned full-mourning clothing for a short white skirt and an orange print top with matching orange flip-flops. Aside from the neon-pink highlights, she looked exactly like a typical Grantham college girl. Interesting...

Penelope leaned out the kitchen door. "And be sure to ask my father what he's teaching in the fall semester. He is really quite gifted, and I think you'll be excited," she called to Amara.

Then she turned and narrowed her eyes at Nick. "That was very thoughtful of you to call Amara's school."

"Only trying to heed your advice." He passed a champagne glass to her and picked up one for himself. "Chin, chin." He offered the traditional Italian toast as he clicked the rim of his glass to hers.

She nodded in acknowledgment and sipped the sparkling wine. She always felt it was the epitome of summer weather. "You know, you should be careful building up her expectations about things you can't follow through on. You barely have her trust now," she reminded Nick.

"You're talking about her suggestion to go on vacation together?"

Penelope nodded.

He glanced out the kitchen window to the sound of voices drifting in from the backyard. "I didn't know what to say. I mean, I'm pretty booked, what with my shooting schedule and editing."

"That's not exactly what I meant."

"Okay, I'll look into it. See how much I value your advice?"

Penelope took another sip of wine. The bubbles tingled the roof of her mouth, and the gentle sweetness teased her palate. She stepped toward him, the thin material of her sundress close to the cotton of his checked dress shirt. The heat wafted off his body in dry waves. She regarded his face closely, noticed he must have recently shaved because there was a small nick under his jawline, and his skin smelled subtly of menthol. He had taken out the small hoop earring in his left lobe. The tiny piercing looked vulnerable. Had he done it for her or because he was going to meet her parents?

Either way, she smiled. "Why do I get the feeling that you're acting the role of the good father because the lure of sex with me is a powerful motivating force?"

He raised his eyebrows. "You're objecting?"

She smiled slyly. "Not at all. It's just that the more important reason for following up would be a sense of parental obligation."

"Excuse me, you're looking at the man who's always paid his daughter's bills on time—even in the lean years. Duty is practically my middle name."

She twirled the stem of her glass. "But is it duty based on love or duty based on guilt? Though, I suppose even the latter is better than doing it because it gives you a sense of self-satisfaction—that you're such a noble and caring father."

Nick stared at her. "You speak from personal experience?"

Penelope shook her head. "It's not as if I have children of my own." Then she twisted around and placed her glass on the tiled countertop. She did the same with his.

He slanted his head—a silent question.

She responded by placing her hands on his shoulders. "I believe you were in the middle of something when we were interrupted earlier?" She raised her chin.

"You know, there's something to be said for a woman with a good memory," he replied and lowered his head.

"I know." And her lips met his.

He tasted of wine and freshness, and he applied pressure here, then a nip there with the skill of a pro, but with the heart of a true believer. With each twist and turn, each exploration of her tongue, Penelope found herself in a process of discovery. She had anticipated the expertise.

She hadn't counted on the depth, the complexity, the feeling.

When they finally broke the kiss, Penelope realized she had backed up against the counter. His body was pressing into hers. The signs of his own arousal were noticeably evident.

"Oh, wow," he said. He exhaled through his mouth. "I think I might need a moment to regroup before we join the others."

She pushed back her hair from her forehead. Her skin felt hot, damp. "Yes, I know what you mean. Still, we mustn't take too much more time. After all, the first course is waiting." Penelope took a large breath, then picked up their wineglasses. She purposely led the way outside so as not to be tempted to pull him back into the kitchen and into her embrace.

He took a large stride and bent down to talk into her ear. "And here I thought that was the first course."

CHAPTER SEVENTEEN

THERE WAS SOMETHING magical about Penelope's
place, Nick thought. Take the coral-colored roses
climbing up the walls of the cottage. Or the beds of
blue and pink flowers, whose names he didn't know,
girding the foundation like an undulating shawl. Not
to mention the emerald-green grass sloping down
to the still water of the lake below. It could be rural
England. Or, better yet, a fairy tale.

For someone who professed to have zero social
skills, she was a natural hostess who seemed to
know how to make everyone feel comfortable and
important. He wouldn't have been surprised to find
tame animals shyly venturing forth from the woods
to partake of the food. Snow White had met her
match in Penelope.

It was pure magic, but then, he was purely smit-
ten.

And, boy, did her food contribute to his bliss.
The antipasto with the thin slivers of salami goodness and the tangy dark olives? Then there was the
swordfish pie, a delectable Sicilian mixture of sweet
and sour with raisins and olives again. The crust?

Talk about flaky. And one slice through its buttery goodness released an aroma as heady and sensual as the finest perfume. And, hey, you could eat it— no, savor it to your heart's content. As a food writer he could have gone on forever. As someone totally captivated with Penelope, he wanted to get up out of his chair at the foot of the table, push away the plates, dash aside the candlesticks and the center- piece of flowers from her garden and crawl animal- like across the white tablecloth, only to ravish her on the spot.

But seeing as Amara was sitting to his left and Penelope's parents to his right, that scenario might prove a bit awkward.

Speaking of awkward, did her father have to tell everybody what a hotshot professor he was? About all his awards and grants and books? Several times, no less?

Amara, bless her impressionable soul, lapped up Stanfield's stories. He could tell that she was en- tranced that she—not even a college undergradu- ate—was able to talk directly to a bigwig Grantham professor. Correction—that she occasionally was able to get in a word or brave a question before Pe- nelope's father launched into a soliloquy about yet another in the list of wonders that he'd achieved.

Nick wanted to pull his innocent daughter aside and explain that there was more to a person than the number of publications he had or how many

170   A RARE FIND

students he'd taught who were now CEOs or professors themselves. Sure, it was great to be smart and all. But things like decency and humility and caring were so much more important. Things that Penelope possessed in spades and her father never would.

Of course, until a few days ago, Nick had never considered trying to emulate these qualities. If only he could.

Penelope wasn't a tiny, lesser chip off the old paternal block, as Stanfield kept insinuating with his sly, underhanded digs. She was on a pedestal that stood far above him. And Nick wanted Penelope and Beatrice, but mostly Penelope's father, to recognize that.

"You know, your mastery of Italian cooking is really quite remarkable," Nick said.

"Coming from a professional chef, that's really quite a compliment, dear," her mother noted. She launched into her second serving of swordfish pie.

Nick quickly filled Beatrice's wineglass again. He had learned a happy Beatrice was a slightly tipsy one. "It tastes highly authentic," he added.

"Thank you. You're overly kind," Penelope replied. "I was lucky enough to live in Rome for two years after I finished graduate school. I was on a fellowship, and in between doing research at the Vatican Library and taking their paleography course, I managed to pick up a few pointers from acquaintances," Penelope said modestly.

Amara leaned toward her father. "Paleography is the study of old handwriting," she told him knowingly. "That's why Penelope can read all those ancient manuscripts."

Nick smiled at his daughter. She understood how special Penelope was, after all.

"Not just any fellowship—you won a Prix de Rome from the American Academy," her mother gushed. Her cheeks were turning a rosy-pink from the wine. "That's very prestigious." She nodded at Nick and Amara.

"We were all very pleased," her father chimed in.

For once, Nick thought the old man might be giving his daughter her due.

"Especially since I've been a Fellow of the Academy for years. So it's essentially as if she continued my tradition," Stanfield added.

No, the guy was an unmitigated schmuck, Nick reevaluated. He wasn't about to let Penelope be pushed to the side. "And your interest in southern Italian food? I seem to recall Justin or maybe it was Lilah saying that you had a house in Calabria?"

Penelope seemed to pause. "Yes, one of my classmates in the paleography program owned a house in Capo Vaticano. That's a promontory in the deep south that juts out into the Tyrrhenian Sea. Very spectacular and undeveloped, unlike much of what's happened along the coastline." She looked down at her empty plate—the fork and knife neatly laid side by side at a forty-five-degree angle. Then she raised her head. "He died rather unexpectedly and, quite surprisingly, willed the house to me. At the time, dealing with the Italian bureaucracy was rather interesting." She looked around the table. "Anyone for seconds or thirds? I warn you, there's dessert."

Nick figured there was more to that story than she was letting on. He was sure of it. He was curious about "the classmate." No, dammit, he was jealous, and he intended to get to the bottom of it. But not now. He'd bide his time. "It was delicious, but even I couldn't stuff any more in—especially with the prospect of dessert."

"But, Dad, I thought you didn't like sweets?" Amara commented.

"Seeing as Penelope has made it, I'll make an exception." And that's when Nick realized his daughter knew his eating preferences, but he didn't have the faintest idea about hers. For someone who placed a premium on eating and food, that was a sorry comment. He racked his brain for a memory, something he could link Amara with. Eureka! Pleased, he looked at his daughter.

"I seem to recall an incident with you and several slices of cheesecake at Carnegie Deli. Topped with blueberries, I believe," he said. Carnegie Deli was an institution on the Upper West Side of Manhattan.

"Da-ad," Amara wailed like only a child could, making her seem every one of her tender years. "I was ten at the time. And it was cherries, not blueberries." Then she turned to Penelope and ventured, "I don't mean to pry, but your house in Calabria? I saw a photo in the study, when I put my stuff down. Was that taken there?"

"Why, yes." Penelope looked pleased, even relaxed as she cocked her head. "I took it from the pool on the hill above the house. You can see the tiled roof of the house, then the edge of the cliff and the private beach below. In the distance is the island of Stromboli."

"Stromboli? Like the Rossellini film with Ingrid Bergman?" Nick had a thing for Ingrid Bergman, and now as he looked at Penelope, he could almost see a resemblance. Not the features, per se, though her nose had the same long line and slightly flared nostrils. The real similarity came when she smiled. Her mouth turned up with the same mixture of innocent gaiety and wily seduction. Then there was the way the light of the setting sun ringed her head and gave her this luminescence. Her wonderful, crazy-colored eyes almost glittered and her pale skin glowed.

Jeez, he was a goner.

"Did you know that the volcano of Stromboli was mentioned back in ancient times?" Stanfield broke through Nick's reverie. "In fact, the name Stromboli is actually a corruption of the ancient Greek *strongule,* meaning a round, swelling form."

At the mention of round, swelling forms, Nick found himself staring at Penelope's breasts. Embarrassed, he lifted his cloth napkin and patted his lips. He furtively glanced around the table to see if anyone had noticed. Stanfield seemed to be engrossed in himself. Beatrice was slowly sipping wine and gazing out over the lawn. Amara was dutifully stacking the dirty dishes. Then he turned to Penelope.

Penelope rose slowly from her chair. He could tell that she was aware of where his eyes and thoughts had strayed. And he could see she wasn't flustered, nor did she pretend to be embarrassed. Instead she breathed in and out slowly and evenly, her chest rising and falling. She wasn't shrinking away by any stretch of the imagination.

"The house sounds fantastic," Amara prattled on, oblivious to the sexual tension. She stood to carry the plates inside. "It would make a great vacation, don't you think?" She looked at Nick.

He shook his head, breaking the spell, and focused on his daughter. "We'll talk about it later. For all we know, Penelope is staying there herself or has booked it for the summer. By the sounds of it, she must have plenty of takers, with that spectacular location."

"And don't forget the open-air shower in the center of the house," Penelope added.

She was killing him. And from the glint in her eye she was enjoying it.

Stanfield cleared his throat dramatically.

All heads turned. It would have been impossible not to.

CHAPTER EIGHTEEN

"PENELOPE, BEFORE WE GET sidetracked with things like infinity pools and vacation homes—mind you, our family has never been acquisitive in terms of property, so the whole idea of a vacation home is quite a mystery to me—I think we need to get back to our conversation from before this dinner," Stanfield insisted. "I'm referring of course to the search for an associate professor at Berkeley."

"Let me just finish clearing the dishes, and then I'll bring in the dessert and coffee, Father," Penelope responded in an even-tempered tone.

The woman was a saint, Nick thought, and he followed her into the kitchen along with Amara. "Where do you want these?" He looked around the limited counter space.

"Just put the dishes and silverware in the sink. I'll rinse them and load the dishwasher."

"I think I can handle that." He looked at his daughter. "Why don't you bring in whatever else is left on the table—and don't forget the salt and pepper shakers."

"Gee, you act like you own a restaurant or something." Amara headed back outside.

"Cheeky little thing," he said to her back.

"She's a wonderful girl. You should be very proud," Penelope declared.

Nick twisted the water spigot on and held a plate under the faucet. "You know, I am. It's a work in progress, but I *am* actually a proud father. And you're a very good influence on me." He bent down and lowered the door to the dishwasher.

He'd never seen a more meticulously organized space in his whole life. He whistled. "This is incredible. You've separated the forks and spoon and knives into separate baskets. I've never seen that."

"It's one of my peculiarities. You'll also observe that I separate the dessert and dinner forks into two different compartments, as well as the soupspoons from the teaspoons." She moved next to him and pointed.

He investigated further. "I notice that the front basket holds serving utensils." He glanced up at her. "Even though they're all serving pieces, doesn't it bother you to mix the forks with the spoons?"

"You're right. Unfortunately there aren't enough baskets to separate them," she explained frankly. As he bent upright, their noses practically touched. "Oh, you're making fun of me?" She didn't seem hurt nor particularly surprised.

"Only a little, and in the nicest way possible." If he moved an inch, he'd be able to kiss her. Again.

She handed him a spatula. "Please, wipe the plates down first in the garbage can under the sink before you rinse." She straightened up.

He got the cue, and straightened up himself. Still, there was a broad smile on his face. "You know, I would have loved to have filmed this dinner for my show."

She boxed up the leftovers and put the containers in the refrigerator. From a top shelf, she removed a bowl of crème fraîche and took off the plastic wrap. "No, you wouldn't have, not with my father."

"You're right."

In companionable silence, they worked side by side. He scraped and loaded the rest of the dishes. She filled a creamer and placed it on a tray along with a sugar bowl and several neat rows of demitasse cups. A small vase held the tiny spoons.

Amara returned with the basket of bread, with Beatrice close on her heels.

Penelope took the basket. "Oh, thank you, Amara. If you'd just bring this tray to the table, I'll be out as soon as I put up the coffee."

"My goodness, what have you made for us?" Beatrice stuck her nose close to the dessert and sniffed. She poked one of the pieces of fruit in the golden-colored cake with her index finger.

"It's a *torta alle prugne,* a cake with prunes," Penelope answered. "The dried prunes are poached in a syrup of red wine. Speaking of which, Mother, do you think you and Father would like some *vin santo* to go with dessert?" She referred to the sweet dessert wine.

"Not for me, dear. I've probably drunk enough."

Not nearly enough, Nick thought.

"But I'm sure your father would enjoy a glass. Meanwhile, I'll take the cake out for you," Beatrice offered. She wobbled a bit as she reached for the cake stand.

Penelope shot Nick a glance behind her mother's back.

Nick put down the dishcloth and rushed to Beatrice's side. "Why don't I do that, Beatrice? That way you can tell me all about your plans for this summer," he said deftly.

"What a gentleman. Let's see, of course we'll be in Oxford again," she began, tripping from the kitchen into the living room as she toddled back to the table outside.

Nick, holding the cake and a stack of dessert plates, looked over his shoulder.

"Thank you," Penelope mouthed. She made drinking motions.

He nodded vigorously.

She smiled, then a few minutes later she joined them with another tray with a tall Italian coffee-maker, a bottle of dessert wine and three small wineglasses. "Coffee? *Vin santo?*" she offered as she poured. "I know you'll have both, Father." And then in almost the same breath, she added, "And as to your earlier comment about the opening at Berkeley, I'm not comfortable teaching in front of a class." She handed him a cup first. "I believe the sugar and milk are on your right."

She picked up another cup. "In fact, when I was originally asked to give a short talk during Reunions in conjunction with the exhibition, my first reaction was to refuse. But then I had an inspiration and invited my student assistant to give it instead."

Amara perked up. "Press is talking?"

"Yes, Saturday afternoon," Penelope answered. "You might be interested to know, Father, that the Grantham Galen has pride of place in the exhibit."

"That's good to hear." Stanfield downed his coffee then tackled the dessert wine. "I still remember purchasing it at that strange antiquarian book shop in Italy, the same place I got the map that hangs in our dining room. I specifically recall negotiating the price of the map down to ten thousand lire from twenty, roughly ten dollars in those days. I said I was just a poor student and wanted to give it to my professor." He chuckled at his ruse.

"I know you always recount that story, Stanfield, but it suddenly occurs to me that you may have bought it in Berlin, or rather West Berlin as it was known back then." Beatrice touched her lips with her finger and frowned. "Do you remember how we took a side trip from Rome so you could work in the library? There was a little curio shop in the Dahlem district, of all places—where the American troops were housed."

Stanfield shook his head. "No, I'm quite sure I got it in *Napoli*." He used the Italian name for Naples.

Lousy accent, Nick thought.

Beatrice made an undulating dismissive hand motion. "You are probably right, dear. I'm afraid the alcohol has gone to my head. Though, I do remember the Dahlem neighborhood. How could I not? Quite leafy, with some lovely homes that the Nazis had confiscated from the Jews during the war. So sad." She blinked with concern.

"Yes, well, history, as I know only too well from my studies, is full of distressing moments," her husband said. "Still, it's nice to hear that you appreciate my gift to the university. Nevertheless, Penelope, I will not be sidetracked. I wish you'd reconsider, about Berkeley, that is."

For the first time, Nick saw Penelope sigh. But then she straightened her shoulders. "At the risk of repeating myself, I'm not gifted in the way you are, and I believe it is ill-advised for me to pursue that position," she replied.

"You're just gun-shy because you didn't get

tenure at University of Chicago," Stanfield argued. "Not that they didn't have a reasonable case, seeing as you had yet to publish your thesis." He slapped the table with his palm.

Penelope, who was sitting at the head of the table with her father on her left, didn't blink. "It might interest you to know that I have just signed a contract with Grantham University Press. And you should be doubly interested because it's for an annotated monograph on the Grantham Galen."

"My, my." Her father seemed taken aback.

"And now I think it's time for a celebration," she announced, opening a small box of party candles that were on the tray. She placed them in the cake in a perfect circle, then took the box of matches and lit each one in order.

"Goodness, how sweet," Stanfield concurred, looking quite jovial. "It's a wonderful idea to celebrate the fact that my donation will finally get the recognition it deserves." He leaned forward and blew out the candles.

There was silence.

Finally Beatrice, blinking rapidly, cleared her throat and turned to her husband. "Actually, Stanfield, if I remember the date correctly, I think the candles might have been in honor of Penelope's birthday."

"You never mentioned it was your birthday," Nick uttered.

"It's no big deal," she said. "In fact, Father's right. It really is a celebration of multiple events—the future publication of the manuscript you donated, Father, as well as Amara's matriculation to Grantham. Besides, I don't usually make a fuss over my birthday, but it was sweet of you to remember, Mother."

Beatrice touched her cheek. "How could I forget? The timing, you see. I remember how worried I was that you'd be born before your father's classes and exams were over. But as it turned out, you arrived right after he'd finished grading the last exam booklet. You were always such a cooperative child."

Nick didn't know whether to hug Beatrice or weep in his *vin santo*. Somehow Penelope's birthday—her birth for that matter—had ended up being all about her father. And yet she handled it so calmly. If it had happened to him, Nick could have easily imagined a torrent of obscenities, coupled with some rash, if ill-timed, blows.

"Maybe you could light the candles again and we could all sing 'Happy Birthday'?" Amara suggested.

"That's all right." Penelope laid a hand on the tablecloth next to Amara's. "I think I'd prefer to celebrate by cutting the cake. And as the youngest person here, you deserve the first piece. Shall I cut a big one?" She picked up the cake knife. "You tell me where to cut."

Amara leaned over and the two practically bumped heads as Amara murmured instructions.

As he watched the two women in his life, Nick sensed a very contented feeling settle over him. It was something he wasn't accustomed to.

All of a sudden, Beatrice stood up and announced, "I'll be back," and she floated into the living room, returning a moment later with a canvas satchel. The words Recording for the Blind and Dyslexic were stamped in large letters on the front of the bag.

"Here you are, Penelope. A copy of my book on the wildflowers of Crete. For your birthday."

Penelope finished cutting the next piece of cake for her father, then calmly placed the cake knife on the plate. She took the slim hardcover between her hands and glanced through the book. "Why, it's lovely, Mother. I've always admired your watercolors so much. Now please, have a seat and I'll cut you a piece of cake. The cream to go with it is somewhere on the table, I believe." She glanced around. "Yes, I see Father is one step ahead as usual and has already located it."

Stanfield spooned a large dollop on his serving. "This doesn't look like whipped cream." He sniffed at the bowl.

"How very observant." Penelope went back to placidly cutting the rest of the cake. "It's crème fraîche, a unique variation on the traditional recipe that I decided to try out for tonight."

Stanfield grunted, but that didn't stop him digging into his cream-laden portion with gusto. Then he lifted his head, unaware that there was a dab of white on the corner of his mouth. "Penelope, I still think—"

Nick couldn't take it anymore. Penelope might have been a saint when it came to her parents, but no one had ever accused him of showing any heavenly tendencies. He pushed back his chair. "Excuse me for interrupting, Professor, but I think this wonderful meal and special occasion calls for a toast. Here, let me fill your glass again so you can join in properly." He generously filled Stanfield's glass to the brim before raising his own. "To Penelope and all her unique variations. She makes giving a splendid dinner party seem as effortless and as welcoming as she makes old manuscripts seem relevant and exciting to even an ignoramus like myself."

"Hear! Hear!" Amara bounced to her feet, as well. Only, she raised a water glass.

Penelope shyly nodded in acknowledgment to everyone around the table and raised her own glass in return. "Thank you all for coming. I know I'm not particularly good at registering people's emotions, but I do believe that the evening has been a success." She looked at her father. And before he could say anything, she added, "You need more dessert, Father. Another piece?"

Stanfield's eyes brightened and his thick eyebrows waggled. "Don't mind if I do."

Catering to her father's sweet tooth. Maybe that was her way of winning an argument, Nick realized.

CHAPTER NINETEEN

"THEY DON'T APPRECIATE her enough. Not even remembering it was her birthday," Amara said from the front passenger seat. Her father needed to work out the arrangements for tomorrow before he drove off. But first she just had to comment on the dinner conversation. "It was so thoughtless," she added vehemently.

He drummed his thumbs on the steering wheel and glanced over. "You're pretty smart for a kid, you know that? You must take after your mother."

Amara rolled her eyes. "Why do you say things like that? I hate it. *You're* the Grantham alum. I'm pretty sure the smarts come from your side of the family."

"I'm the Grantham dropout, and don't underestimate your mother. She successfully raised you as a single parent, went back and got her degree, a job and, by all accounts, a swell second husband. Anyway, I think that most women are smarter than men—at least they're not as clueless."

"Yeah, Penelope's definitely smarter, even when it comes to people," Amara agreed. "You know that book her mother gave her? Her drawings of flowers?"

"Yeah." Nick put the keys in the ignition and turned on the engine. It was pitch-black outside except for a street lamp at the end of the block. With the car in Park, he turned on the overhead light. "Kind of an unusual birthday gift," he added.

Her father's face was cast in shadows. He was kind of handsome as dads went, Amara confessed to herself. Still, what she wanted to say wasn't about him. "Well, when I was looking at her books in the study, I saw that Penelope already had two copies. You think her mother forgot that she'd already given them to her?"

Nick seemed to consider the question. "I think you could be right. Her mom probably has boxes of copies from the publisher. Beatrice just seems a little flaky, but I'm sure she meant well, though."

Amara nodded thoughtfully. "Penelope was so good about it—the way she didn't say anything. I mean, if it had happened to me, I'd have probably mouthed off about that being the only present my mom ever seemed to give me. I'd probably even go get the other two copies."

Nick chuckled. "Yeah, I can't see you standing silently by."

"Penelope's a good daughter, isn't she, Dad?"

"You're right about that, sweet pea."

He hasn't called me that since I was little, Amara thought.

He reached up and rubbed her cheek with the back of his knuckle. "But you're a good daughter, too. You know that, don't you?"

"Even when I screw up like getting thrown out of school?" she reminded him.

"Even then." He hesitated as if searching to say something more. But all he said was, "You better hop out now. I don't want you to keep Penelope up too late in there. She's had a long evening and still has work tomorrow."

"About tomorrow. I had promised Noreen Lodge, back when I was staying at the pool house, that I would babysit her daughter, Brigid, in the afternoon. She only has a half day of school this time of year, and Noreen has work. But if you need me to be with you…"

He shook his head. "No, why don't you do that. It'll be a good change from hanging around with me, bored out of your skull. Just give me a call, and I'll come and drop you off at the Lodges', say, eleven. That's before this lunch thing I'm shooting."

"Okay, sounds good." Amara squeezed her lips together. Did he expect her to kiss him good-night? she wondered. But then he flicked the light off, and she figured it was her cue to leave. No kiss. She was surprised it bothered her a little.

She pushed down on the handle and opened the

car door. Then she jumped down and turned to close it shut. She hesitated. "I'm glad you're letting me stay with Penelope, by the way. I'll appreciate her. You will, too, right? I mean, you'll figure out something to give her for her birthday? It's only fair."

"I'm gonna try, sweet pea. I'm gonna try."

CHAPTER TWENTY

"So, DID YOU CATCH the six o'clock news, then? The segment I filmed with Mimi Lodge and Vivian Pierpoint?" Georgie buttonholed Nick as he opened the door to his hotel room. Georgie's own room was right next-door, and he stood there in bare feet, pajama bottoms and a Knicks T-shirt that stretched across his round stomach. Without waiting for an invitation, he padded into Nick's room.

Nick threw his key card on the console table and turned down the thermostat to kick the air-conditioning up a notch. He was still thinking about how awful Penelope's father was to her. Stanfield seemed to think that Penelope had done nothing her whole life but please him, including when she was born.

And what did she get in return?

A third copy of her mother's book on wildflowers and criticism from her father that she wasn't his clone. All Stanfield wanted was a professional Mini Me as justification for his own existence.

What an ungrateful bastard. He should be dancing for joy that he had such a talented and loyal daughter. If Nick had had a daughter like that…

Nick paused that thought in midsentence. *Hang on.* He *did* have a daughter like that. Amara was smart and sensitive. And even when she screwed up it was with good intentions in mind. She just fouled up on the details. But then, she was a kid.

And as Penelope had pointed out, he was the adult. And he was the one who regularly screwed up—and it wasn't just in the details. He didn't remember Amara's birthdays, he never went to see her in school plays. He didn't know who her friends were. Had never read her bedtime stories. Hadn't taught her to swim or ski, let alone how to drive.

So the question was, what had he ever done to deserve her?

Nick tapped on the thermostat dial. "What's that?" he asked Georgie, only half-aware that his friend had said something.

"Jeez, Nick. I ask you about something that's important to me, and you can't even pretend to pay attention? I thought spending time here with old friends and Amara and even that wacky librarian lady—"

"Penelope's not a wacky librarian lady. And you can think what you want, but for a change, I wasn't being self-absorbed—more like self-eviscerating." Nick turned. "So tell me, what's so important?"

"This segment I shot for the evening news with Mimi and Vivian Pierpoint? You know, the woman who's running for governor of Connecticut?"

"Oh, yeah, the hoagie lover. She's a big mover and shaker at the University, too. Mucho successful, obviously. Those diamond earrings she wears—she practically needs scaffolding to hold them up they're so big."

Nick saw the scowl form on Georgie's face and realized he had overstepped in his comments. Apparently Georgie thought highly of *La* Pierpoint. Somehow he didn't think that it was a shared vision of cutting healthcare costs that was driving this closeness.

"Sorry," he apologized, plopping on the end of the bed. The chambermaid had already pulled it down for the night. A complimentary chocolate waited for him on a pillow.

"It's been a long evening," Nick confided. And since his daughter got to be Penelope's sleepover buddy and not him, it was a long evening not culminating in any benefits. "What about Ms. Pierpoint? You mentioned something big? I hope she's all right?" Nick's inquiry sounded lame even to his ears. But just making the effort seemed to mollify his producer.

Georgie sat in the desk chair and rolled it closer to the bed. "You know she's married, right?"

Nick dredged through his memory. In general, he took no notice of political machinations. If he was being honest—which he seemed to be at the moment, *finally*—it was because he had always

194

been too selfish to think about the common man and what he could do to make any difference. He was ashamed to say that he couldn't remember the last time he'd voted.

But now, with Georgie sitting there in obvious distress, he closed his eyes and willed himself to recall what he could. "Isn't her husband some bigwig French businessman who's also an animal-rights activist? Saving porpoises or something?"

Georgie gripped the arm of the chair. "He's Belgian. And it's bears. Saving bears in Russia. Problem is, his efforts closer to home aren't so tremendous. It seems the bum was *shtupping* the live-in dog walker—who is not of legal age, to boot."

"What? The louse was doing it with a minor? That must be illegal in any number of states—even Connecticut."

"Especially Connecticut, but apparently not in France where the two were headed when Vivian notified the girl's parents, who in turn notified the authorities. Can you say, 'Stop this flight from taking off in the name of the law'?"

Nick shook his head. "No, but apparently, federal officers can. So Ms. Pierpoint must be devastated?"

"I'd say she's moved beyond the stunned stage. I'd say that *white-hot anger* is more apt."

"So she's not planning on standing at her husband's side during his arraignment?"

"Are you kidding? No, that's why I was called in

to film the interview with her and Mimi Lodge. It was preemptive."

"Glad to know that Mimi can go from foreign battleground to marriage battleground."

"Hey, Vivian asked her to do it as a favor—friend of the family and all."

"Some family." Nick shook his head.

"Anyway, Mimi asked me on the spur of the moment since she knew I was in Grantham and she wanted the scoop. So, live on the evening news, Vivian went on about wanting to seek justice, especially to protect the rights of a minor. She's even offered to pay for a legal team to represent the girl in the event that Monsieur Renard's team of high-priced lawyers try to smear her."

"And here I thought this Grantham gig was going to be a snooze fest." Nick attempted to take it all in. "Boy, was I ever wrong. The thing of it is, I'm still trying to figure out how we can work what you're telling me into our episode."

Georgie rolled the desk chair away. It banged against the edge of the desk. "Hey, I don't want you making snarky remarks on the show about how the mighty, especially Vivian Pierpoint, have fallen."

"I don't know why you're all hepped up over Vivian Pierpoint. She's an adult with plenty of resources at her disposal. I'd be more worried about the girl. I mean, think of it. She's somebody's

daughter, you know." Strange—or not so strange—
where his mind seemed to have wandered.

"Well, Vivian might be all grown-up and have
money to burn. But that doesn't mean *she's* not
somebody's daughter, too. At times like this, she
needs all the support she can get."

If Georgie didn't look so sincerely upset, Nick
would have made one of his usual wisecracks.

Instead he thought of Penelope. By any stretch of
the imagination, she was all grown-up—certainly
professionally accomplished and financially secure.
Yet even she was subject to abuse, well intended as
it might be, from her father. Her father of all people!

So in the end, Nick actually tried to demonstrate
a modicum of understanding, which, surprisingly,
wasn't as difficult as he might have expected. "It
makes you wonder who you can trust, doesn't it?"
he asked.

To which Georgie nodded philosophically.

"Tell you what," Nick continued. "Let me know if
there's anything we can do for her. I know she says
she's more concerned about the girl, but she doesn't
deserve such a raw deal."

Georgie glanced up, a look of surprise on his
face. Then that softened. "Thanks, buddy. I'll let
her know."

For a few moments, the two sat there in silence.
Georgie thinking whatever he was thinking. Vivian
and what he could do to help her, was Nick's best

guess. And Nick? He was still thinking of Amara and what he'd missed. But mixed with the guilt was the sense of urgency—an urgency having to do with Penelope.

She was tied up all day tomorrow at the Rare Book Library, including helping Press prepare for his talk at the exhibit. But she had promised that the night was his.

They were scheduled to film at Lion Inn. Besides the usual kick-off dance for Reunions, the club was also sponsoring a Beer Pong contest. It promised to make great television.

And if he had anything to say about it, it would also make the perfect prelude to a great evening.

CHAPTER TWENTY-ONE

"YES, LADIES AND GENTLEMEN, behold Beer Pong—
the sport of tipsy college kids everywhere and, it
appears—" Nick pointed at the Reunions throng
crowded around a long piece of plywood atop two
wooden sawhorses "—of today's captains of in-
dustry and financial wizards. Come to think of it,
maybe this explains something about why our economy is in the state it is."

Nick stood in the games room on the second
floor of Lion Inn, a spacious stucco, half–timber
and stone building that combined architectural ele-
ments of a Tudor manor and an old-world hunting
lodge. The cameras were rolling.

From downstairs, the sound of the band carried
through the thick plaster walls and wood paneling.
The festivities were just getting started. Members of
this year's graduating class and the corresponding
tenth-year Reunion alums were yet to arrive since
they were still in the grips of the annual softball
battle. Nick was only glad his weary body would
not be required to do anything more strenuous than

attempt to throw a Ping-Pong ball in a plastic cup. How hard could that be?

"As many of you may know from reading such illustrious publications as *The Wall Street Journal* and *Time*—not to mention *ESPN The Magazine*—Beer Pong is practically a national pastime," Nick went on, looking askance at the camera. "Alas, owing to my previous insistence of not diluting my drinking with any form of physical activity, I have not yet had the privilege of playing. This omission is about to be remedied."

He turned to two men standing next to him. They both looked mildly embarrassed. "With me, I have here two Beer Pong experts who are going to explain the rules of the game. The only reason they've agreed to be on camera is because they had the misfortune of being two of my freshmen advisees when I was a junior at this institution. That was before persons in authority realized I was not to be trusted." Nick mugged for the camera. "Anyway, since I am privy to information from their pasts that would be damaging to their current careers, they basically had no choice."

Nick held up his hand. "Welcome, Justin and Hunt. Since you're both ex-jocks, I know you must be experts at this, right?"

Justin rolled his eyes, and Hunt nodded his head.

"So give me some insight so I don't make a complete fool of myself," Nick instructed.

Justin gingerly walked closer to the end of the table. "Basically there are two teams that stand at either end of the table, and the object of the game is to toss a Ping-Pong ball—" he picked one up "—into one of the cups of beer at the other team's end." A triangular array of six red plastic cups was positioned at each end. Beer filled each cup about halfway up.

Justin demonstrated by shooting the ball down the length of the table. He missed. "Oops."

"Hey, I may actually stand a chance!" Nick observed.

Hunt scooped up the ball before it bounced off the table. "I think I may need a new partner," he joked.

Justin ignored him. "Now, if this were an actual game, I'd have to drink one of the beers at my end since I missed."

"So what happens if a ball actually goes in one of those?" Nick asked.

"If Justin managed to put one in," Hunt remarked, "then someone from the other team would be obliged to drink that cup of beer."

Nick rubbed his hands together. "This sounds like my kind of sporting event. So, if I understand correctly, the winning team is the one that has at least one beer cup remaining on their side while the other team has had all theirs knocked out?"

"Exactly," Justin said. "So shall we get started?" He picked up a ball and started bouncing it on the table, catching it neatly on each rise. "My suggestion is that Justin and I play as one team. That way we just need to find someone for you to play with, Nick." He peered around the room for likely suspects.

"How about I play with Hunt and you look for someone?" Nick retorted.

"But Hunt and I *always* played together as a team back in college. Everybody knows you can't break up a team." He looked at Nick with an expression that declared there was no room for compromise.

"Why do I get the feeling I'm being set up here?" Nick joked for the camera. Nick sought out Georgie with his gaze. The producer never seemed to tire of seeing his on-air talent make a fool of himself, and he didn't bother to restrain his obvious glee.

Irritated, Nick shifted his eyes around the room. Spectators watching the filming leaned against the walls or lounged in the tired-looking leather chairs. He tried to see if Mimi Lodge was in the audience. He remembered that she'd been a jock in college, and she clearly was no novice in front of the camera. Mimi was nowhere to be found.

But that's when he saw whom he wanted.

Without breaking stride, he maneuvered around some onlookers and zeroed in on a slim figure trying to disappear into the bank of photos displayed on the walls. They portrayed the members of Lion Inn Social Club through the successive years, dating well back to the forties when young men posed in suits and ties, in stark contrast to today's coed and multicultural members.

"I pick you," Nick announced. He shot out a hand and pulled the unwilling person toward the lights.

"Why on earth would you choose me?" Penelope protested under her breath. The soles of her black patent-leather ballet shoes slipped across the hardwood floor. In preparation for the potential for spilled liquids, the ancient Persian rug had been rolled up against one wall.

Penelope looked at him with abject fear in her eyes. "As I am sure you have already guessed, I am not an athletic sort of person. Unlike my brother, I might add." She nodded in Justin's direction.

"Don't worry. We have a secret weapon," Nick confided.

"We do?" She looked at him dubiously.

Larry moved the camera closer to her face.

She sent a panicked glance to Nick. "We do?"

"Sibling rivalry," he declared in a stage whisper. "There's no way you're going to lose to your little brother, now, is there?"

She narrowed her eyes. "When you put it that way."

Frankly it was the only way that Nick could think of at the moment. What he wanted to say, he couldn't. The reason he'd asked her to come to Lion Inn this evening—insisted, really—was that all day he'd been thinking of her. No amount of locally farmed orange-colored beets, or veal from grass-fed calves that had been kissed on the nose before being slaughtered, could command his attention.

Because he knew, just like he knew she knew, that tonight was the night they would be together.

So, all right, a round of Beer Pong humiliation was not his usual form of foreplay. But then, Penelope was not usual. And, come to think of it, up until now, he had never really thought about the whole concept of "romancing." He'd always just somehow fallen into bed, smoothly or, admittedly in some cases, awkwardly. But the notion of wooing had never entered the equation. Until now...

Maybe that's why Beer Pong seemed about as good a place to start as anywhere.

"C'mon," he coaxed her. "It'll be fun. Well, maybe not fun, but at least potentially amusing. Trust me."

And seemingly she did.

CHAPTER TWENTY-TWO

THIS WHOLE BEER PONG competition was just the type of activity that Penelope had shied away from her whole life. When it came to conquering tough intellectual challenges she was more than eager. But anything that involved physical competition or team play? Not so much. Homeschooling under her father's ever-watchful eyes might have produced a prodigiously gifted academic. But it did nothing for this kind of event.

Scared out of her wits, Penelope realized the sudden pain in her right temple was due to the way she was maniacally grinding her teeth. "Nick," she said, unhinging her jaw.

"C'mon, it'll be fun," he said with a wink.

Yes, a wink. And like that, Penelope felt her heart flutter. And that's when she knew. Here in the overcrowded, noisy, hot games room of Lion Inn—a place she had never set foot in all her four years of college—she had found love.

How else to explain the way Nick gave her the courage to do the impossible? And that's when she also realized that she didn't want to let him down. Because for some reason, she trusted him.

So, albeit nervously, she shook her head and stepped toward the Beer Pong table. "All right. 'Damn the torpedoes. Full speed ahead.'" She quoted Admiral Farragut.

"Just so long as they don't bring in the big guns," Nick joked. He positioned her close to his side, then looked across the table at Justin and Hunt, who were confidently grinning. "Okay, hotshots. Seeing as we're strangers in these parts, we'll let you go first."

"Great." Justin picked up a Ping-Pong ball and dipped it in another cup of amber liquid—presumably beer—that was positioned at the side of the table. He shook it before holding it aloft.

"Hey," Nick protested. "Is that legal?"

"It's all according to house rules," Hunt assured him. He folded his hands over his T-shirt, a faded Grantham Lightweight Crew shirt. With almost zero body fat the strength of his sinewy arms was intimidating. The easy smile, which seemed all nice and friendly, paradoxically added to the fear factor.

"Why do I feel we're being suckered?" Nick said out of the side of his mouth to Penelope.

"You're only figuring that out now?" She put one hand to her mouth as she studied the board and her brother's motions. Justin bounced his shot in the middle of the table. It ricocheted up, arcing over their triangular array of cups. As the white ball descended in flight, it ticked off a rim of one cup, just missing its target.

The crowd oohed.

Nick held up his hands in protest. "Hey, now I know we've been hoodwinked. You never mentioned anything about bouncing the ball."

Justin laughed and began drinking one of the beers. "I happen to prefer the bounce shot, but you can make your pitiful attempts at our cups any way you want—a fastball or slow pitch. Whatever." Then he leaned forward. "House rules say we alternate. So it's up to one of you." He looked at his partner, bobbing his head confidently. "Like we have anything to worry about."

Hunt nodded. "Damn straight. Isn't Nicholas Rheinhardt the candy-ass television host who was left crippled after some massage?"

"So now it's come down to trash talk, huh?" Nick responded. "If you really want to go there, that's something I excel at." He spoke to Penelope. "Any advice here would be extremely welcome."

She tapped her lips with a finger. "Let's see. The cups appear to be sixteen-ounce with an approximate diameter of three and one half inches. Given the configuration of the vessels and size of their top openings, I believe that in the early stages of the game it is best to throw the ball with a high arc."

"And what, pray tell, makes you say that?" Nick asked, not looking totally convinced.

"How can I explain this?" She paused. "Let's just say it's similar to an approach shot in golf. A good one has a nice arc that allows it to drop down without moving too far. In effect, we're talking about a trade-off. Even though an arcing shot may be harder to control in regards to accuracy, it will come down practically vertically. Ergo, I recommend an arcing shot while there are still a number of cups on the board because such a ball dropping vertically has a better chance of making it into the cup."

She held up her finger when Nick was about to speak. "I'm not done." She was in full lecture mode. "By contrast, toward the end of the game, when there will be fewer cups on the table—thus reducing the total size of the target—I recommend a lower arc. This path requires less force and therefore provides the possibility of greater accuracy."

Nick stared at her dumbfounded.

Penelope was perplexed. "You disagree?"

"I'm still working on your use of *ergo*." He shook his head. "And you postulate all this because…?"

"Because it's based on classic laws of motion, of course." When that didn't seem to satisfy him she added, "I took a course in introductory fluid mechanics in college."

"*You* took a course in fluid mechanics? Why?"

"The professor had won all sorts of teaching awards. I thought it might come in handy one day."

"Did it?"

She shrugged. "We'll see, won't we?" She handed him a Ping-Pong ball. "Since I'm stronger on theory than practice, I suggest you go first."

He studied her a moment before taking the ball. He bent his elbow and held his upper arm upright. The ball was between his thumb and forefinger.

She leaned toward him with her shoulder. "Remember, a high arc."

He dropped his hand. "I got that part." He set himself again.

"Hold it," she shouted. She reached out for the cup on the side of the table. "Dunk the ball first."

Justin and Hunt watched amused from the other end of the board. "To think my brainy sister needs to imitate me," Justin joked.

Penelope addressed her brother. "It's not a matter of imitation so much as aerodynamics. Wetting the ball increases its mass, thus lowering the effects of air resistance on the trajectory." She pushed the cup in Nick's face.

"And here I thought it was just some Lion Inn superstition." Hunt laughed. "Like giving the ball good juju."

Nick sniffed the cup. "This is beer? Is water any better?"

She frowned again in thought. "No, it shouldn't make any significant difference since the mass of both liquids is essentially the same."

Nick dunked his Ping-Pong ball. "If a Grantham University professor recommends this course of action, who am I to question it?" He readied his throwing stance, making a couple of practice arm movements.

"High arc," Penelope repeated with a whisper.

"Penelope," Nick snapped. He let the ball go.

As one, the whole room leaned forward, arching their necks to mimic the flight of the ball. Up it went before dropping in a perfect parabola.

Plop. It landed in the center cup.

"All right," Nick shouted and turned to high-five Penelope, who needed a second to register just how to respond.

"How embarrassing. That's the first time I've ever given a high five," Nick admitted.

"For me, as well," Penelope confessed.

Their eyes locked.

From across the table, Hunt removed the ball and chugged the beer. "Not to worry, bro. That was merely beginner's luck." He wiped the ball on a paper towel, then dunked it carefully. "Now you'll see what happens when the pros take over." He raised his arm, and tossed a perfect, arcing ball.

Plop. It landed in the left cup of the row of three.

Penelope looked down, then back at Hunt.

He smiled knowingly. "Not only was I captain of an undefeated crew my senior year, I majored in chemical engineering. Ergo, I *also* took introductory fluid mechanics." He turned to Justin.

Hunt and Justin shared a well-coordinated high five.

Penelope gulped. She spoke in a low voice to Nick. "I think that, given the competition, you should drink most of the beer. Even sober, I will definitely be the weak link in the group." She daintily removed the Ping-Pong ball and passed the cup to Nick.

"No way, sis. House rules state you have to alternate drinking," Justin informed her.

"Oh, dear."

"Don't worry." Nick smiled encouragingly. "Drinking a few beers will relieve the tension in your arm. You'll throw even better. After all, Don Larson pitched a perfect game in the 1956 World Series with no memory of doing so, supposedly because he was still drunk from the night before."

"The World Series of what?" she asked innocently.

Nick rubbed his brow. "This could be a very quick night." He chugged down the cup of beer, then tossed it backward into the audience.

Out of the corner of her eye Penelope saw the camera follow the action.

There was a loud cheer that Larry and Clyde recorded before returning to the game.

"Go for it, Penelope," Nick encouraged her.

"The worst that can happen is total humiliation and shame."

The thing of it was, as the game wore on, Nick was right. Not the part about humiliation, but that alcohol seemed to free up her muscles.

Or maybe she wasn't used to drinking this much beer?

The game was nip and tuck. Both Justin and Hunt were natural athletes and, while rusty, they were clearly the more experienced players. Nick proved to be no slouch, either.

There was only one cup remaining at their end, and two at the other. It was Hunt's turn. He shot the ball. It fired through the air, heading on target. The little ball found the edge of the cup. It circled the rim.

There was a collective holding of breath.

Nick leaned forward.

Penelope covered her face. She couldn't look.

Then, as one, the crowd groaned.

Penelope lowered her hand to see the ball rolling on the table. Breath returned to her lungs.

Then it was Nick's turn again. Two cups remained across the table. The one closest to them, and the one on the back right.

"Fastball," Penelope coached. She wavered slightly on her feet, the beer making her a little wobbly.

Nick picked up a ball. "No worries. This is going

to burn up the radar gun." He gave her a large, slightly tipsy smile. "I'll explain that to you later." Without waiting, he pitched the ball forward on a near-straight line.

Plop. It found the back cup.

Cheers went up.

Nick beamed. "I do believe we are dead even. Your turn, amigo," he said to Justin.

Justin confidently picked up the Ping-Pong ball. "Sayonara, suckers." He made a dartlike throw with his wet ball.

Penelope pressed her fist to her mouth. Nick rocked on his heels and looked as if he expected defeat.

The ball overshot.

"Ouch." Justin winced.

Penelope clapped. She hadn't felt such relief since successfully defending her Ph.D thesis.

Nick retrieved the ball and placed it in her hand.

"Oh, no, can't you do it?" she protested. "You're so much better." It was true. He was the only one on their team who had successfully landed the ball in any of the cups.

"House rules," the whole room roared.

Nick cupped her hand in his. "Don't worry. Just throw it without even thinking."

"I never do anything without thinking."

"So, maybe it's time you started." He kept his

face close to hers for a moment more. "No think-ing," he mouthed silently.

Penelope wet her lips and nodded. She faced the table and, barely registering where the cup stood, tossed the ball with a quick flick of the wrist. "Oh, no," she called. "I forgot to dunk—"

Then a miracle occurred.

The ball rocketed to the cup and, like a beer-seek-ing missile, found the center.

Plop.

The crowd roared and started jumping up and down. Downstairs the music from the band sud-denly seemed to up in volume and the bass prac-tically shook the floor and the walls. The photos rattled on their hooks. Larry barely managed to pro-tect his camera from a stray hand or two. Clyde's sound boom swayed precariously above it all.

Penelope stood there blinking. She pointed to where her ball had landed. Then she looked up at her brother, who seemed as stunned as she was.

After a moment, Justin recovered with a broad smile. "You're not going to rub this in, are you?" he asked before picking up the cup and downing it. Half the contents poured down his cheeks. He tossed it over his shoulder. "Well done, Penelope. Well done," he congratulated her.

"There you have it. Not only survival under fire, but victory," Nick declared with a fist pump. "What can I say but never underestimate the prowess of a rare-book librarian." He put his arms around her shoulders and gave her a gentle squeeze, as if it was the most natural thing in the world.

Penelope decided to return the favor—in her own natural way.

She placed one hand on the side of his head and angled it downward. Then she went up on tiptoes and kissed him fully on the lips.

He responded immediately, deepening the pressure, parting her lips and letting his tongue tango with hers.

Penelope breathed in the smell of cheap beer, shaving cream and lust.

There came the sound of wolf whistles and clapping. Was it coming from the people gathered around? Or could there be a joyful band in her head?

Did it matter?

CHAPTER TWENTY-THREE

HESITANT, AMARA TAPPED her fingers on the handle-
bar of Penelope's bicycle propped against the garage
wall.

Her father had stopped by the house earlier and
had tried to get Amara to go along with them to
Lion Inn. Despite his seeming eagerness to have
her join them, she had watched the way his eyes
had followed Penelope around the living room as
she neatly placed a bookmark in her hardback copy
of *War and Peace*. "I'm trying to improve my Russian," she had explained. "It's pretty rusty."

Rusty or not, Amara was pretty impressed that
Penelope hadn't needed to use a dictionary. She
would have needed one just for the English translation.

Anyway, given the way her father looked at Penelope, Amara had no desire to be the proverbial
third wheel. "I'm kind of tired after babysitting all
afternoon," she'd said, making excuses. "Besides,
I haven't slept that well since…well…you know—
the whole getting kicked out of school bit." It was a
cheap move, but not entirely inaccurate.

Penelope had seemed genuinely hurt. She'd immediately taken Amara by the hand and guided her to a tin of biscotti.

"I understand completely. You know, I find that puttering around the kitchen is useful when I have trouble sleeping. In fact, I made these at three in the morning just as a distraction. When I was younger, I used to decline irregular Latin verbs, but then I learned them all..." She'd almost seemed embarrassed at that last admission.

"I'll be fine. Don't worry," Amara had assured her, practically pushing the two adults out the door. The truth was, she had other plans.

Press.

She'd gone to the Grantham University website and looked up the schedule of the Reunions activities for the weekend. There was the annual softball game between the graduating class and the tenth-year Reunion members. Since Press didn't have to work, she figured he'd be there. The only problem was that by the time her dad and Penelope had left, the game was already underway.

She looked down at her watch. By now it was probably in the fifth inning. The university's baseball field was a fair hike from Penelope's house. If she walked—even ran—she might miss him. But if she had wheels...

She squeezed the bike's hand brake and considered her options. The obvious choice was the vin-

tage sports car. Amara had already noticed that
Penelope, being the superorganized person that she
was, placed all her keys in a small wicker basket
on the small table in the kitchen. But she'd already
gotten into trouble borrowing a car without permission.

So the bike was her best bet. Besides, Penelope
had said that Amara could borrow it whenever she
wasn't using it. True, the implication was for trips
like going to the library or tooling along the towpath
by Lake Vanderbilt. Probably a mission to lose her
virginity would not have been included on that list.

Amara hesitated. Then she noticed the bike lock
in the front wire basket on the bike. And sticking
out of the lock was a key.

It was karma, Amara figured. Or Penelope's or-
ganizational skills.

Whatever. Amara whipped around and raised the
garage door. She wheeled the bike out the driveway,
leaned it against the house and turned to close the
overhanging door. Penelope might insist on bolting
her bike, but she didn't bother locking her house.

"Except for the bike thieves, Grantham is so
safe," she had informed Amara. "Besides, what are
they going to steal? My complete works of Ovid?"
Penelope had chuckled. "That was a joke, wasn't it?
I made a joke." She had seemed very pleased with
herself.

In that instant, Amara thought that Penelope looked truly beautiful. She had laughed in response.

Amara wasn't laughing now. But she *was* determined. She swung her leg over the bike and straddled the frame. Penelope was a few inches taller, so she'd have to stand on the pedals the whole way. She pushed out the driveway and headed up Henderson Street. It was slightly uphill, and her calves started killing her within five minutes. Amara decided to ignore the pain. What she couldn't ignore was the feeling of the slim packet slipped into her back jeans pocket. The packet with the condom.

PRESS STOOD NEXT TO THE on-deck circle, metal bat in one hand and a plastic cup of beer in the other. "C'mon, throw strikes," he jawed at the pitcher. "It's past bedtime for your teammates in the field, so just put 'em outta further misery."

It was the bottom of the last inning, with his team trailing by one run. Every ball counted. Big time. A man, or rather, a woman, was on first, with Press's class president up at bat. The guy already had an analyst's job lined up at a private-equity firm—and what looked like a good eye for balls and strikes.

His classmates hooted from the sidelines and stamped their feet on the metal stands. The "Game" was a long-standing tradition at Grantham Reunions. Last year, the ten-year Reunion members had uncharacteristically won—a situation that was not about to happen again this year.

Frankly, Press didn't give a hoot about being some kind of athletic hero. To his father's dismay, he'd refused to play football, despite being courted by practically every Ivy League school. Even Big Ten Stanford had scouted him in prep school. Instead he'd been a walk-on for the tennis team his freshman year, and confounding expectations, had actually made varsity.

Yet Press had found himself chafing at the hours of practice and the hefty chunk of travel time required for away matches. And his enthusiasm for competitive sports began to wane as he found his love of learning begin to blossom. Talk about out of the blue. His old man had just about freaked when he informed him he was majoring in biology with a concentration in paleontology.

"Lodges don't dabble in living organisms," Conrad Lodge III had announced in his lockjaw accent between sips of his single-malt scotch. "We establish investment banks, and we serve our country by being ambassadors."

"Of course," Press had sniggered under his breath.

Screw the whole Masters of the Universe thing, Press had thought that day as he'd gotten up and walked out of the Grantham Club. The local institution was famed for WASP deal making over Yorkshire pudding and gray slabs of roast beef.

His half sister Mimi liked to tell him that he had a problem with authority. *As if she didn't?* In fact, he figured she was about as mixed up as he was. But that hadn't stopped her from becoming a leading journalist. Just the way he intended to become a groundbreaking paleontologist.

In the meantime, when it came to his turn at bat, he just wanted to knock the cover off the ball. To wipe those smug grins off the alums, all so comfortable with their well-paying jobs at "white shoe" law firms and elite hedge funds.

Press breathed in loudly. Actually some of them seemed really nice. One guy who was an engineer for Schlumberger in Papua New Guinea thought being a paleontologist was just about the "neatest thing ever." So, it wasn't as though the need to win was personal. No, there was something else involved besides his put-it-to-people-in-positions-of-authority attitude.

Something had been bugging him for a couple days now. It was akin to an itch between your shoulder blades or an invisible hair that kept getting in your mouth. He figured it was just senioritis. Four years was a long time to be in school, and it was definitely time to move on.

The class president finally connected with a ball. It was a weak grounder to second base. Despite the fact that the second baseman was standing with a beer in his bare hand, he managed to put down the cup, field the ball cleanly, step on second base, thereby forcing the lead runner, and throw to first in time. A double play—all without knocking over his cup.

Press looked back at his teammates who were booing. "What gives?"

"He played Triple-A ball at Pawtucket before he ruptured an Achilles tendon," his friend Matt Brown informed him from the sidelines. Matt was a year younger and was also a local. The two had met when they worked during a summer in high school at a local country club. Press had taught tennis, and Matt had manned the cash register in the pro shop. Even though Press gave Matt a hard time for going to Yale, he admired him—a lot.

It was a long story, involving Matt's mother dying and his coming to live with the father he'd never known. But Matt had survived that crisis, and this summer he'd be heading off to Congo for the second time to work for Lilah Evans and her nonprofit organization. If anyone deserved to have a good time right now, it was Matt.

"Pawtucket?" Press repeated. "Isn't that a Red Sox affiliate?"

Matt nodded. His tall, lanky body seemed dwarfed in his faded khaki shorts and Yale T-shirt.

Press made a face. He was a diehard Yankees fan. "Yet another reason to annihilate these guys," he declared and took another gulp of beer. Then he rolled his shoulders to try to loosen up that nagging feeling.

That's when he saw her. And he stopped moving his shoulders.

CHAPTER TWENTY-FOUR

HE WATCHED AMARA HOP OFF this bike that looked way too big for her and come walking toward the sidelines. He saw her scan the crowd—and finally spot him.

She waved.

He gave her a nod. That pain between his shoulder blades? It just got worse. Another gulp of beer. A short swing of the bat. "Here comes trouble," he said to Matt with a nod of his head in Amara's direction.

The kid—that's what he kept telling himself she was—locked the bike against the fence and headed in his direction. She didn't run, thankfully. She took her time slowly, her hands next to the sides of her jeans. She had a tight smile on her face as she passed Matt.

She's nervous, Press realized. Out of the blue, he felt protective. That was the weird thing about Amara. She stirred up these emotions he didn't know he had. And which he didn't particularly want. She rattled his sense of who he was and what he wanted or, more appropriately, what he expected out of life.

And she was a kid, he reminded himself. Barely out of high school. Jailbait. And despite her tough-girl look—which he couldn't help noticing she had abandoned in favor of jeans, boat shoes and a white T-shirt. Even her hair didn't look so coal-black as before, but rather a dark brown, the waves gently caressing her shoulders and spilling down her back.... *Not good,* Press chided himself. She was innocent, clearly not in his sarcastic, dim-view-of-the-world league.

Someone offered her a beer, but she declined. Yeah, she was a good kid.

The guy in the on-deck circle had moved to the batter's box. So far he'd hit a couple of fly balls. "Hey, Matt," Press called out as he moved into the on-deck circle. "That's Amara. She's coming to Grantham University next year as a freshman. Think you can entertain her while I'm busy?"

Matt shuffled his feet around and held out his hand. The guy was hopelessly shy. That didn't keep Amara from smiling more broadly as she returned the handshake, Press noticed.

He tried to refocus on the game. "C'mon, Doug," he encouraged the batter. The guy had been his freshman lab partner in Organic Chemistry. "Enough with practicing your swing. Put the ball in play."

Doug glanced over his shoulder. "You always did like to order me around."

"Hey, you got an A thanks to my efforts," Press reminded him.

The pitcher went into his slow pitch windup. Their teammates clapped. The opponents heckled. He threw the ball.

Doug made contact, hitting a seeing-eye single that the third baseman—an up-and-coming bond trader—made a diving catch for, but missed. He got up and dusted his shirt off. "Just don't come looking to me for a job when you graduate," he called over to Doug who was standing on first base and taking bows.

Press was up next. He put his beer down and stepped into the batter's box. He took a few more practice swings. Out of the corner of his eye he could see Matt and Amara chatting away as if they'd known each other for a lot longer than a few minutes. Matt had even taken his hands out of his pockets. Amara's hair blew in the light breeze, and when a strand caught in her mouth, Press saw her reach up, separate her lips and slip it out.

Matt, he saw, noticed that little gesture, too.

Press narrowed his eyes and concentrated on the batter. A line drive to right field would bring in the tying run.

The pitcher delivered. Press swung. A screaming line drive whizzed past the first baseman. Press took off.

"Foul," cried the alums.

His classmates moaned.

Press trotted back to the batter's box and picked up the bat. He tapped it against the insides of his sneakers.

The breeze picked up. Again, Amara's hair blew in front of her face. This time, Matt reached over and brushed it aside for her.

Press ground his teeth. *What the hell is Matt doing? She's a kid.* He narrowed his eyes and stared down the pitcher.

He delivered.

The ball arced slowly toward home base. The sound of a girl's giggle infiltrated his brain. Amara. He swung, a sudden surge of adrenaline fed his muscles and the bat made contact with the ball. *Thwack!* He followed through, twisting from his hips. Then took off, his head down. The hoots of the spectators reverberated all around him. But still he heard that little giggle as he raced toward first. He was rounding the bag and halfway to second when he nearly ran into Doug.

"Hey, slow down, buddy." Doug held up his arms. "You can go into your home-run trot. Didn't you see it? You hit the thing out of the park."

For the first time, Press looked up and saw the

right fielder turned with his back to the crowd as he watched the ball sail over the fence.

People were jumping up and down. Clapping. Screaming. The one-time hot prospect at second base even high-fived Press as he eased up into a sedate jog.

Press rounded the bases and headed for home, jumping on the bag with two feet. He raised his hands and did a little dance.

His classmates crowded him, slapped him on the back, patted him on the head and doused him with beer.

He looked frantically around. For Amara.

The next second she was next to him, being pushed up against his body by the crunch of people.

"You were incre—" she shouted.

Press shook his head. Her words were drowned out in the din. He reached for her shoulders and pulled her close. "What? I couldn't hear you," he said. He pointed to his ear and turned his head sideways. His hands were still on her shoulders.

She went up on tiptoe and spoke into his ear. "I said, 'You were incredible.'" She looked into his eyes.

He studied her face, the alluring combination of innocence and yearning etched on every feature. He waited a beat.

She parted her lips. Breathed in sharply through her mouth.

And then he let his hands drop and stepped back. He shook his head. "No," he said.

"But...but...I thought that...that...maybe we could spend time together tonight? You know, even celebrate? You and I? And...and..." She took another deep breath. "I just want to do something special—make it special between us."

Press knew immediately where she was going. He moved his jaw. *Whoa.* He'd figured out already that she had a crush on him. But this was taking it to another level.

He went to pull her away from the crowd where it would be easier to talk. They'd only moved a few feet when the class president lunged between Amara and him. "Hey, Press, way to go, bro."

"Oh, yeah. Lucky hit," Press responded. Right now a softball game was the furthest thing from his mind.

"Luck, nothing. It's unanimous. This belongs to you for the year." The president plunked a Grantham baseball cap on his head with a straggling lion's tail pinned to the back. "This year, you get 'tail,'" he said with a guffaw, then hurried back to the celebration by the keg.

Press slipped the hat off his head. It was sweat stained and faded. The polyester lion's tail looked as though several real animals had chewed on it. The annual tradition of passing "The Tail" to the game's

MVP was usually a joyous moment. On Press, it was lost.

He paused and made eye contact with Amara. *Jeez.* The kid looked as if her whole world depended on what he was about to say. "Listen," he said. "I like you. You're nice. More than nice. But you're also a kid."

"Like I said, though, I'll be eighteen in August." There was a hint of desperation in her voice.

"And I'll be twenty-two on August twenty-seventh. Don't you see? That's a big four years."

She suddenly perked up. "Me, too. My birthday's the twenty-seventh. Don't you see? It's like we're fated to be together."

Press shook his head. "I don't believe in fate."

"What do you believe in?"

"Science. Friendship, I guess."

"Not love?"

"No." He swallowed. "And that's why you deserve someone better than me. For you first time, especially. I'm right, aren't I? It would be your first?"

She tossed her hair. "I mean, it's not like it's a big deal."

"No, it is a big deal. I just don't want to see you get hurt."

She studied the ground. "Like you care," she said under her breath.

"Yes, I do. Like I said, I like you. But as a friend." He searched her profile for a reaction.

She emitted a sarcastic laugh. "Please. That's like saying I have a nice personality." Then suddenly, her expression changed. She waved.

Press swiveled his head to follow her line of vision. Matt was heading toward them.

"Hey, there, hero of the day. Why am I not surprised to find you with a pretty girl?" Matt stood awkwardly next to Amara and offered his usual tense smile.

Maybe it was just as well that Matt had showed up when he did, Press thought. What more did he have to say to Amara? *Nothing. Right?* It's not as if he could see himself sitting down with her at some quiet coffee shop having this heart-to-heart, divulging his innermost secrets—like how his father barely spoke to him, or if he did, it was with total disdain. *I mean, what kind of person turns out normal with a parental role model like that?*

Nah, that wouldn't be something he would do. Which just went to show how wrong he was for someone like her.

So he took the easy way out. Acting as if the whole encounter with Amara had never happened, and he asked, "So, Matt, you're staying for the pig roast that's on now, right?" He pointed toward the picnic tables and the meat roasting in a large pit. "Seems just about ready."

Then he glanced casually—*really* casually—at Amara. "You're welcome to stay, too." It was a pathetic move, he knew. *But she'll thank me in the long run,* he rationalized.

Amara merely gave him a forced smile. "No, thanks. I just came by to check on the game," she said in an easy-breezy manner.

Matt had his phone out. "I gotta go, too. Promised Katarina I'd meet her and Dad and the baby at Babička's for dinner soon." He looked at Amara. "Katarina's my stepmom and Babička's her grandmother—she's just the greatest, especially her cooking."

"But you'll come back to Lion Inn later for the dance?" Press purposely didn't look at Amara.

"I'll try. Otherwise, I'll catch you tomorrow afternoon at your talk."

Press groaned. "You would have to bring that up."

Matt swiped the cap from Press's hand and plunked it on his friend's head. It sat at a lopsided angle. "Hey, it doesn't look bad. Only you could get away with wearing the stupid thing."

Press saw the way Amara looked at him, and he did something he didn't think was possible. He blushed. But then he cleared his throat and adjusted the bill of the cap so that it was positioned correctly.

Doug waved to him from near the roasting pit. "Hey, Press. You got to come over and have some of this. It's fantastic." He held up a sagging paper plate to demonstrate.

Press waved. "I'll be there." Then he shifted his

attention back to Amara and Matt. "So I guess I'll see you guys around, then." *You guys.* Would she get the message?

Amara left without bothering to say goodbye. Just a wave, no big deal, and she headed toward the bike.

"Hey, wait up," Matt called. "I can walk with you, if you don't mind not riding?"

She flipped her hair.

She frigging flipped her hair, Press screamed internally.

"Sure, why not? It's too big for me anyway." Amara slipped a key from her back pocket and undid the lock. Matt waited while she'd stowed it in the basket, and then the two of them walked off with Amara guiding the bicycle between them.

Press shook his head when he saw Matt catch himself from stumbling on the uneven grass. "Isn't the hero of the game supposed to get the girl, not some nerdy political-science major who wants to save the world?" he mused to himself.

Then he stopped. Because he'd just noticed something—something shiny that was peeking out the back pocket of her tight jeans. The one that she'd slipped the key from.

There was no mistaking the foil packet. Press watched the way it moved back and forth, bobbing with the sway of her hips as she sauntered off into the sunset.

With his best friend, no less.

CHAPTER TWENTY-FIVE

PENELOPE AND NICK SAT in Nick's rental car, a Ford Explorer. Each stared ahead, out of the window. The engine was running with the air-conditioning blasting. The car was still in Park.

"Sorry, I get a little jacked up," Nick explained. He drummed his fingers on the steering wheel.

"That's understandable. Being on camera, knowing the whole production rests on your shoulders is a stressful situation. Furthermore, the direct relation between stress and secretions by the adrenal glands is well documented, with the net effect not only a rise in blood pressure but an elevation of heart rate."

Penelope furrowed her brow and turned to him. "I realize you are very good at what you do, but excessive levels of adrenaline have adverse effects on your health," she said earnestly. "Perhaps, therefore, you should take up more restful activities such as yoga or meditation to help relieve the pressures of your work?"

Nick raised his eyebrows. "Yoga?"

"You're right. That might be a stretch."

Nick slumped back on his seat. "You entirely misread the source of my stress."

"I did? I mean, unlike with most people, I seem to be able to judge your verbal and nonverbal cues more easily." She folded her hands in her lap.

Nick turned to face her. "You're the reason I'm stressed out."

"I am?" Penelope squeaked. Then she cleared her throat. "I am," she repeated, her tone lower. She hesitated. "And that's a good thing?"

Nick smiled. "It could be. Most definitely." He reached over and picked up one of her hands.

She stared at her small slender hand in his large one. His knuckles were large, and she noticed scars from various cuts and burns, hazards of being a professional chef, she presumed.

"Tell me something, Penelope. Not to pry, but did you ever stop to analyze why you feel awkward with most people?"

"Yes, of course. When I was in graduate school at Oxford I went to a psychiatrist. I wanted to find out if I had Asperger's syndrome—you know, a mild form of autism."

"Asperger's?" He turned her hand over in his and ran his index finger along one of the lines. "And what was the diagnosis?"

"He said he needed multiple sessions before making a firm diagnosis. Unfortunately we never got that far."

Nick stilled his finger. "And that was because?"

"Actually, it's something of a source of embarrassment for me, if you must know the truth. You see, he informed me that over the course of the one session he had observed that I was already starting to experience transference, that is, where the patient believes he—or she—is falling in love with the doctor."

"Yes, I know what transference is."

Penelope nodded, glad to proceed as quickly as possible with her story. "He then went on to explain that this feeling was perfectly natural. In fact, he said that was a good thing because he had observed that he was also attracted to me."

Nick looked up. "So what did you say?"

"Why, I didn't say anything. I merely stood up, picked up my backpack and then I socked him around the head with it. After that, I left."

Nick threw back his head. "You're fantastic, you know that?"

"Frankly I find it strange that you have a positive reaction to the fact that I used physical violence."

He shook his head. "If only you knew." Then he brought her hand to his chest and laid it flat against his shirt. "Do you feel that?"

"You mean the quality of the cotton of your shirt?" She paused. "That was a joke." She cocked her head, pleased. "I made a joke."

"Indeed you did." Nick emitted a light laugh.

Penelope found the lines radiating from the corners of his eyes highly attractive.

"And, furthermore, in the view of Dr. Rheinhardt—*moi*—that is clear evidence that you couldn't possibly have Asperger's or any other form of autism."

"And what medical-school degree allows you to make that judgment?"

"The proverbial school of hard knocks, or in my case, the years of being a line cook. Trust me, nothing tells you more about people than working in a restaurant. Take the organization alone. The hierarchy is rigid, starting with the *chef de cuisine,* then the *sous-chef,* on down to the *chef-de-partie* or line chef, which in turn has its own order of first and second cook, not to mention areas of expertise like fish chef or sauté chef or pastry chef."

"It sounds similar to the bureaucracy at the Vatican."

Nick nodded. "Could be." He lightly kissed her hand before guiding it to his lap. "Anyway, as I was saying, you quickly learn in a kitchen where you stand in the pecking order and who the head honcho is."

"This is all very informative, but I'm still not sure what it has to do with me and my...my social failings."

Nick shook his head. "You don't have social failings."

Penelope stiffened her back. "I beg to differ. You should have seen my teaching evaluations. They were hardly glowing."

"So a bunch of snot-nosed kids didn't appreciate you. In my opinion, whatever failings exist are not yours but your father's. Asperger's my ass. Okay, you're a little shy. I'll grant you that. But what you're really manifesting is Stanfield's syndrome."

Penelope straightened her shoulders. "Stanfield's syndrome? You're saying my father—"

"Deliberately separated you from society by insisting on homeschooling you. Then he molded you in his image, like some Mini Me. And you, being a good daughter who wanted to please him, went along willingly."

"I'm not sure about the Mini Me reference," she responded. "Nor, from personal observation, am I entirely convinced that you are an expert on good daughters."

She held up her free hand, pointing with her index finger. "Here, let me digress by saying that Amara is a very good girl, despite her recent problems." That point made, she lowered her arm. "Now, regarding your evaluation of my relationship with my father— you make it sound like he tried to brainwash me."

"Well, isn't that essentially what he did?" Nick asked.

"Without his time and encouragement, I never would have excelled in the Classics. Staying in school could never have afforded the same advantages."

"But were you happy?"

"That never came into question," she replied swiftly.

"Did you ever kick a soccer ball with friends on the weekend? Have sleepover birthday parties? Deal with nasty girl cliques? Go to the Senior Prom?"

"Of course not. I didn't have any friends, and even if I did, you must remember that I used to wear glasses with lenses as thick as the bottom of Coke bottles. I wasn't exactly a prize catch." She stared awkwardly at the floor of the car. A gum wrapper was lying, half-folded, on the mat next to her feet.

Nick reached over and, applying pressure to her chin, turned her head so that she had to look at his face. "I'm sorry to admit it, but in college I was one of those immature, superficial males of the species who didn't know any better than to look behind those glasses. Because what's there is amazing."

"It is?" Penelope blinked rapidly.

He slanted his head this way and that, as if memorizing each contour, each nuance of her face. "Indeed it is—now more than ever."

"Oh, that's because of the laser surgery. It's remarkable. I can actually get up in the morning and be able to read my alarm clock without having to put on my glasses."

"It's more than the glasses, Penelope," Nick insisted.

"It is?" She experienced a fluttering of hope in her stomach, which, truly, was a physiological impossibility, but which she nonetheless accepted with a sense of cautious anticipation.

"Very much so. Because I believe you have finally stopped being that very good, very obedient daughter."

"You're saying I'm no longer good?"

"Of course you're a good person." This time, he held up his hand. "You know what? Let me get back to my universe once more—cooking. I kind of got sidetracked before. Do you remember how I was talking about being a line chef?"

"Of course."

"Well, a line chef is supposed to master all the fine techniques of true cooking by unfailingly following the orders of the *sous-chef* and the *chef-de-cuisine* over him. But the thing of it is, the only way for someone on the bottom to make a name for himself is to find his own voice—to buck the system. He needs to break away from slavishly following what the authorities above him have taught him to do."

"Are you saying I need to do that? I need to break away from my father's yoke?"

He shook his head vigorously. "No, don't you get it? You've already done that. You took the curator's job and are sticking with it despite your father's harassment. You've found something you love. That makes you happy."

"I guess I was starting to become more independent, as well as subconsciously finding myself, when I took the library-science degree, too," Penelope thought out loud. Then she looked at him. "I guess this makes me something of a late bloomer."

"Some of the most beautiful flowers are late bloomers. And waiting for them to blossom fully only enhances their allure."

"It does?" She found herself mesmerized by his lips, and not just the words coming out of them. She thought how wonderful they might feel against hers.

"So, I take it that you agree with my diagnosis?" Nick asked.

She pictured his mouth moving from her lips to her cheeks, then her neck and parts even more sensitive.

Penelope shook her head. "I suppose what you say might have some academic merit. After all, it is a well-documented psychiatric finding that the desire to garner favor from a person of authority—be it familial or otherwise—is not necessarily a wise one. You know, you really do have an amazing mouth…" she said, her voice trailing off.

Nick grinned. "I'm glad you think so. I intend to use it in ways you never dreamed of—or at least my overdeveloped male ego likes to think so. If you have no objections, that is."

She breathed in. "None whatsoever."

He leaned closer. Then stopped. "Tell me, you said a friend of yours in Italy taught you how to cook?" he asked hesitantly.

"Yes?" She was confused.

"I ask not just out of curiosity, but quite possibly out of jealousy."

Penelope smiled, pleased. "Really, you have nothing to be jealous about. My friend's name was Giovanni, or Gigi, as he was often known. I knew him when I lived in Rome. He was a brilliant historian, mind you, an expert on Franciscan theology and the papacy. But he also had a very playful side to him. Always joking. I understood him, too, much the way I can read you."

"You're saying nothing to relieve my jealousy," Nick admitted.

"I'm sorry. I thought you understood. Gigi was gay. And unfortunately, he didn't practice safe sex and developed HIV. Medication kept it in check for a number of years." She faltered. "By the time I met him, that was changing. In the last year, I had him move in with me so I could help take care of him. His family, you see, was very conservative, very religious. They had rejected him because of his lifestyle. Can you imagine?"

"Can I imagine some people acting that way? Unfortunately, yes. But you? Never."

She wet her top lip with the tip of her tongue. She heard him groan softly, an indication of the power she had over him. That made her feel good, made her feel feminine. "Anyway, to make a long story short, Gigi was a very proud man, and he wanted to pay me for what he called my kindness. Obviously I refused any money."

"Obviously."

Penelope recognized that he wasn't being sarcastic. "So, instead, I suggested he give me cooking lessons in return. His specialty was Calabrian food—apparently the love of his life had been a Calabrian—very dark, passionate, an architect. Anyway, Gigi would sit in his chair, bundled up no matter how warm the weather, and instruct me in how to prepare various dishes. I use the term 'instruct' loosely. Often, it was more like a screaming match." She laughed.

"I can imagine." Nick nodded.

"Then he died." Penelope stopped to collect herself. She covered her mouth.

"Take your time." Nick brushed her cheek.

The gesture reassured her. She cleared her throat. "After the funeral, while I was getting ready to come back to the States and my job in Chicago, I was contacted by an Italian solicitor. She informed me that Gigi had left me a house he owned in Capo

Vaticano—a house I never even knew he had. The gift came with instructions. I was to take his ashes down to the villa and spread them in the sea by the little beach. I went. And I fell in love with the spot, the house—designed by Gigi's former lover, I found out later."

"So you found happiness?" Nick observed.

Penelope reflected. "I guess you could say I did. Through Italy, through friendship and through food—a lot of it was through food. It was the start of my transformation and, I guess, my independence from my father. True, my first job was as an assistant professor of Classics—something in his mold, but I believe I took it because that's what I had been trained to do, not solely to please him. Yet, when I didn't get tenure, he was the one who was devastated. I was actually somewhat relieved."

She laid her head against the headrest of her seat. "This has been a most enlightening conversation." Then she lavished him with her most genuine smile. "But then I would have expected nothing less from a bestselling author, three-star chef, travel authority and television host, not to mention a champion Beer Pong player."

"Is this where you throw yourself at me in awe and yearning?" Nick asked playfully.

"And you're even funny," she reflected. "Remarkable." She shifted in her seat, kicking her bag that rested on the floorboards. The toe of her shoe made contact with something solid. "My goodness. I almost forgot." She bent down and lifted out a large bundle covered in butcher paper. She handed it to him.

Nick held it aloft. "I'm confused."

"It's my 'nduja," Penelope announced. "I brought it tonight as a present for you. I also have some minitoasts in my bag—you know, the ones from France—and a spreader in case your hotel room doesn't have any utensils."

She went to search through her bag again, but Nick held her back.

"Did you say my 'hotel room'?" he asked.

"Yes, of course. Don't you think that the comfort and privacy of your room would make it easier for me to throw myself at you in awe and admiration? Besides which, in all the years I've lived in Grantham, I have never been to a hotel room in our quaint, if overpriced, community."

He grabbed her and kissed her hard and fierce before swiveling around and putting the engine in Drive. "Then, let me be your first."

CHAPTER TWENTY-SIX

NICK ROLLED OVER ON HIS back and flopped with his arms on either side of his head. "Oh, my God, that was positively mind-blowing." The twisted top sheet clung to his lower body. His bare chest heaved with each deep breath, a few gray hairs sprinkled among the dark ones.

Penelope licked her fingers. She was sitting up against a mound of pillows, seemingly oblivious to the fact that she was totally naked, exposing her lovely rounded breasts. To Nick's eye, they seemed like barely ripe, lush peaches—minus the fuzz, of course. Her rosy-red nipples pointed slightly upward, firm and erect, a testament to her recent arousal.

Nick sighed. He didn't do that very often.

"Yes, I think it was a good batch of 'nduja, if I say so myself. I will have to compliment Mike for providing such succulent, tasty pigs," she said with amusement stamped across her face.

Nick flipped to his side. He reached for her hand and licked her fingers himself. They tasted of the piquant sausage—hot and smooth. Just like Penelope. "You've become a regular verbal minx, as they would say," he noted. A few crumbs from the cracker on which she'd spread the 'nduja sprinkled down between her breasts.

She looked up thoughtfully, holding the rest of the cracker in her hand. "Minx. I like that. I've never heard that used in conversation."

He slid up and took her in his arms. "Another first. I feel all-powerful." He bent his head and licked the crumbs off her skin.

Penelope closed her eyes and purred. "I never knew that homemade sausage could be such an aphrodisiac."

Nick looked up. "The 'nduja was truly inspirational, but do you think that was all?"

Penelope placed a hand on the side of his head and gently stroked his wavy hair. "I like how you've gone gray," she said. "And, no. I don't think it was just the 'nduja. I love you, you know." She said it simply, directly.

So like Penelope, Nick thought. Honest and open. "I know. And I think I'm in love with you, too."

"Think? I thought you told me it was sometimes better to feel?" She stilled her hand.

He brought his head close to hers, angling it just so. "As usual, you are correct." His lips meshed with hers in a sensuous, exploratory kiss. His hands found her face, her shoulders, her breasts, and even before he had rolled on top, they became oblivious to the crumbs on the bed.

CHAPTER TWENTY-SEVEN

"WE SEEM TO SPEND A FAIR share of our time in the front seat of a car," Nick observed hours after their lovemaking. Once more he sat in the driver's seat, Penelope to his right. The dashboard was lit up in the darkness of night, the engine running and the headlights streaming against her garage door. He had just pulled into her tiny driveway.

He didn't want to let her out of his sight. Didn't want to think about anything but being with her and doing all sorts of things with her. Mostly sex. *So sue me,* as his late grandfather Lou would have said to his fellow retirees after trouncing them yet again at canasta. It was a wild bunch at his nursing home in Englewood, New Jersey.

Penelope looked at him with a sly smile that turned up one corner of her mouth. He wouldn't put it past her to know what he was thinking.

But being Penelope, she just smiled, and then said, "We're doing the right thing. This is what's called discretion and being the parent of an impressionable teenager."

Nick turned off the engine and killed the headlights. He had the feeling this conversation was just the beginning. "You don't think Amara isn't aware that certain things go on between a man and a woman?"

"I think she probably knows more than I."

Nick frowned. "That's supposed to be reassuring?"

Penelope laughed. "I think Amara is more than aware of what goes on, as you say. But that doesn't mean she's experienced. So that makes it even more imperative that I go home now. Your relationship with her right now is, shall we say, tenuous?"

"At best," Nick admitted.

"In which case, why complicate an already complicated situation? And besides, if I am here with her, I can make sure she is up in time for The Parade tomorrow morning." A traditional part of Reunions at Grantham University was the Saturday-morning parade of alumni from all the returning classes, as well as the soon-to-be-graduating class. All the participants marched in outrageous outfits picked out by each class.

"Wait a minute. You're coming, too, aren't you?" Nick detected a note of anxiety in his voice.

"I don't usually march with my class, no. Large gatherings of that nature have never been my style."

"You don't have to march with *your* class. March with *mine*. You can accompany Amara. It'll be fun." Or so he hoped. "For me," he added for emphasis.

"All right. If not for you, then for Amara. After all, we daughters of successful but emotionally remote fathers have to stick together. *Sisterhood is Powerful*—or so goes the title of the classic anthology dating from the second wave of radical feminist writings, I believe circa 1970…though, it could be 1971. I need to check that."

"You do that. And in the meantime, I'll get Georgie to scrounge up a costume for you." He knocked the side of his head with the heel of his hand. "That's right. Amara will need one, too. I don't want to be the only member of the family to look totally ridiculous, you know."

She patted him on the leg. "No, don't bother Georgie. Amara and I are perfectly capable of coming up with color-coordinated creations of our own. Besides, I think I like the idea of being able to make fun of you." She leaned over the hand brake. There was a glint in her eye.

"What kind of a monster have I created here?" Nick moved toward her and wondered if he could get her to do more than neck. After all, it was dark. It wasn't as if anyone was up and about this time of night in the quiet residential neighborhood. He was sure that with a little coaxing… His lips touched hers, warm and by now familiar, yet a mystery at the same time…

And then he heard the squeak. He shifted and decided to ignore it. But it only grew louder.

He lifted his head and reached for the headlights mechanism on the dashboard. He flicked them on, and in the sudden glare, saw a dark figure coast a bike to a stop in front of Penelope's garage door. "What the..." He sat up straight, then pushed the driver's side door open.

"Amara, what's going on?" He confronted her on the driveway.

Amara hopped off the bike and turned around. She shaded her eyes from the glare of the lights.

Nick glanced at the illuminated dial on his overly expensive watch, a present to himself after the one-hundredth episode of the television show. "It's freaking two-thirty in the morning. You said you were going to stay home and go to bed early because you were tired. Now I find you sneaking home." He loomed over her.

Amara shook her head. "It's not what you think, Dad."

"You don't want to know what I think," he shouted. From behind him, he heard a car door open and shut.

Penelope joined them. "Perhaps we'd all be more comfortable if we went inside?" She pointed toward the door.

"Thank you." Nick could control himself enough to be polite. After all, it wasn't Penelope's problem that his daughter had the judgment of a gnat and the hormonal urges of...well...a randy teenager.

He tried to calm his anger. Unfortunately he was so rattled by what appeared to be Amara's poor judgment that there was no way he could keep his cool. "That's kind of you, but I don't see any reason to make things easier for Amara. It wasn't enough for you to take your mother's car. Now you steal Penelope's bike?"

"I said she could borrow it." Penelope came to Amara's defense.

"But I bet you didn't say she could borrow it to meet up with Press at all hours of the night?" He saw Penelope flinch, but there was nothing he could do about it at the moment. He was too upset with Amara. He would smooth things over with Penelope later.

Amara stuck out her chin. "Okay, I snuck out to see Press, but that was at some lousy softball game."

"You know the one between the graduating class and the ten-year alums?" Penelope said, trying to be helpful.

It wasn't. "A lousy softball game doesn't last this late at night. You were with him, weren't you? He put the moves on you, didn't he?"

Amara shook her head, purposely avoiding his glare. She pulled back her narrow shoulders. "You'd think you know everything. But you're wrong. I was the one to put the moves on Press. And he rejected me. That's right, he essentially told me I was a baby."

"Those wouldn't have been my words, but you'll thank him for them one day, trust me," Nick said, searching for a note of sensitivity.

"Trust you? What have you ever done to make me trust you?" Amara shot back. "Besides, if you really want to know, when Press rejected me I went off with his friend Matt. I was with him until now."

"So now you're telling me that you let that little twerp in your pants instead?"

Out of the corner of his eye, he saw Penelope cover her mouth with her hand.

"What!" Amara screamed back.

This was not his finest hour. *How do people get through the teenage years anyway?* Nick wondered. He tried to pull himself together. "Keep it down, would you?" he ordered.

"I'm supposed to keep it down when you're allowed to shout all you want?"

"That's right, because I'm the parent."

"The parent who doesn't know his own daughter enough to trust her? What kind of parent is that?" she spat back.

Father and daughter stared each other down.

Penelope stepped between them. "I think it's getting extremely late. And it's probably better to continue this discussion after a good night's sleep, when cooler heads can prevail."

Nick and Amara looked at her as though she was speaking gibberish. Finally Nick inhaled slowly and worked the base of his neck. "Okay. Penelope's right. That's probably enough for now." Then he pointed a stubborn finger at Amara. "But this discussion is not over, young lady. I have to prepare for filming The Parade in the morning, pretty early, but I'll come by to pick you both up before the thing starts."

"It would be easier on everyone if we make our own way over to the staging area," Penelope suggested. "There's no need for you to be running around on our account." She held up her hand. "And, no, Georgie doesn't need to chaperone us, either. We are perfectly capable of getting there on our own."

Nick's blood pressure was still elevated, but at least it had come down from near-stroke point. "All right, but be there. I don't want to find out about any other extra-curricular activities going on behind my back." He eyed Amara critically. "And I don't want to hear you've taken advantage of Penelope's kind nature. She's predisposed to please other people."

"You make me sound like a loyal bloodhound," Penelope said archly.

"And what does that make me? The criminal on the run?" Amara asked.

CHAPTER TWENTY-EIGHT

AFTER HE GAVE PENELOPE a quick peck on the cheek, Nick drove off. Penelope reasoned he had regained sufficient control of his emotions that he was not a menace to himself or anyone else on the road. To Amara she said, "Come inside. It's late, and you must be chilly in nothing but that T-shirt." Penelope put a hand around the girl's shoulder and guided her up the stone walkway to the front door. A cascade of climbing roses framed the top.

"Despite what you appear to want your father to believe, you didn't have sex with Matt, did you?" Penelope asked, opening the door. She waited for Amara to go through first, then closed it behind them. She switched on a small table lamp. It cast a glow over the wood floors. The colors of the books on the shelves came alive.

Amara stopped.

Penelope stowed her bag under the table and waited patiently.

Amara looked away. Then she returned Penelope's stare. "No. He invited me to have dinner with his parents and baby brother at his great-grandmother's. She lives in town, near the Engineering School. It was great. They were great. A real family. Then afterward we just sat out in her little backyard, and he told me things hadn't always been terrific. But that he and his dad had gradually figured things out—at least most of the time. And that his stepmom and her grandmother sometimes gave him grief, but only when he deserved it. And he told me how he's gonna be a senior at Yale, but in the summers he goes to Congo with this nonprofit organization started by a Grantham alum."

"Yes, Sisters for Sisters. The founder, Lilah Bigelow, is married to my brother," Penelope responded.

"Wow. It's a small world. Anyway, we just talked about stuff—you know. And I kind of told him about my life and my problems, which all seemed sort of trivial compared to what's going on in Congo, but how I still couldn't help being worried and stuff." Amara stopped, finally coming up for air. "Is this making any sense?"

"I think it makes a lot of sense. You're at a stressful point in your life, with significant changes on the horizon, including going off to college. You can't help but feel overwhelmed. Having a shoulder to lean on, someone sympathetic to talk to at such a time would seem a real comfort. And you're certainly not blind. Any woman could see that Press is attractive. I don't know Matt, but he sounds as if he has his own appeal. But you have a good head on your shoulders. You are obviously bright and clearly much more sensible than I was at your age."

"But you heard about my screwup, right?"

"Yes, well, we all screw up at some point in our lives. I've learned the hard way that it is better to screw up early on. That way you learn that life still goes on despite all. That the most important thing is to assess the problem, take responsibility and then execute the logical next steps."

Amara sighed. "Penelope, you are so wise."

Penelope laughed. "Hardly. But at least I'm trying to overcome my weaknesses. Now, what do you say to a grilled cheese sandwich?" She slipped off her ballet shoes, placed them neatly next to her purse and headed barefoot to the kitchen.

Amara padded after Penelope. "I had a big dinner with Matt's family. I don't know."

"Come, now. The world always looks brighter after a grilled cheese sandwich, especially with fresh tomato." Penelope opened the refrigerator.

"I guess you're right." Amara leaned against the doorjamb. "Do you think my father will ever believe me if I tell him what really happened tonight? It's not like the two of us have this outstanding track record, you know. And you heard him when he left. He was spitting bullets. Although, after the stunt I pulled back at school, I'm not really surprised."

Penelope looked over her shoulder as she squatted down to get the panini maker from a lower shelf. "He'll get over his anger in the morning. He's just tired and under a lot of stress himself. Besides, even though he's been absent for so much of your life, I get the feeling that he's trying to rectify that situation."

"I guess he did say he was going to call my headmistress to fix things up at school. It never occurred to me to ask him how that went."

"You'll be able to ask him tomorrow, but I'm sure everything will be fine. As for your father, sometimes you just have to cut a person a little slack in the early phase of the learning curve. Besides, you more or less baited him, the way you mentioned Matt, now, didn't you?" She plugged in the griddle.

"I suppose so. But I was mad. I didn't think."

"Hmm. Somehow that behavior sounds familiar."

"Are you telling me I'm my father's daughter?"

"We're all someone's daughter, but most of all we're ourselves, don't you think?" Penelope buttered the slices of bread. Then she stopped and turned around. She leaned against the edge of the tile countertop, the knife still in her hand. "Tell me, Amara, do you have an idea of why your father and I were together tonight?"

"Duh. I can see the way he looks at you."

"You can?"

Amara shrugged. "Listen, as far as I can tell,

you're both consenting adults who aren't in another relationship. So what's the big deal?" Amara gathered up her hair and let it fall down her back.

Penelope squeezed the knife. "But does that bother you? I mean, it's your father we're talking about after all."

"No. I mean, it's not like I'm used to seeing my father with my mother—so you're not busting up anything on that front. Besides, from the way my mother talks every once in a while...you know...because my dad's a celebrity and all, I didn't picture him living like some monk." She paused. "But, I gotta admit, I am a little surprised about one thing."

"You mean that your father would go out with me?" Penelope turned back and picked up the tomato. She sliced it and placed the thin rounds atop the pieces of American cheese.

"No, that's not it at all," Amara said emphatically. "The surprise is that he had good enough taste to go out with *you*. I know it's not very flattering to be critical of your own father, but I guess I tend to think of him as being kind of superficial. You, on the other hand? Like Press says, you're totally cool."

Penelope opened the panini maker and placed the sandwiches on the griddle. It hissed on contact with the buttered bread. "I've never been cool in my life."

"You definitely are. Trust me."

Penelope wanted to—to trust her, that is—to

get over all her old insecurities. She listened to the
sizzle of the cheese melting outside the bread crusts.
After a few moments, she lifted the lid and checked.
The bread was toasted with chestnut-brown tracks.
The cheese dripped in molten globs from the edges.
"Perfect," she announced to herself as much as to
Amara.

She reached up and got down two plates. She
placed the sandwiches in the center of each plate,
and cut them diagonally into perfect right triangles.
"Here you go." She passed a plate to Amara. "Why
don't we go sit outside and munch on these and
watch the fireflies? You can get two napkins behind
you—and maybe get a sweater if you're chilly."

Amara nodded. "That's okay. I'm fine."

Penelope watched the girl bend over to get the
napkins, her long straight hair sliding over her
shoulder to fan her cheek. She looked so young, so
sweet. "Amara, you are the one who's cool—you
and Press, actually, for looking past my idiosyncra-
sies, shall we say."

Amara held out a napkin. "We clearly just have
good judgment—unlike other people. Actually,
speaking of other people, meaning my dad—can
I just say that I'm surprised that you would even
consider going out with him? I mean, he's famous
and maybe even good-looking. And he's done all
this stuff. But, come off it. He doesn't listen, and he
makes up his mind before he gives you a chance to

explain? I mean, really. How can you trust someone like that?

Good question. Good question, thought Penelope.

CHAPTER TWENTY-NINE

MIMI SPED DOWN THE grand staircase of her family's
home early Saturday morning. The sun streamed
through the two-story Palladian window, casting
oblong expanses of sunlight on the needlepoint
bench on the landing and the Persian carpet runner
on the stairs. In the old days when her mother was
still alive, she used to slide down the polished ma-
hogany banister, past the portraits of generations of
Lodges, screaming with joy at the thrill.

Today she barely glanced at the paintings. And
the only screams came from her little half sister,
Brigid, who was throwing a temper tantrum before
going to The Parade.

Mimi shook her head. She felt bad about Brigid,
but she had to go. Needed to go. She glanced down
at her trusty tank watch—it had seen her through
wars, torrid jungles and frigid arctic temperatures.
It had never failed her yet. She still had a couple
minutes before the limousine would arrive—time
to get a quick cup of coffee.

She stopped next to one of the Hepplewhite chairs
in the foyer. There was a certain irony to having

grown up in a house that was furnished with museum-quality antiques, only to spend most of her adult years in what could only be called hellholes. And it wasn't by accident, she admitted to herself.

She bent down to place her small duffel bag on the floor. That's when she saw Press pacing back and forth in the dining room. She had been hoping to avoid this encounter, but that no longer seemed possible.

Mimi straightened up and walked over to join him, stopping at the wide entrance to the dining room. Press was texting madly on his cell phone, his face contorted in a frown. He wore khaki shorts, well-worn boat shoes, and over his white button-down shirt, his class's jacket—a loose-fitting sports coat with rows of lions marching on their back legs and holding pennants saying Grantham. It was an eye-popping fluorescent orange.

Mimi caught herself from sighing. To think, her little brother was graduating from college. She remembered when he was born. She had been eleven years old, still a baby herself really. His appearance on the scene, and the attention he soaked up from his mother, Adele—Mimi's former nanny—had been an immense source of jealousy. It had taken years for her to forgive him for things he had no control over, like being born and having a mother who was a social-climbing cow.

"Hey, Press," Mimi called out. "Can I interrupt for a sec?"

"Let me just finish. I was…ah…catching up with Matt." He texted some more before pocketing the phone in his shorts. Then he glanced at Mimi's attire. "I guess you've come to tell me you're not marching in The Parade?"

She glanced down at her usual uniform of jeans, a multipocket tan jacket, black T-shirt and a scarf draped loosely around her neck. "You're right. Anyway, the gaucho costume that my class chose never did anything for my figure."

"I never figured you to be a member of the fashion police," he scoffed. He eyed her contemptuously. "I suppose this means you won't be coming to my graduation on Tuesday?"

She shook her head. "No, I'll be back. I promise. It's just this story's come up…"

"Yeah, I know. The Vivian Pierpoint thing. I saw it on the web. 'Dog Walkergate,' they were calling it."

Mimi rolled her eyes. "Must everything be reduced to a sound bite? And do they have to imply it was the girl's fault? The husband's a major sleazeball, in my opinion."

"It's always the guy's fault in your opinion."

She pursed her lips. "Actually this is something new. Something really big."

"Bigger than your brother graduating from college?" He dismissed her gesture when she went to object. "Don't worry. I understand. It's not like this family is known for being there for one another. You get used to it, you know?"

Upstairs, Brigid's wails could be heard even louder. They both looked up.

"What gives?" Press asked.

"Oh, Brigid's throwing this fit because I won't be there to hold her hand during The Parade. I let her have my sunglasses—Oakley's, no less—thinking that would mollify her. She's been bugging me about them ever since I got home. Anyway, she threw them on the ground and would have stomped on them if Noreen hadn't picked her up and told her to have a time-out."

"She might as well learn early on that she shouldn't always count on members of this family. Though, I gotta admit, Noreen seems a lot more savvy about dealing with her than my mom ever was with me."

Absent from his statement was any mention of their mutual father, Mimi noted. Noreen, Brigid's mother and their father's third wife, for some reason loved the bastard. And miracle of miracles, he appeared head over heels in love with his younger bride. In fact, in deference to Noreen's demands, he had slowly become more of a factor in Brigid's life—certainly more than he'd ever demonstrated with his two older children.

The sound of his firm voice carried downstairs. "Five minutes, young lady," he declared. The sound of a closing door followed. Brigid's cries grew more muffled.

Mimi whistled softly. "Gee. In the old days, he would have spanked me, come down to his study to have a scotch then headed out without waiting. Times *have* changed."

Press looked at her. "For some of us maybe."

"I thought he actually came to your aid after your court appearance last year, admitting it was all his fault." An overly ambitious local policeman had charged Press with disorderly conduct for kicking a garbage can. He'd been pissed that after working his butt off all day and night at last year's Reunions, he'd been forced to drive his drunken father home.

"True—thanks to you, I discovered from Noreen," Press replied.

"And he did his community service, right?"

"Kind of. You should have seen the way he carried on ladling out food at a soup kitchen for a few nights—like it was more than a high-flying finance king should have to endure."

Mimi pressed her lips together. "Yeah, I know what you mean. Which is why we're both screwed up, I guess." She paused, debating how much to say. In the end, she figured Press deserved some explanation for why she was skipping out. "Listen, this is all pretty hush-hush…"

"Like I would say anything to anyone?" Press asked.

"No, of course you wouldn't. I know I can trust you." Mimi believed that Press was one of the few people she *could* trust. "I'm going to New York to set up a contact—for a big story in Chechnya."

"Chechnya?" Press repeated the name of the remote region of Russia. It was the scene of ongoing fighting between the Russian military and local revolutionary groups who wanted independence. "Isn't that where your mother was from?" he asked.

Mimi nodded swiftly.

Neither mentioned the fact that Mimi's mother had committed suicide shortly after their father divorced her to marry Press's mother.

After an awkward moment of silence, Mimi stepped toward him. She raised her arm as if to touch his shoulder, but stopped short. The Lodges were not big on displays of affection. "You're a good kid, you know," she said, dropping her hand.

Press shrugged. "I don't know about that." Upstairs, the sound of a door being opened and the murmur of voices could be heard. He turned his head to listen. "I guess peace has once more been restored to the household and we'll be able to get to The Parade after all—only twenty minutes late."

"It never starts on time anyway. You know that." Mimi glanced down at her watch to check the time.

"Besides, you're still early. I don't even have ten o'clock."

Press pulled out his phone. "I don't think so." He showed her the time on the display.

That's when Mimi knew that her trusty watch—the one that had never let her down through thick or thin? The one that had belonged to her late mother?

It had stopped.

Mimi didn't believe in omens. She believed in dead batteries. The obvious, short-term solution was to get an intern in the news department to run out and get a new one.

The long-term solution? Mimi studied the older watch. She wasn't ready to give up on it quite yet. Not when she was about to get closure on the part of her life that seemed to haunt her on a daily basis.

She glanced out the long windows of the dining room. The limo was waiting in the circular driveway. *See, I might be a psychological basket case, and my watch might be kaput, but some things still functioned without a hitch.*

Mimi shook her head. *Nah.* She didn't believe in omens.

CHAPTER THIRTY

"I STILL DON'T KNOW WHY I have to go to The Parade anyway, especially after what Dad said last night," Amara complained. She sat on the bed in Penelope's bedroom. Dormer windows placed between the slanted rafters bathed the attic room in morning sunlight.

Penelope finished tying an orange scarf in her hair and turned from the mirror to face Amara. "Not to go would be childish. I expect greater maturity from you. And along with maturity comes forgiveness."

"You sound like a fortune cookie. Some trite suggestion for how to live a better life."

"Really? I've never been called a fortune cookie before." Penelope didn't take offense. She smoothed the side of her hair that billowed out behind the rolled scarf. "So do I look all right?"

Amara cocked her head. "Just move the bow a little to one side…." She indicated with her finger. "Yeah, that's good. Anyway, not that it makes a big difference. You look terrific. You should wear bright colors more often."

"You think?" Penelope had rummaged through her drawers and found a cream-colored fringed shawl. She'd tied two ends at the back of her neck, and twisted the rest around her body, holding the whole thing together with a piece of braided gold cord that she'd borrowed from the windows in the downstairs study. "You sure I don't look like a reject from a Hummel factory? You know, one of those quaint gypsy figurines?" She studied her appearance in front of the mirror and jiggled the square knot on the cord, making sure it held fast.

"Believe me, nobody would ever associate you with anything made out of clay."

"Porcelain, actually, which is made by firing clay to temperatures in excess of two thousand degrees Fahrenheit." Penelope stopped speaking and focused on Amara's reflection in the mirror. "You know, this is the first time I've ever talked to another female about, you know, girly stuff." She twirled around.

"You're kidding me? Sometimes I wish my mom wasn't so concerned about the way I look or dress," Amara admitted. "When I was little, I guess it was okay. Like the way she always picked out a new dress for me to wear the first day of school. But even then, it always bugged me the way she kept tucking my hair behind my ears. What is it with mothers and ears anyway?"

"I wouldn't know. I don't think my mother has even noticed that I have ears."

"If you pierced them with four holes in each she would." Amara shook her head. Her tiny silver hoops shimmied back and forth.

"However many piercings you have, I'm sure your mother would think you look absolutely lovely now. I know I'm very pleased to be able to be seen in public with you."

Amara rose and rubbed her hand down the fine material of the tangerine-hued silk sari that Penelope had lent her.

She had bought it for the wedding of a former colleague at the University of Chicago. The bride and the groom were both from Sri Lanka, and the invitation requested traditional clothing.

"You know, with your dark coloring, you are much better suited to that. You should definitely keep it," Penelope offered.

"Oh, I couldn't." Amara left her mouth open.

"Nonsense. It's not as if I plan to wear it again." Penelope picked up a small evening bag from her dresser. "Shall we go, then?"

"Gosh, I don't know what to say," Amara replied.

"Say you're coming."

Amara gazed down at the sari, obviously overwhelmed. "Okay, I guess. Even if it means I'll have to deal with my dad." The cell phone she'd left on the bedspread began playing a moody rock song. She retrieved it and looked at the screen.

"It's my school," Amara blurted. She bit her lip.

"Maybe I should let it go through to voice mail and listen after The Parade?"

"No, take it now. We have plenty of time. I'll wait downstairs if you'd prefer."

Amara reached out. "No, stay. I definitely need the moral support."

"In that case." Penelope nodded at the phone.

Amara answered the call. "Hello," she said meekly.

Penelope watched silently as Amara responded in monosyllables to the person on the other end of the line. She felt the urge to rush over and listen in, offer advice, encourage her to show more enthusiasm, more engagement with the caller—but she didn't. This was Amara's responsibility to handle. Penelope would have to trust her to know if and when she needed a concerned adult to join in the conversation. Until then…well…until then, Penelope was beginning to understand the limits of her extrastrength deodorant.

After what seemed an eternity, Amara rang off. She raised her head. Penelope couldn't tell from her expression whether the news was good or bad. Then all of a sudden, Amara let out a whoop of joy. She raised her hands and did a little jig around the room. Then she threw herself in Penelope's arms and hugged her fiercely.

Penelope awkwardly put her arms around Amara. She felt the teenager's trembling shoulder blades. And she did what seemed right. She hugged her tightly. "I presume this reaction means it was good news?" she murmured.

Amara pulled back. She sniffed and wiped away the tears of joy. "It's better than I could have hoped. They'd decided I could graduate next week. While they don't condone how I took the car, they now seem to understand that there were extenuating circumstances. I mean, I'll have to do some tutoring this summer at a local learning center, and the director will have to send a letter to the school, confirming I did what I was supposed to. But I don't mind. I like kids."

"That's wonderful. So you can graduate?" Penelope asked.

"Yup. I mean, as further punishment I won't be able to take part in any of the senior-year festivities going on before the ceremony next Friday, but who cares? I'm doing Grantham University stuff. That's way cooler than any dancing around a maypole, don't you think?" She looked heavenward and sighed.

"Way cooler," Penelope said with a smile. "You see, you have to trust that people will do the right thing. It definitely sounds as if your father called and explained the whole situation to them, just like he promised. Once they got all the details, they were able to come to a just solution—especially because deep down, they realized what a caring person you really are."

Amara's eyes were bright. "You must be right. I never really thought he'd call. And here I acted like such a spoiled brat last night. I'll have to make it up to him somehow."

Penelope held out her hand for Amara to lead the way down the stairs. "I don't think you need to do anything special but act yourself, which means, of course, you will thank him sincerely."

Nick will be so pleased, she thought. Yes, he had overreacted last night, but he had clearly done the correct thing earlier in the afternoon by speaking with the headmistress. Parenthood was a learning process, but his heart was in the right place. And she knew where she'd placed hers.

Amara stopped halfway down the stairs. "I'll give him the biggest thank-you ever. You're right, Penelope. You have to learn to trust people—even when they're not perfect."

"It's the flaws that make people interesting," Penelope responded. "After all, think how dull life would be if we only had perfection."

CHAPTER THIRTY-ONE

NICK NERVOUSLY RUBBED his mouth as he scanned the collective Ivy League masses for his daughter and Penelope. The staging area for The Parade was one of the large campus parking lots. According to the information packet for Reunions, everyone was supposed to group around the flags designating their classes. This directive appeared to be more of a suggestion. Alumni from one class chatted away with members of other classes, their various costumes mixing together.

"Like the look," Clyde, the soundman, teased him. He rested his boom on his shoulder

"Anything for television, right?" Nick pretended not to care that he was dressed in orange-and-black as a low-rent toreador. He figured he was ripe for goring by any passing bull, irate or otherwise.

"Georgie is having a field day," Clyde went on. He pulled a cigarette pack out of a vest pocket and scanned the crowd.

"Why wouldn't he? He has color, a festive atmosphere and a whole lot of wealthy people making fools of themselves on purpose. Talk about filming the ultimate sociological experience," Nick commented.

He watched Clyde tap the pack. "Icks-nay on the igerette-cay. The antitobacco bloodhounds will pummel you to a bloody pulp. And speaking of bloodhounds…" He nodded to their right.

Vivian Pierpoint had just descended on the throngs of Grantham alums and family members. "If anyone can carry off wearing an orange-and-black wide-stripe blazer cut for your basic blockhouse body, it's La Vivian," Nick observed. Supporters immediately surrounded her, and if his eyes didn't deceive him, his erstwhile producer was leading the charge.

"To be totally accurate, I believe we're not dealing with bloodhounds here. If I know my canine breeds, she's holding a bichon frise. One of those white, moplike dogs."

"Hypoallergenic, I'm sure." Nick watched Vivian lean toward Georgie and, with her hand covering her mouth and the top of the dog's head, say something to him and him alone.

Georgie smiled sheepishly—a reaction that Nick had never witnessed before. Then he raised his eyes and, petting the dog, whispered a reply. The dog licked Georgie. And Vivian touched the base of her neck. *Interesting,* Nick thought.

This little interlude ended almost immediately with Georgie glancing frantically around and motioning to Clyde to hurry over. Larry, the camera-man, who even on this seventy-five-degree day wore a down parka, was already on the move.

Clyde sighed. "I believe that's my cue." He pocketed the cigarette pack. "Care to join the circus?"

"That's okay," Nick replied. "I'll keep my distance. I learned long ago that good food and politics don't mix. Besides, it looks like the lady has enough well-wishers." It was true. Alums of every age, male and female, were giving Vivian hugs, shaking her hand and offering high fives. "I wouldn't be surprised if most of them move to Connecticut and vote her into office in the fall."

"She's got my vote, but then, I'm a dog lover." With equipment in hand, Clyde sashayed his way through the crowd, miraculously without injuring anyone.

"Just remember that you guys are supposed to be shooting *my* episode today," Nick called out, without bothering to kick up too much fuss. He was more intent on tracking down his own lady—ladies, if you counted his daughter. He craned his neck past a line of tubas. They were warming up before the start of The Parade, making concentration a little difficult. And he would need all the concentration he could muster, he figured, after royally screwing up last night.

Out of the blue, he had become an overly protective father. That still didn't excuse him for jumping to conclusions before he'd heard Amara's side of the story. Besides, even if she had spent the night doing the dirty with some horny though undoubtedly over-achieving boy, who was he to criticize? He had done his fair share of crazy things by the time he was his daughter's age. And he supposed that she, too, had to learn by making mistakes.

If only they could happen on somebody else's watch.

Um-pah-pah. Um-pah-pah. The tubas were working away.

"Nick, buddy. Oh, ruler of the Beer Pong table!" With a slap on the back, Justin greeted him from behind.

Nick held his hand to his ear to indicate the difficulties in carrying on a conversation. "I'm glad to see you're not a sore loser," he shouted. He gave Justin the once-over. He was dressed in an orange-and-black stretchy yoga outfit. "That getup could be very iffy if you had any kind of a paunch." He patted his own small mound. He really would have to get a gym membership, he told himself.

"Don't I know it!" Lilah appeared next to her husband. Her hand fondled her round belly. A gap of skin showed between the tank top and the loose pants.

"Is it possible that you've gotten bigger just since I saw you at Hoagie Palace?" Nick asked.

She turned to Justin. "See, I told you. It makes it

even more urgent to find a bigger apartment before
I get stuck trying to negotiate our narrow hallway."

Justin squeezed her shoulder. "I'm already one
step ahead of you. I emailed my sister yesterday to
see if she'd heard of anyone at the university going
on sabbatical in the fall semester who might want
to rent their house."

"Wouldn't it have been easier to call your father?
He might know more people since he's on the faculty," Lilah suggested.

"Please, it's not like I'd ever call him for anything," Justin replied.

"I've met your father, and no offense, but I'm with
you all the way," Nick agreed.

Justin held up his hands. "No offense taken at all.
Anyway, I must have had some ESP thing going because Penelope got back to me earlier this morning,
saying there was a possibility that we could rent her
place next semester. I'm sure she'll give us a deal."

Um-pah-pah. Um-pah-pah. The tubas kept it up.

Was she already thinking of moving in with him?
Nick wondered. If any other woman had sent out a
signal like that, it would have sent him scurrying
to a distant country with no means of reliable communication. But this time, the thought that Penelope could...or would... He found himself smiling.
So this is what love is all about? he couldn't help
musing.

"Everyone, please gather at your respective stations," a voice boomed over the loudspeaker.

Um-pah-pah.

"Oops. Better follow orders," Justin said and waved goodbye. He grabbed Lilah's hand, and the two wandered toward their fellow classmates, Justin greeting one and all, Lilah stalwartly at his side.

Um-pah-pah. Um-pah-pah.

"Oh, when the saints. Oh, when the saints…"

The blare of the tubas now competed with a Dixieland jazz band on a float that was billowing suspicious gray smoke. The march at last got underway.

"Where the…" Nick was nervous. Penelope did say that she and Amara would join him, right? He pressed the tip of his tongue against the inside of his top teeth and craned to look around the growing melee.

"Da-ad! Da-ad! Here we are!" Amara pushed through the crowd that was slowly working its way up a campus road toward Main Street.

Amara launched herself at her father. "I'm sorry I acted like such a brat last night. I let you jump to all the wrong conclusions. I should have just been honest with you." She hugged him tight.

He closed his eyes, savoring her warmth, her energy—her love. Life didn't get much better than this.

"I'm sorry I blew my stack last night, too," he apologized. Here, he'd been prepared for a long and drawn-out exchange where he'd have to regain Amara's confidence in him while still reaffirming the importance of parentally established limits. One of those grown-up talks that no one liked giving or hearing, but apparently were essential for a family to survive.

And now? All that angst that he had built up about it? Poof. Gone. He'd have to learn not to question the good times and just accept that life was indeed wonderful sometimes.

"It's okay, Dad. I get it now. You have a lot on your plate, me included," Amara continued. "And before you say anything, I know I shouldn't have taken off last night without telling you where I was going. And, yes, I've already apologized to Penelope for taking her bike."

"Which was completely unnecessary because you'd had my permission," Penelope said from off to the side.

Nick slanted her a grateful look.

She returned it with a dazzling smile.

Yup, life couldn't get any better than this.

After she gave her father one more tight squeeze, Amara stepped back. "So, aren't you going to say anything about how we look?" Amara held her hands out to her sides and stepped next to Penelope.

They looked like exotic birds—Amara in a dazzling mandarin-orange sari that somehow went with her fuchsia highlights. And Penelope. Ah, Penelope.

He wondered what would happen if he pulled on one end of the gold braid at her waist. Would all that fringe slither down her body, leaving her standing delectably naked?

"Well, what do you think?" Amara prompted him, doing a quick twirl.

He picked his jaw up off the ground. "I think you look fantastic, both of you. I was just worried when I didn't see you earlier."

"I know. I was a bit concerned about how long it took us to walk here—there was no point in driving since there's no place to park," Penelope admitted. "But Amara convinced me that it was okay to arrive fashionably late. It's a first for me, you realize, and I have your daughter to thank." She gave a nod of her head to Amara and a knowing smile to Nick.

"It seems like we all have a lot to be thankful for." He stepped between them and reached for their hands. He leaned toward Penelope and whispered, "Thanks, I couldn't have done it without you." He kissed her lightly on the lips until he remembered that his daughter was there, too. "Oops." He pulled back.

"That's okay, Dad. Penelope and I talked about that, too, and I'm all right with it," Amara assured him. She took his hand in hers and swung their arms. "Shall we?" she offered as his class gradually swelled forward to join the others.

CHAPTER THIRTY-TWO

EACH CLASS MARCHED IN ORDER, with the oldest first
and the year's graduating class bringing up the rear.
The alums and families, including numerous pets,
celebrated the gigantic display of kinship with their
alma mater and each other. It was an orgy of colors
with the costumes, banners and balloons waving
in the breeze. The motley assortment of loud bands
and dubious floats added to the festivities as the
marchers made their way through the campus. All
along Main Street, townspeople lined the sidewalks.
Some were even waiting in beach chairs. The sale
of Grantham University pennants and fake lion tails
was big business. That and a bilious orange-colored
cotton candy.

The whole thing was corny as hell. But the thing
of it was, Nick actually found himself enjoying it
immensely. Celebrations were good, he recognized,
whether it was for the birth of a child or a wedding
or winning the Super Bowl. There was something
fundamental about people needing to get together
in a common bond of goodwill and good memories.
These were the moments that helped lessen life's

problems that invariably touched everyone in some fashion.

The pace of the march was slow enough that he could easily look around and think these grand philosophical thoughts without worrying. In fact, he didn't worry at all—a rarity when he was filming. One, because he caught sight of Georgie on the rampage, orchestrating Clyde and Larry to catch as much good stuff as possible. And two—a big number two—why worry when he had his girls on either side?

He tipped his chin down and pressed a kiss atop Penelope's soft hair and nuzzled up against that absurd bow. Immediately he had the wicked idea of taking it between his teeth…. He smiled. Then glanced up, catching the camera's lens right in his face. That would definitely have to be edited out, Nick mused.

"Hey, Amara." Press jogged up next to Nick's daughter. "I tried to text you, but you didn't respond." He glanced over and noticed Nick. "Actually maybe now isn't the best time."

Amara kept cool. "That's all right. My dad knows about everything."

"You mean everything?" Press opened his eyes wide.

Nick felt Penelope squeeze his hand a little too tightly. He got the message. He looked at Press. "I know you did the right thing, kid. So, as a father, what can I say but thank you?"

Amara looked at him sternly. "His name's not 'kid.' He's called Press."

Penelope leaned around Nick. "Hi, Press. I'm glad you could make it to The Parade before the talk this afternoon. I'm so looking forward to it."

"Yeah, I hope it goes all right. I've never given a lecture before. I'm a little nervous."

"You'll be wonderful." Penelope glanced at Amara. "Won't he?"

"If you say so." Amara was hardly enthusiastic.

Penelope narrowed her eyes. "What did we agree to about forgiveness?"

Amara sighed. "Sorry."

Press kept up with the flow by skipping backward, occasionally looking over his shoulder to make sure where he was going. He didn't look as though he was in any hurry to leave.

His doggedness seemed to do the trick. "Listen," Amara finally said. "How about we just forget about everything that happened. You know, with you and me."

"Sure, no problem. It's forgotten." Press jumped over a loose brick. "But at the same time, I don't think we should just forget about each other—pretend like we never met. I mean, I don't intend to forget you. You're terrific."

Nick, who was acting as if he wasn't listening to

286   A RARE FIND

the whole conversation, couldn't help empathizing with the guy. Press didn't stand a chance in the face of his daughter. That was for sure.

"And I know we just agreed to forget about... well...the stuff that happened last night. But I still want to apologize for the way I brushed you off. I mean, it wasn't right...you know?" He gave Nick a furtive look.

Amara touched Press's arm. "I know."

"Which is why I'm glad you met my friend Matt. You see, he's really a decent guy." Press landed awkwardly coming off a curb, but he didn't let that stop him.

"Then you know that we just had dinner and talked?" Amara asked.

"Yeah, he texted me this morning. Not that I wasn't worried when I saw the two of you leave together." Press bit down on his lower lip.

Amara suppressed a smile.

The kid really didn't stand a chance, Nick thought with amusement.

Press scrambled along some more. "Listen, I wanted to let you know that Matt's someone you can trust, someone for the long haul, someone with his heart in the right place."

"And you're not?" she questioned.

"Listen, I better get going," Press said, ignoring Amara's question. "I'm supposed to be back with my classmates. So…" He pointed to the rear of the procession.

Amara grabbed him. "Wait, Press. Matt *is* nice, but strictly just as a friend. Anyway, right now, I need time just for me. And you, Press Lodge—" she pointed a finger at the center of his jacket "—you need to take some time to figure out who you are, too. Stop pretending that you're some noble lone wolf who feels he needs to protect other people from getting close to him. I mean, talk about an attitude."

Press looked down at her finger. Marchers around them were moving forward. Nick lingered. Penelope held back.

Press opened his mouth, but nothing came out. Finally he shook his head. "So maybe I'll see you this afternoon at the talk, then?"

Amara checked dutifully with her father. "Is it okay if I go to Press's talk this afternoon? Penelope will be there."

"And you may consider me the perfect chaperone. Think of me as a maiden aunt, a Miss Havisham without the wrinkles," Penelope contributed, referring to the character in Dickens's *Great Expectations.*

"Penelope, you made a joke!" Press was stunned.

"She makes them all the time," Nick chimed in. "And, yes, you may go to the talk, Amara. But now, *Press*—" he emphasized the young man's name to prove that he remembered it "—it's time you headed back to your class. I am understanding up to a point. I prefer you in small doses. Nothing personal, you understand."

"I got it. See you this afternoon, then," he said with a jump before surging to the back of the line.

"He's sweet," Penelope announced.

"I guess." Amara turned away. "Oh, is that the new residential college that we're passing?" she asked ever so casually.

Nick turned to Penelope. "I think she's trying to tell you it's none of your business."

"I may be socially inept, but I'm not stupid," Penelope said with a harrumph.

Amara went on tiptoe and whispered in Penelope's ear, "You're right. He is."

Nick pretended not to notice. Instead he just let himself enjoy the sunny June day, the company, the music—the total experience that had a way of making life seem utterly simple.

"I have a big confession to make," he admitted.

"You do?" Penelope asked.

"You have?" Amara inquired.

"Right now, I am a very happy man." He angled his head to catch sight of the crew, and signaled he wanted someone to zoom in.

"So, Amara." He put his arm around his daughter.

The tubas started blaring again, this time with a rendition of the "William Tell Overture." Larry danced around with his camera on his shoulder, filming Nick in the middle with Amara and Penelope on each side.

Nick made a show of brushing off an invisible piece of dust from the braiding on his short little toreador's jacket. "It isn't every day a man gets to look a total fool and still enjoy being in public with his daughter."

The tubas blasted away.

Amara laughed and leaned into his arm. "I'm glad that I could be here, too, even if the reason behind showing up was pretty depressing at the time." She skipped by his side, oblivious to the camera and sound boom wavering overhead.

"Tell me, daughter," he began. "Other than the fact that you are clearly more mature than I was at your age, how come you're feeling generous enough to forgive my failings as a parent? Are you caught up in this festive spirit, or are you simply taking pity on me because of this ridiculous outfit?" He held his arms out and mugged for the camera.

"You do look pretty bad, but, c'mon, Dad, you know." Amara teased him.

Nick shook his head. "Actually I don't." He glanced over at Penelope. "Do you?"

She smiled. "I was very pleased with the news."

Now Nick was *really* confused. "News?"

They continued to walk along at the leisurely pace.

Um-PAH-PAH.

"About my school? About being able to graduate after all?"

Nick opened his mouth. *Oh, my God.*

"Isn't it wonderful," Penelope agreed. "Amara will be able to go to the ceremony next week after all, along with all her friends."

"I can't thank you enough for calling. It clearly made all the difference," Amara gushed.

Nick stopped dead in his tracks. His sudden lack of movement forced Amara and Penelope to halt, as well. On both sides, the marchers swarmed past them.

Pah-pah-pah, PAH-PAH-PAH. The tubas ended with a flourish.

"But I didn't call. I forgot." Nick caught the startled look on Amara's face. "I'm so sorry. What with everything going on with the filming yesterday at the restaurant, and then later with…with…"

"Me," Penelope said, her voice flat.

Nick saw the color drain from Penelope's face. Then he turned back to Amara. "But, believe me, I'm so happy for you, that everything worked out at school after all. Clearly they must have decided to cut you some slack, which means any input on my part would have been a waste of time, right?"

He reached for her hand again.

Amara pulled it back, nearly tripping against a

toreador-clad classmate of Nick's. "You don't understand. They just couldn't have changed their mind.
The headmistress knew all about my friend and everything. If you didn't call, who did?"

Nick shrugged. "I don't know." He glanced at Penelope. She shrugged, too.

"But…but…you promised you'd call. I trusted
you."

Nick could see the tears forming in his daughter's
eyes. She looked so small and vulnerable with the
boisterous revelers pushing all around her. And that
the whole world seemed to be crashing in was all
his fault. "Amara, I know I've disappointed you. I
should have called. I was wrong to forget. But promise I'll make it up to you." He reached out again.

She shook her head. Now the tears were streaming down her cheeks. She didn't bother brushing
them away as she turned and ran.

"Amara, Amara, come back," Nick shouted to her
retreating figure. He pushed his way against the on-
coming tide.

Penelope yanked his arm. "No, you stay here.
She's hurt and will only run farther if you try to
follow. I'll go after her."

"But I should go," Nick protested. "It's all my
fault."

"Yes, it is." As usual, Penelope didn't mince
words. "But she needs some distance right now. Be-

sides—" she looked around "—don't you have an episode to shoot?"

And that's when Nick realized the sound boom was still hovering overhead.

CHAPTER THIRTY-THREE

"AMARA, AMARA, WAIT UP."

Amara could hear Penelope shouting, but she kept running, veering onto some campus road that led past the tennis courts. She didn't have the faintest idea where she was. All she knew was she had to get away. From The Parade. From the people. From her father.

"Amara," Penelope called again from behind. "Running away doesn't solve anything."

Amara twisted her neck and looked over her shoulder. Penelope was still holding her own, not looking winded at all. If anything, she was gaining on her. *It must be all that bike riding*, thought Amara dejectedly. She tried turning it up a notch to shake her. She wasn't angry with Penelope. It wasn't her fault her father was an ass. Still, that didn't mean Amara wanted to face her.

She pumped her legs faster until her calf muscles burned and her throat became sore from breathing heavily. With each stride, she felt her broken heart rip a little further.

"Amara, stop," Penelope shouted.

Amara looked over her shoulder. And realized she couldn't lose Penelope. Finally she did stop. She didn't bother to stem the flow of tears.

Penelope drew up next to her. She stood up straight and tightened the knot around her waist. "Good," she announced when it was secure. "I had visions of doing a Lady Godiva about fifty yards back, there."

Despite everything that had happened, Amara almost laughed. "Try running in a sari, if you want excitement. If it hadn't started slipping, I'm sure I could have outrun you," she replied. She wasn't so sure at all.

Penelope, to her credit, didn't contradict her outright. Instead she spoke in gentle tones. "Speaking of running, I remember when I was a little girl I had this favorite book. I'm sure you're too old to remember it. It was called *Runaway Bunny.*"

"No, I remember it. I loved it, especially the pictures—like the blue cover with the white rabbit."

"Yes, the illustrations are lovely, aren't they? There's something very charming about them even now. And the story has the same timeless appeal. Do you recall? No matter how far the bunny ran, his mother rabbit found him." She stared directly at Amara. "I'm like that mother rabbit. No matter how fast or how far you run—and regardless of potential wardrobe malfunctions—I *will* run after you and I *will* find you."

"Except you're not my mother."

Penelope pursed her mouth. "Very true. I'm not that lucky. Nevertheless, that doesn't mean that I can't have a mother's instincts." She paused. "Come home. Come home with me."

Amara breathed in slowly. She mulled her options—basically none. "All right," she surrendered. "But this time a grilled cheese sandwich is not going to solve the problem."

"I know."

"You said I could trust him. You lied."

"I didn't lie. I truly believed it myself."

"And now?" Amara shot back.

"Now?" It was Penelope's turn to breathe in slowly. "Now I don't know." She seemed thoughtful for a minute, then straightened her shoulders. "One thing I do know, however, is that our good friend Press is giving a talk this afternoon. I intend to be there—as should you. So let's go home, get refreshed—calm down, at least outwardly. He needs our support, and we will concentrate on that for now."

"But what about my dad? How can you forget about what just happened? Especially after you lectured me earlier today."

"I'm not sure *lecture* is the correct word," Penelope qualified.

Amara tossed her head. "Whatever. I'm pretty sure you *talked*—" she emphasized the word sarcastically "—about the importance of trust—how you have to forgive people—that they can change, do the right thing. And I'm pretty sure my father just demonstrated that he's beyond change. Don't you agree? Or are you going to ignore his pathetic behavior and pretend it doesn't have any impact on your relationship with him?"

"Hardly. But I am capable of compartmentalizing my life, not having emotions overwhelm me. That way I can deal with what's most immediately important."

"I don't get it. Doesn't that amount to another form of running away?"

"Not exactly. I will make my decision as to your father with quiet, timely deliberation. I'm not what you might call a spontaneous person. I prefer to evaluate the events fully. But once I do that, I'm not afraid of making decisions. So, no, I would not call that running away."

Penelope adjusted the knot of the shawl behind her neck to make sure that didn't slip any further. Then she pointed in the direction of her house. "Beyond that—say what you will. I definitely need a grilled cheese sandwich. But I might team it with a large glass of wine."

CHAPTER THIRTY-FOUR

PENELOPE APPROACHED PRESS once all the questions after his half-hour presentation were done. "Press, that was a terrific talk. I was particularly impressed with the way you handled the queries about preservation."

After the emotional roller coaster at The Parade, she felt reassured that at least this part of her life was under control.

Even though the exhibit talk was in the same time slot as a symposium on world economic markets by two Nobel Prize-winning economists, Press had managed to draw a crowd of forty to fifty people. It was particularly encouraging to see that it attracted people of all ages. Perhaps the written word would not die out despite the onslaught of technology.

Perhaps even more gratifying was the sight of her father walking in halfway through. They may have had their differences over dinner the other night, but it just went to show, family will out, she thought.

She'd tried to make eye contact during the talk, but as he stood at the back of the group, his hands crossed behind his back and his black-and-orange bow tie perfectly centered at his neck, he focused intently on Press. When the subject of the Grantham Galen came up, she was glad to see it pleased him.

With Press's fine performance now over, she shook his hand, one colleague to another. Both of them had switched out of their Parade regalia, Press in a blue blazer and striped tie, she in black trousers and a moss-green linen jacket. She kept the orange foulard in her hair in deference to the school colors and to cheer herself up.

Things had not gone the way she had hoped this morning. She felt for Amara. She really did. The relationship between a father and daughter was a special one, and she was afraid that Nick might have jeopardized it seriously for the near future.

At least Amara looked better. Before the talk had started, she had taken a seat next to a thin young man, and the two had chatted amicably. He must be the Matt Penelope had heard mention of. The two had waved to Press before he'd started, and he'd acknowledged them with a nervous nod.

Now they were quietly making their way to the front, and she was sure he would want to join them. "I don't want to keep you any longer than necessary," Penelope spoke to him, "but I just want to let you know what a difference it made having you by my side, helping out all year. I don't know what I'll do next year without you."

"That was a great talk, Press. I was impressed," the young man said.

"Like it's hard to impress a Yale man," Press joked. He held his hand out to Penelope and introduced Matt. Then he turned to Amara. "I'm glad you could make it, too." Some of the bravado had gone out of his voice.

"Your presentation was inspiring," Amara told him. "It makes me even more excited about coming to Grantham in the fall."

Penelope sent her a pleased smile. No matter how much she must be hurting inside, Amara was doing the right thing.

Press snapped his fingers. "Hey! I've got a great idea. Amara will be a freshman. You can employ her."

"Oh, my gosh. It would be a dream come true." Amara touched her chest, clearly moved. She, too, had switched out of the sari and was wearing the shirt and skirt she'd had on the night she'd come to dinner.

"What a good idea." Penelope beamed, wanting to encourage her positive attitude.

And she would have said something more but she noticed a small, frail-looking man making his way to the front of the room. His dry skin showed a web of fine lines and was very pale, except for several conspicuous age spots. Atop his head, he wore a black baseball cap emblazoned Class of '43.

"Excuse me, I was wondering if I could have a closer look at the Grantham Galen?" the man asked. He had a wisp of a German accent. "I've only seen one other like it."

"You must mean the manuscript in the Vatican Library. I remember studying it years ago, but I believe this one is finer," Penelope said.

"Penelope." Press touched her shoulder. "If it's all right, I'll take off?"

"Absolutely. You three go and celebrate, enjoy yourselves." She watched them leave and give their goodbyes before turning to aid the man.

He had rested a metal cane against the cabinet containing the manuscript and was peering close to the glass. He murmured something that Penelope couldn't catch.

Then she saw him reach, grabbing the corners of the wooden frame of the cabinet to steady himself. She rushed to his side. "Can I get you a chair?" she asked. "A glass of water? It's been warm today and perhaps with the crowd…"

"No, no, I'm fine. I'm just…ah…overwhelmed." He pointed to the typed label next to the manuscript. "This indicates how the university came to possess the document, correct?"

"Yes, yes, that's right," she responded. "As you can see, it was donated by Stanfield Bigelow, Class of '71. He's a professor here, quite renowned."

The small man stared at Penelope, taking in her

words, before returning to gaze at the manuscript. "You know him well, this Professor Bigelow?"

Penelope nodded. "Very well. He happens to be my father. In fact, I believe he's in the room now, looking at some of the other pieces in the collection. I could get him." She struggled to find him among all the people still lingering around the exhibition space, admiring the objects on display.

The man touched her sleeve lightly. "If you please, would you wait just a minute?"

Penelope glanced at his withered hand atop her jacket. It seemed to be formed by weightless bird-like bones. Her gaze met his. His eyes were rheumy, behind glasses with thick bifocal lenses. Still, the force of the gaze was sharp, piercing.

"Yes, Mr…Mr…?" she asked.

"Himmelfarb. Daniel Himmelfarb. My father was Jacob Himmelfarb? Perhaps as a curator of rare books you have heard of his name?"

"Jacob Himmelfarb?" she repeated. "The famous Berlin collector and dealer in rare books?"

"The same. Unfortunately he died in the camps during the war. Auschwitz."

"Yes, I remember that from the biography I read. I can't tell you how sorry I am."

"There is no need for you to be sorry. You weren't even born then. Luckily I was already in the United States, studying physics at Grantham. My father, ever the patriot, insisting on staying, convinced that Germany—*his* Germany—would see the light. When I signed up to fight for America, naturally the army in its infinite wisdom stationed me in New Guinea. Not particularly pleasant. But I survived, unlike my father—or my mother or sister…" His voice trailed off, his gaze once more lingering on the manuscript. "Tell me, your father? He is a good man? An honorable man?"

Penelope automatically nodded. "Yes, of course."

"In which case, I am sure there is some kind of explanation. You see, this manuscript, which somehow came into his possession and which he subsequently donated to Grantham—I must tell you—" once more he shifted his gaze from the display case to Penelope "—it belonged to my father. That is, until the Nazis confiscated it, along with the rest of his holdings, before they sent him to Auschwitz."

Penelope was stunned. "Are you sure? Perhaps you are mistaken? Perhaps it was another manuscript?"

He shook his head. "Perhaps, but I don't think so. I still have the inventory of my father's holdings. He had mailed it to me before he was killed. At the time, I couldn't understand why. And this manuscript, I am sure, is among those listed. I even remember him showing it to me before I left for America. It was one of his favorites. In any case, there is a simple way to verify if it was his or not. On the next-to-last folio of the manuscript—the recto side, to be precise—he always made a faint black mark of the Hebrew letter *hei*. I don't know if you know it? It has two vertical lines, and one horizontal wiggly line at the top. It stands for the sound of an *h*—as in Himmelfarb."

Penelope felt the encounter take on an almost out-of-body experience, as if she were hovering somewhere above the floor, watching a woman, who looked very much like she looked, talking to a man in his late eighties, who clearly had deep and sad memories. And then she heard this woman in the room—the woman who looked and sounded like she—speak. "There's no need to look. I know the mark is there."

CHAPTER THIRTY-FIVE

PENELOPE LOOKED DOWN at the business card that Mr. Himmelfarb had given her before he left, obviously shaken. She had promised she would get in touch with him as soon as possible. He was staying at the Grantham Inn across from the university, so setting up a meeting would be no problem.

She anticipated more than one.

She made a beeline toward her father in the corner of the room. He wasn't so much standing out of the limelight as holding court—attracting a coterie of former students and admirers. He glanced up when he saw her approach. A pleased smile was on his face as if to say, *You see, it may be your exhibit, but I am the one they all came to see.*

Or maybe she was simply feeling critical just then. Who could blame her? Nonetheless, what she was about to do wasn't personal. It was necessary. For her. For the university. But mostly for Jacob Himmelfarb and his descendants.

She nodded politely as she sidestepped a middle-aged couple. "Father, I need to speak to you privately."

"I'm busy at the moment. Perhaps later in my office?" he said, focusing again on the couple. He launched into a story Penelope had heard many times about how he first discovered his love of the Classics as a young boy in Indiana. A neighbor, a retiring high-school Latin teacher, had offered him a copy of Caesar's *Gallic Wars* when he was helping clear out her classroom. "Even though I didn't know a word of Latin, somehow the text spoke to me—not to mention the gory bookplates that accompanied the edition."

The little group chuckled.

They always did. Penelope remembered doing the same, many times.

"Father, this can't wait," she interrupted.

Stanfield stared at her, his eyes wide. Then his expression softened as he addressed his admirers. "If you'll excuse me, please. This is my daughter, and as I am sure you know, a father's job is never done, even when children become adults."

The middle-aged couple nodded knowingly.

Penelope guided her father to a small office off to the side of the exhibit room. It contained a metal desk and chair, stacks of library catalogs and the unforgiving light of overhead fluorescents. They hummed accordingly. The obligatory poster of an illuminated-manuscript show at the Morgan Library hung on the wall.

"Father, I need to talk to you about the Grantham Galen," she said, closing the door behind them.

He waited silently.

She didn't let this behavior intimidate her. She carefully chose her words. "Up until dinner at the house last week, I had always assumed you found the manuscript while you were in Italy after graduate school. But then Mother mentioned her recollection of the time you visited Berlin."

"West Berlin," he corrected. "And I am sure your mother is mistaken."

"Perhaps you are mistaken," Penelope went on. "Perhaps you think you remember purchasing it in Naples, but in fact, Mother is correct. In which case, if you were to find such a rare manuscript in Germany—West Germany," she modified before he could change the subject, "surely you would have suspected that it might have been unlawfully confiscated from a Jewish collector during the war?"

"Penelope, I have never known you to mangle the English language in such a fashion. But to answer what I believe to be your question, even if hypothetically I were to find such a rare manuscript, the logic does not necessarily follow that it would have been taken by the Nazis."

Penelope nodded thoughtfully. "Tell me, Father. You know of Jacob Himmelfarb?"

Stanfield made a *tsking* sound. "Please. Any classicist worth his salt has, of course, heard of the great collector."

"And would you also be able to recognize the distinguishing mark he always made in his acquisitions?"

"You mean the Hebrew letter *hei?* As a learned man, naturally I know Hebrew. But I have yet to see why this discussion warrants pulling me away from talking to one of my former students. He owns a very successful commodities-trading company, and I'm sure the university's Development Office would much rather I spend my time charming him than verifying my academic capabilities with you."

Penelope refused to back down. "Father, the elderly gentleman talking to me a few minutes ago turns out to be Jacob Himmelfarb's son. The Grantham Galen, which you purchased in what I believe now to be Germany despite your recollections, belonged to his father. There is no question. It has the letter *hei* that Jacob Himmelfarb always marked on a particular folio. Surely you must have recognized it as such. You must have realized that it is a stolen artifact that rightly belongs to the Himmelfarb family." Her eyes never left his face.

She saw the tendons in her father's neck grow taut. He cleared his throat. "No, I didn't know." His eyes blinked rapidly.

"You didn't ask."

He raised a disdainful eyebrow. "Neither did you."

Penelope breathed in. "You're correct. I improperly assumed the provenance of the piece based on my respect for you. It was only as I was putting the exhibit together that I noticed the ink mark. It didn't register at the time. A subconscious attempt at denial, I can only assume. In retrospect, I believe I am also responsible for what very well could be a crime."

"If you feel culpable, then you have only yourself to blame. The fact that you question me offends me as a scholar, a moral person and your father."

"I'm sorry, Father, but regardless of your professions of innocence and my own judgment in the matter, the fact remains—indeed, the law states—that the work is the property of Jacob Himmelfarb's family. The university will have to make restitution as soon as possible. As a courtesy to you, I am letting you know that I will be contacting university counsel and the president's office as soon as we finish speaking. I will also let the University Press know about the development, since it has a direct bearing on my book contract."

Penelope realized that she would also have to let Nick and Georgie know that they couldn't use the footage they had shot involving the manuscript.

"If that's all" was her father's only reply.

"Isn't that enough?" she asked. "If it makes you

feel any better, Mr. Himmelfarb's son appears only to be interested in the rightful return of the manuscript. He made no mention of pressing charges of illegal trafficking in stolen merchandise."

"I'm not the least bit concerned about the interests of Mr. Himmelfarb's heirs. My only interest in the manuscript was as a scholar and as a loyal member of the Grantham University community."

Penelope winced. "I'd like to think so. Because if I can't trust my own father, who can I trust? Certainly, it seems, not myself."

CHAPTER THIRTY-SIX

NICK CHECKED HIS MESSAGES. Yet again. Nothing. He
threw the phone on the bedspread.

"Amara hasn't rung back?" Georgie asked calmly.
They were lounging in Nick's hotel room. Georgie was drinking his umpteenth cup of black coffee
with three Sweet'N Lows. Nick was nursing a bottle
of beer.

Nick shook his head and took a long sip. "It's like
she's gone completely off the grid, which frankly
I can't blame her for. But I've also been trying Penelope a bunch of times, and she hasn't answered,
either. I just get put straight to her voice mail. It's
not like her."

"Maybe she's got her phone turned off or is talking to someone? She had that talk at the library,
right? The one that college kid is giving?"

"Or maybe she just doesn't want to talk to me,"
Nick acknowledged with frustration. "You haven't
heard anything since her text about the footage at
the Rare Book Library, right?"

Georgie shook his head.

"Humor me. Look again?" Nick asked semipolitely.

Georgie pulled the BlackBerry from his pants pocket and checked his messages. "Nothing."

Nick screwed up his face. "It was not my finest hour at The Parade, as you and the boys captured so brilliantly on film."

Georgie shrugged. "Don't sweat it. That's what editing's for. What's more important was Penelope's text saying that she was taking Amara to the talk. Things can't be all bad then, am I right?"

"Wrong. I finally called Amara's headmistress, like I should have done days ago, and I find out the reason things are now hunky-dory with Ms. I've Even Got Starch In My Underpants headmistress is because Amara's friend went in and confessed the whole thing." Nick held up his hands, palms up. "A frigging sixteen-year-old knows to do the right thing while I make a hash of it."

"You've had a lot on your plate. Give yourself a break," Georgie consoled him.

"Like in the midst of everything else you would have forgotten to do something for your kids?"

"Did I ever tell you about the time I forgot to pick up my eldest from nursery school? I got this call from her teacher, saying little Betsy was beside herself. Talk about feeling guilty. Marjorie didn't let me forget it for weeks, no, years," Georgie confessed.

"I hardly think that forgetting to pick up your

daughter from nursery school is on equal footing with neglecting to make sure your daughter graduates from high school."

"At the time, you wouldn't have thought so." Georgie reached over to place his coffee mug on the desk. "Listen, you made a mistake. Accept responsibility and apologize profusely. Whatever you do—don't try to bribe her with money."

Nick blinked. "That never would have occurred to me."

"See? That just goes to show you're not as superficial as you think."

"I *think* you're putting too positive a spin on it. Listen, we're not shooting this dining scene at the student center until six, right? That still gives me time to hoof it over to the library and try to catch her there."

"Which 'her' are you talking about?"

Nick didn't answer. He wasn't sure himself.

Georgie waved him off. "Sure, go. No problem. I promised I'd discuss some campaign-advertising strategies with Vivian, anyway, this afternoon."

"So it's 'Vivian' now?" Nick asked.

Georgie scowled. "Did anyone ever tell you you're a smart-ass?"

"Yeah, you. All the time."

PRESS HEARD THE TAPPING on the glass door at the entrance to the exhibit hall. It was Amara's dad, probably coming to bust his chops about doing something he hadn't even done. From what Amara told him over strawberry ice cream after the talk, the guy sounded like a total loser.

Press lowered his head and pretended he didn't see Nick standing on the other side of the locked door. He had just removed the Grantham Galen from the locked display case to transfer it back to the vault, as per Penelope's instructions.

She'd phoned him when he'd been sitting with Amara at the picnic tables outside the ice-cream shop.

"You need me to do what?" Press had asked his boss to repeat her words. And when she did, he said, "I don't get it. Is something wrong?"

"I'm not at liberty to discuss it now," Penelope had responded in a clipped fashion.

Press started to feel guilty even though he couldn't imagine why. "I didn't do anything wrong at the talk, did I?"

Penelope had laughed, but it hadn't sounded particularly jolly. "Press, we should all be as virtuous as you." Then she'd told him to print up a card to place in the case, announcing that the manuscript had been temporarily removed.

Tap-tap-tap.

Annoyed, Press looked up. The guy clearly wasn't about to take no for an answer. He locked the transfer box with the manuscript and pocketed the key.

Then he walked to the glass door, undid the dead bolt and inched open the door. "I'm sorry, the exhibition is now closed. It will be reopened later." He went to shut the door.

Only, Amara's dad used his foot to block the door from being closed.

"Ow," he complained when the heavy door pressed into his foot. "I'm not here about the exhibit."

Press looked aside before glancing back at Nick. "Somehow I didn't think so. Did you suddenly remember you had a daughter maybe?"

"Okay," Nick stated matter-of-factly, "I deserved that. But as long as we're on the subject of Amara…"

Press lifted his stubborn chin. "She's not here. She went back to Penelope's house."

"And Penelope?" The question hung in the air.

"I don't know. You'll have to ask her. Now, if you don't mind…" He again put his hand on the door to close it.

Nick angled his head. "Something's up, isn't it? Is it something I did?"

Press frowned. "You know, sometimes not everything is about you." This time he closed the door without any problems.

PENELOPE GLANCED DOWN at her cell phone and saw the list of calls from Nick. She did the only logical thing.

She turned off her phone.

She would have unplugged the home phone, too, but she needed to leave a line open in case the university's lawyer called back. She had also left word with the president's office, but the lawyer said he would also speak to him directly. There was also the chance that Press would need clarification regarding her instructions to remove the Grantham Galen. But she doubted it. She had trained him well. He was smart. Unlike most people, he didn't feel the need to ask too many questions.

She sank into a wooden chair by the small table in the kitchen and slipped the scarf off her head. She didn't feel festive anymore. She breathed in slowly. The only thing she had eaten all day was half a grilled cheese sandwich, and she contemplated the options without much enthusiasm.

As she reached into the pantry to get a box of Stoned Wheat Thins, the phone rang in the living room. Before she got there, it rang again, obnoxiously loud, and she stared at the caller ID. Her parents. She sighed and picked up the phone. It was inevitable.

"Hello," she said as she headed back to the kitchen.

"Penelope, this is your mother."

As if she couldn't recognize her mother's voice. "Hello, Mother." On the lowest shelf of the small pantry was a clear bottle. Grappa—Italy's version of white lightning. Highly effective for cauterizing wounds, opening up the sinuses and achieving a rapid buzz.

"I'm calling because your father is deeply hurt by what happened today at the library exhibit."

Penelope could sense her father standing next to her mother, hanging on to every word as she spoke. "Imagine how I feel." She plunked the bottle on the counter and opened an upper cabinet. There was an array of drinking glasses, including decent wine and sherry glasses. *Screw it,* she thought, and chose a cheap juice glass. She tucked the phone under her chin, wrestled the top of the bottle free and poured herself a generous three fingers.

"Did you have to talk that way to him in front of all those people?" her mother asked.

"There was a sense of urgency to our conversation, but I discreetly pulled him to the side, to an office." Penelope sipped the liquor. It burned her throat. She heard some murmurings in the background. She'd been right. Her father was there, using her mother as a shield.

"You know he feels ashamed, don't you?" her mother went on.

Was he now admitting what he had done? She felt sad, but at the same time a sense of relief. "I'm glad he is willing to accept his part."

"No, dear, I don't think you understand. He's ashamed that you would accuse him of doing anything so unscholarly. He feels it demonstrates a level of insensitivity on your part. That you just don't know him."

Penelope stared at the glass on the counter and the box of crackers next to it. She shook the box. It was nearly empty. She breathed in deeply. "I'm sorry to hear you say that, Mother." Her voice showed no emotion. Though did she ever show any emotion when talking to either of her parents? That revelation seemed rather sad, even to her "insensitive" ears.

In the end, she said the only thing she could say. "I'm sorry, but on the advice of the university's attorney, I can't talk about this matter any further with anyone, including you or Father." She waited.

There was silence from the other end. And then her mother spoke, her voice clearly shaken. "I want you to know, Penelope, that regardless of this little episode…"

Little episode? Penelope wanted to scream out loud. Instead she chomped on a cracker.

"Your father and I love you very much."

Penelope didn't respond.

"Penelope? Are you there, Penelope?"

Penelope detected someone coughing in the background, followed by low voices.

"I'm not sure, but I think she hung up," she could hear her mother say.

"Nonsense. The daughter *I* know would never hang up on her mother." That was her father.

The absolute certainty in his voice did it.

Penelope hung up.

Startled by her own action, she stood there, her hand still touching the cradled portable phone, wondering if her parents would call back. They never did.

Her father was a bully *and* a coward, and her mother would never think of challenging his judgment, Penelope realized. She turned to the chair by the fireplace—the one that her father always occupied when he came to her house.

"How can you talk about the daughter you know, Father, when the truth of the matter is, you've never known me—not really." She directed her question to the armchair. "And if you've never really known me, how is it possible for you to have ever loved me— the real me?" She paused, deliberately wet her lips then set her jaw. "All I can say, Father, is it's your loss. Because I'm worth knowing—and loving."

CHAPTER THIRTY-SEVEN

AMARA FOUND PENELOPE sitting on the grass in the garden behind the house. In her hand she held a drink. Amara walked closer. "That doesn't look like Prosecco," she observed, peering at the bottle of alcohol on the stoop by the French doors.

Penelope looked up. "This is not a Prosecco moment."

Amara slid to the ground across from her. "Something wrong?"

Penelope took a slow sip. "Something that even a grilled cheese sandwich can't cure."

Amara made a face. "That bad, huh?"

"That bad."

"It's not because of anything I did, like with what's going on with my father?" she asked. The last thing Amara wanted was to drag Penelope into her family's mess.

Penelope reached across the small space of lawn and patted Amara's hand. "No, it's nothing to do with you. If anything, you've been a breath of fresh air in my life—a reminder of all of life's good and exciting possibilities." She smiled weakly before removing her hand. Then she took another contemplative sip. "I believe my father has done something terribly wrong," Penelope said in her straightforward fashion.

"He didn't kill anyone, did he?"

"No, nothing like that. But something immoral, nonetheless. Intellectually dishonest."

"It has to do with the exhibit, doesn't it?"

Penelope nodded.

"Press said that you'd asked him to remove the Grantham Galen from the show."

"I really can't talk about it. It's a legal issue, you see."

Amara didn't, but she nodded anyway. She hated to see Penelope so unhappy. She bit her lip, trying to think of something that might help. "Maybe, even if he did do something, he didn't really know what he was doing? I know that's no defense, but…" Her words trailed off.

Penelope blinked slowly and stared off into space. "I try to tell myself the same thing. That's what I want to believe. That he was young and simply too excited to ask larger questions."

"Well, maybe he *is* innocent?"

Penelope refocused on Amara. "I just can't be sure, even if he claims to be so." She paused. "And that's the real crux of the matter. I've arrived at a point where I don't trust him anymore. And without trust, I don't believe you can love someone."

She seemed to wrestle with her words. "I want to love my father, I really do, no matter what. He's my father, after all. But I find I can't. So, you see, in a way, it's my failing. I can't find it within myself to forgive him no matter what. In fact, I also believe that I am complicit in this matter, which makes me untrustworthy, and by inference, unlovable."

The doorbell rang.

Penelope turned her head to the living room. "You don't think he could have come over? My father, I mean."

"Well, there's one way to find out." Amara rose, and strolled into the house

A moment later she returned.

"IT SEEMS TO BE RAINING fathers today," Amara announced.

Penelope glanced over her shoulder.

Nick wiped his brow with the back of his hand. He was sweating, and the short orange jacket of his toreador costume had dark crescents under his armpits. The white T-shirt underneath stuck to his chest. "Sorry for barging in like this. That kid—" he stopped "—Press told me I might find you here, so I ran all the way from the library. I didn't want to miss you."

Penelope unfolded her legs to get up. "Perhaps it would be better if I went inside?"

Nick held out his hand. "No, there's no need. Besides, this is your house."

"In which case." Penelope settled back on the grass. She made a grand gesture to the stretch of lawn before her.

He crouched down. There was the sound of tearing. He swung his head around and felt the back of his tight pants. "That was probably a mistake." He looked at his daughter and Penelope. Neither had a smile. *Okay.*

He settled gingerly on the ground and turned to Amara.

She raised her chin, daring him to knock the chip off it.

He breathed heavily. Then he collected himself. *You can do this,* he told himself.

"First off, I want to say how sorry I am for not calling your headmistress right away. I have no excuse."

Amara crossed her arms.

"I also want to let you know that after The Parade I immediately called her and got through. She verified that you will be able to graduate along with everyone in your class, and that the school would not notify Grantham of the incident. So there's no need to worry on that account."

"She said the same thing to me over the phone already," Amara stated.

"And did she tell you that they came to this decision due to the girl you helped? She knew to step up and do the right thing. That took a lot of courage. Clearly she's a good friend who values you as a good friend, too."

"She's all right, though? I mean, she's not kicked out?" Amara asked.

"There'll be some punishment, but nothing too drastic from what I understand."

"And she'll still keep her scholarship?"

Nick nodded. "As far as I know." He paused. "Listen, as soon as your mother gets back—"

"She comes back Monday," Amara interrupted.

He nodded. "Fine, two days from now, then, *after* you ask her all about her honeymoon, you better tell her what happened. She should hear it from you first."

"I know."

"And when you do, you don't have to sugarcoat my ineptitude in handling the situation—although I don't think that will surprise her." Nick worked his jaw. "Amara, that's about all I have to say, except how sorry I am that I disappointed you. I would like to tell you that it will never happen again, but I don't want to make any promises I can't keep. I'm certainly willing to try harder. And needless to say, I'm more than willing to listen to regular reminders about how I should behave properly. An occasional kick in the pants would also not be out of order."

He looked back and forth between Amara and Penelope.

Amara glanced over at Penelope, but she sat there silently, her hand cupping her glass. Amara scrunched her nose. "Great, thanks for coming by and telling me all that."

"I know it doesn't make up for what I did, but I was kind of hoping you'd…" He stumbled for words.

"Forgive you?" Penelope spoke up for the first time.

He glanced at her. "There is that, although that might be stretching things."

She didn't respond.

Then Amara sighed loudly. "You know, I don't want to have to keep going through this whole thing with you again and again—having you promise to do something, then failing miserably, then me getting all upset, followed by you apologizing, leaving me having to say it's all right."

"I know. That would be really pathetic, especially if I have to keep running around town in this ridiculous outfit. And now I'm sitting here with my pants split open."

Amara rolled her eyes. "Da-ad. This is not some joke."

He shook his head. "You're right. It's not. Sometimes I can't help myself—especially when I'm nervous."

Amara looked shocked. "Nervous? You get nervous?"

"Doesn't everybody?" He raised his hand, shook it, then clenched his fist. "Listen, I don't want you to constantly be disappointed and then later feel obliged to make me feel better, either. I want to take responsibility. I don't want you to have to be the parent. If I do a good job, you don't have to thank me. That's what I'm supposed to do. If I mess up, you don't have to make excuses for me. Just tell me I messed up and demand that I do better."

Amara bit down on her lower lip. "You hurt me bad, you know."

He gave a brisk nod. "I know I did."

"I'll have to think about what you said—the whole 'father' thing. And that's the best I can promise now."

"Then that's what I'll take." He rubbed his open palms against the grass.

"But if we're going to have this discussion again, you've got to lose that outfit," Amara reprimanded him. "At least you're not wearing that stupid hat."

Penelope raised her glass. "Now, *that* is funny."

"But just because I made a joke doesn't mean we're squared away—not by a long shot." Amara gave it to him good.

Finally—finally—he suppressed his smile. "I know. I realize that. But at least let me extend the offer for you to come to my Class Day speech. Let me show you that I do know how to do some things right." He held out a hand.

"I might have accepted, but your timing's bad—as usual. See, Mom and Glenn are coming in on Monday, and I was thinking of going back home tomorrow to make sure that the house was all in order. Maybe get them eggs and milk, or whatever you're supposed to have in the refrigerator."

"Flowers. Flowers are always appropriate—not in the refrigerator, though," Penelope piped up.

Amara bobbed her head. "Good idea. In any case, that means I'll have to take the train tomorrow."

"Perhaps it would be better if I drove you. It can't be that far to go back and forth in one day," Penelope offered.

"Farther than you think," Nick said. He was astounded at her offer.

"No, just to the train station in Grantham Junction will be fine," Amara responded. "In any case, it's time I became a little more independent, don't you think?"

"Independence is always a good idea," Penelope agreed. Then she slowly turned and looked out over the lawn as it fell away to the lake.

Nick knew there was more to that statement, but he needed to concentrate on his daughter now. "If you've already decided, then," he said to her.

Amara nodded once up and down. "I have."

He wished he could have had a chance to be with

her a little longer—to settle things. But this way he'd just have to give her time. "In that case, I'll just say that I'll miss you."

"You know, you can always send me a DVD of the speech. Georgie is filming, right?"

"Georgie is always filming," Nick answered philosophically. He found himself drawn to the lake, as well. The water was like glass. "And now I think I need to talk to Penelope."

"I'll take that as my cue to go to my room and start packing," Amara answered. She waited until Penelope glanced her way. "I'm doing this as much for you as for him, you know."

CHAPTER THIRTY-EIGHT

"Don't you think you should quit while you're marginally ahead?" Penelope asked.

"You're probably right," Nick admitted. "I'd get another glass and join you in…" He reached back to read the label. "I thought it was grappa."

"Mother's milk," Penelope cooed. The alcohol had mellowed her considerably.

"Mother's milk—but with a kick. Unfortunately I still have to film a segment at the student center with alums and their enthusiastic family members. Ah, the joys of institutional food."

"I'm sorry," she said.

"Not nearly as sorry as I am." He pulled at a few blades of grass. "I'm worried."

"Are these worries of a global nature? Professional? Dare I say personal?"

He reached over and laid his fingers atop hers on the grass. "I'm concerned about us."

"From a professional standpoint, I think that concern is not unfounded. As it turned out, I won't be able to film making 'nduja with you after all. I have more pressing matters with the university."

"Does it have to do with what we shot at the Rare Book Library? Georgie told me about your text. I thought we'd gotten all the correct permissions."

"It's related to that, yes. But you can put your mind at ease. You have absolutely no…ah…involvement in the case. Please, let Georgie know, will you, that it's an internal matter."

"But whatever it is, it has an impact on the exhibit, doesn't it?" He cocked his thumb over his shoulder in the general direction of the campus.

She nodded briskly. "That's probably the least of it."

He leaned closer. "Is there anything I can do?" His voice was gentle.

She shook her head, then straightened her shoulders and raised her chin. "It's more what I have to do. It's quite serious, but you'll just have to take my word for it because I'm not supposed to talk about it."

"Of course I'll take your word. You, and probably Georgie, are the only two people in the world that I *do* trust completely."

"What about Amara?"

"I trust her about as much as you can trust any teenager—meaning, wholeheartedly but with reservations."

She studied her glass. The grappa had seemed like such a good idea, but now her stomach was starting to rebel. On the other hand, maybe it wasn't the grappa that was producing her heartburn. Maybe it was her heart.

Penelope coughed. "It's not just the filming that I will have to cancel out on. I also won't be able to see you anymore."

"But why?" Nick seemed genuinely stunned. "You said you loved me."

"Yes, I did," she acknowledged. "But the circumstances are not right. Realistically I can't see any future between us, especially when I'm not sure about my own future."

"No future? Then why did Justin say something about you letting them rent your house in the fall? From that, I was thinking, or maybe hoping…"

"That I planned to move in with you? No, as part of my accepting the curator position, I had negotiated a semester off to work on my next book, which naturally involved travel." She exhaled. "Though, who knows what will become of the book, let alone my position at the library now."

Nick clenched his hands in tight fists. "I'm sorry if there's some problem with your work, and I really want to help. But the only way I know how to do that is by not giving up on us. I'm not willing to accept failure."

"How odd that you would say that. In my father's estimation, I'm a failure."

"Your father should have his head examined."

"Then there's my brother. Justin loves me." She

stopped and squinted. "Yes, I believe he loves me." She looked back at Nick. "But we all know that he thinks I'm weird."

"There's nothing wrong with weird. Like I'm so normal? Besides, who cares what anyone else thinks. This is between you and me. Penelope, level with me. Be honest. That's one of your strengths." He stared her down.

Penelope pursed her lips. Then she polished off the last of her drink. All right, she would be honest, but it didn't hurt to have a little liquid strength. "To be honest, right now my life has suddenly become extremely complicated."

"So the timing sucks. If you wait for the perfect moment, you'll be waiting your whole life."

She smiled to herself. "That's just it. I'm not good at waiting. Unlike my namesake, Odysseus's wife, Penelope, I couldn't possibly spend years weaving and unweaving, waiting for my wandering husband to return."

"I would never ask you to," Nick protested.

"The thing is, it's not about you. It's me, and, yes, I know that's supposed to be the man's line. But in this case it's appropriate."

She took a deep breath and plunged on. "I'm not sure I could trust anyone to be loyal to me. And really more importantly, after what has happened at the library I am not sure *I'm* trustworthy. I can't really go into detail, but suffice it to say the library has in its possession a valuable holding that I should have realized was looted by the Nazis. And I should have recognized that was the case immediately."

Nick was speechless for a moment. "It's the Grantham Galen, isn't it? The manuscript your father donated."

She should have known he would put two and two together immediately. "I really can't comment on it, now that the lawyers are involved."

"Lawyers," he sniggered. "Bottom-feeders. Whatever. I think this is more about your father."

Penelope disagreed. "It's more about me, my role as his daughter. Which is why I also feel responsible for what happened between you and Amara."

"What? You've got to be kidding me. That was strictly my mess-up."

"I'm not so sure. Did you ever think that subconsciously, maybe I wanted to monopolize all your emotional attention? That I was in competition with your daughter for your affections? As an adult, I could have reminded you to follow through with making the phone call. But did I?"

"But it wasn't your responsibility," he replied.

"A child's welfare is everyone's responsibility. And when something goes wrong, I do believe in collective guilt."

"That's bull."

"Tell that to Jacob Himmelfarb's ninety-one-year-old son, who for the first time in more than seventy

years sees the manuscript that had been part of his
father's collection—before he died at Auschwitz."

"It's difficult to say anything in the face of that,"
he said softly.

"I know."

He hesitated and finally looked up. "I guess this
means you won't be coming to the Class Day ceremonies, either?"

"You need to guess?"

CHAPTER THIRTY-NINE

AT THE CLASS DAY CELEBRATIONS on Monday afternoon, Nick slipped on a beer jacket that the president of the graduating year had just given him, making him their honorary member.

Nick adjusted the collar and, looking down at the rows of lions marching across the cotton material, mugged into the microphone. "I can't tell you what a relief it is to have a legitimate excuse to take off my class's toreador jacket, not to mention that ridiculous hat."

The assembled graduating seniors and family members clapped in approval. They filled the folding chairs set up on the green in front of Grantham Hall. The next day, the site would serve as the venue for the Commencement ceremonies.

Up until now, Nick had sat on the dais, smiling and clapping at appropriate times during the humorous speeches by the class officers and the giving of awards to various students for academic and athletic prowess. The award for the highest grade point average in the sciences went to Press Lodge, he noticed. The kid—why did he always think of him that way when he knew he shouldn't—got a loud round of applause. One small group in the family-seating section seemed particularly animated. A silver-haired middle-aged man, dressed in his class's striped Reunions jacket, smiled and clapped with manly vigor while a small girl wriggled around on his lap. A stylish woman with well-toned upper arms brought her hands together with polite vigor, even though her eyes appeared to wander. And a stunner of a redhead stood up. She was hard to miss in an orange minidress. She whistled loudly through her fingers. But he couldn't help noticing that the celebrated Mimi Lodge was AWOL from the family group.

Her loss, Nick couldn't help thinking. And he also couldn't help reflecting, *So this is what I denied my parents when I dropped out of college.*

As Press left the stage, Nick gave him a nod and said, "Good job, Press."

Press seemed startled. "Thanks," he acknowledged. "And give Amara my best."

Don't push your luck, Nick wanted to say but didn't. He was getting soft in his old age.

True to her word, Amara had left for upstate New York. He scanned the crowd repeatedly, but Penelope was also a no-show. Why wasn't he surprised? Still, the disappointment weighed heavily. As did the feeling that there was nothing he could do to help her. Because despite what Penelope had claimed, he was sure he was the cause of the problems.

Maybe not the whole looted-manuscript thing. He'd wheedled out what details he could from Amara, and it seemed to him that once again Penelope was taking responsibility for things beyond her control. The woman who most people thought didn't or couldn't relate to others had a "good daughter, good girl, make the world a better place" complex that was tearing her apart. Making her unhappy. Making him unhappy.

Okay, that last part sounds selfish. Nick looked up and clapped at yet another moment in someone's speech, what exactly he wasn't quite sure, but clearly it was the right thing to do. Besides, he could see the camera focusing on him while Georgie, scooting around the perimeter of the stage and the audience, orchestrated the shoot with a walkie-talkie into Larry's and Clyde's earpieces.

But, dammit, Nick reasoned, a stupid grin plastered on his face, *I have a right to be happy and make the woman I love happy, too.* And that was it, he realized. No matter what, love trumped remorse. It had to. Otherwise he and everybody else might just as well pack it in.

He clapped like a trained monkey as the class president looked toward him with his arm held out. And that's when Nick heard mention of his now notorious massage episode. Showtime.

Nick rose, waving, and approached the podium. "Thank you all for inviting me to be your Class Day speaker. As many of you probably know, I never graduated from Grantham. Unlike you all, I was unable to wrap my head around a certain hurdle known as the Junior Paper."

There were moans and laughter.

"Consequently I am delighted to be experiencing my first Class Day here with you." Nick placed his hands on either side of the podium and paused. He saw Georgie look at him nervously. He also spotted Mimi slipping in through the university gates way in the back. Then he cleared his throat.

"You know, I'm frequently asked to speak at gatherings, so I shouldn't feel nervous today. But I gotta confess. I am. And it's not just because I have to clean up my language in front of a family audience."

More laughter.

"First off, I'm nervous because I'm here at Grantham University. And I've come to realize on my first trip back to my alma mater just what a special place it truly is. There's the obvious—its long, illustrious history, its superb teaching and academic research, its brilliant student body—"

This last mention got a thunderous round of applause and stamping of feet.

Nick waited until it died down. "Not to mention its, shall we say, seminotorious Social Clubs."

If possible, there was even greater applause.

Nick glanced around. "Don't worry, parents. I was merely referring to the all-night study sessions that go on within those walls."

Again more laughter, this time even from the parents.

"But in addition to all those things, I think the thing that makes me so nervous about speaking is what makes this place so important—the people." He pointed all around. "Yes, all of you out there."

He could see they all loved being praised.

"So, with that in mind, I want to talk about certain people who made a difference when I was at Grantham." He went through a litany of amusing anecdotes about his roommates and the antics of his freshman advisees, leaving people shaking their heads and hooting in laughter. "Don't worry. They all lived to become successful adults, but let me tell you, I can still beat them at Beer Pong—as you will see when this episode of my show is televised."

Then he paused. "I suppose at some point, however, you also expect some words of wisdom from me—especially after your parents have spent tens of thousands of dollars on your college-tuition payments."

This time it was the family members who clapped the loudest.

"So let me continue with my theme about the importance of the people you meet here. At the end of the day—long after you can't remember the date of the Norman Conquest—"

"Ten sixty-six," someone shouted out from the audience.

"I guess all the tuition wasn't wasted," Nick acknowledged. "Well, after you can't remember the molecular weight of...I don't know...barium..." He held up his hand. "I know, I know, there're at least several of you who know it. And believe me, I have it on good authority that probably a couple of your parents also know about it in terms of enemas."

There were a few semiembarrassed groans.

"But seriously—" Nick brought them back again "—it's people who make the difference. And I can tell you how I know this for a fact. I came back to Reunions, thinking it'd be easy pickings to make fun of silly traditions and college food. I'd make my usual semiprofound comments about the sociology of universities and why they engender such lifelong loyalties. Well, let me tell you—the joke was on me. I mean, I found silly traditions and bad college food. But I also discovered some truly amazing people. And most of all, due to them, I learned some profound things about myself."

He nodded in thought, because...well...he really was thinking.

"The thing of it is, everyone talks about how resilient people are. And I'm not saying we're not. God knows, look at the wars and the famines and the natural disasters we manage to get through. But at the same time, it's important—very important—to remember that what we hold dear—the love and respect of people we care about—is also very fragile. It's something we can lose in a heartbeat. I know, because I know what it's like to lose that love and respect."

Nick raised his chin and flashed a smile. "So, I suppose this is the moment where I am supposed to leave you with some guidance. And I'll do that, but first, just to prove that a Grantham education was valuable even to me, let me quote what the Red Queen said to Alice in *Alice in Wonderland*. You knew I had to quote something, right?"

"Ri-ight," came the response in unison.

"Anyway, absurdity somehow naturally appeals to me, therefore, let me quote. 'Always speak the truth—think before you speak—and write it down afterwards.' Actually, in this day of YouTube and a 24/7 news cycle, perhaps you can omit the last bit."

There were a few nervous laughs.

Nick paused. He wanted to get this part right, not only for the people here, not only for the show—but mostly for the two people who were not in the audience. "So now, from the profound, let me move to the mundane. Here is my top-ten list of things you should do in life. Granted, the format may be familiar, but I'm betting the actual items are not quite normal…just like me."

He held up his hand to help count off his points. "One. Occasionally pick up your friends' bar tabs. Two—this is multipart. Know how to drive stick shift, swim at least one hundred yards and make an omelet. The last one comes in very handy the morning after, if you get my drift. Three. Work hard. Luck is very handy, and God knows, I've had my fair share. But you can't count on it. Sheer determination and grit go a long way in helping to make things happen. Four. Always strive for the truth and demand truth of others."

He stopped to take a drink of water. "Five." He held up his hand again. "It's okay to act foolishly at times as long as you don't hurt anyone else and assume responsibility afterward. Six. This is kind of a corollary to Five. Try not to hurt anyone you love, and if you do, do everything in your power to make it up. Seven. Be hard on yourself, but not too hard that it prevents you from loving people around you. Eight. Say thank-you and I love you, and never forget how lucky you are to be able to say those precious words. Nine. Write yourself notes so you don't forget to say thank-you and I love you—and anything else you should do."

He let the ripple of laughter work its way through the crowd. "And finally, Ten. Never *ever* give a Class Day speech if you yourself have failed to follow all this so-called good advice, thereby irretrievably losing the ones you love most."

There was an awkward silence.

"Nah, just fooling." He gave a large theatrical wink. "Parents, you can take a huge amount of solace in the fact that your children here will be graduating from an institution that instills a sense of purpose, a sense of excellence and a sense of caring." He held up his arm. "Thank you again for inviting me. And I promise that not only will I be back again for Reunions in the future, I will be back for another Class Day and Commencement. You see, my daughter is an incoming freshman at Grantham University in the fall. And all you parents out there? You may have finished with your tuition payments, but I still have four years to go."

With that, he waved goodbye and stepped down.

PRESS STOOD UP ALONG WITH the rest of his classmates and gave Nicholas Rheinhardt a standing ovation. The guy might be a loser of a father, but he sure could give a speech. And who knew, maybe—if he sincerely believed any of his own words—he might be redeemable.

Though, given his own experiences, Press wasn't entirely convinced.

He felt something bump his shoulder from behind and ignored it, figuring somebody had knocked into him by accident. Then he felt it again. Only, this time harder, frankly, painful.

"Hey, watch it." He turned around, annoyed.

And saw Mimi. She'd kept her word after all. "Is that how you greet your only brother?" he asked, trying to act cool.

"Is that how you greet your only older sister?" she responded.

And then she did something that Press never would have expected. She reached up and gave him a great big hug.

If he didn't know better, Press would think the tears forming in his eyes were due to overwhelming emotion. Still, after they broke the embrace, he needed a second before he could speak. "So you decided to make an appearance after all?"

Mimi nodded. "I told you I'd come."

"To tell you the truth, I didn't think you'd make it. I mean, when I saw the rest of the family sitting together and noticed you weren't there..."

"You're surprised I'm not sitting with the rest of the family?" She raised her eyebrows.

Press shook his head. "I guess not. Are you coming to the Commencement ceremony tomorrow? You know, Noreen is throwing me a graduation party right afterward."

"You bet I'll be at the ceremony. I wouldn't miss seeing you in a cap and gown. After all, as a journalist, I need direct confirmation that you're honestly graduating before going out into the cold, cruel world." Mimi grinned.

Press groaned. "You make it sound so inviting."

"It's not…well, sometimes it is. Anyway, you'll find out." She reached up and touched his shoulder. "I'm proud of you, you know."

Press squinted. He could tell she was finding this conversation difficult. He swallowed. "Thanks, thanks for coming."

She nodded.

He wasn't sure what he was supposed to say. "So you're coming to the party?"

Mimi shook her head. "I have to take off right after the ceremony tomorrow."

"Your interview?"

"Yeah, it looks like it's going to happen."

"You'll be careful. I mean, you're the only big sister I've got—even if you are a royal pain most of the time."

Mimi laughed. "Don't worry. You can't get rid of me that easily."

"Yeah, but I have it on good authority that it's a cold, cruel world out there." Somehow, he didn't feel much like laughing.

IT TOOK A LOT LONGER than Nick would have wished for his day in the spotlight to be over. There was the handshaking and the photo ops and the autographing. But when they were all done, when Clyde and Larry were packing up and Georgie had removed his earpiece, and when the patter of big and small feet had left the grassy area, Nick slumped his shoulders.

The sun had begun to dip beneath the spire of Grantham Hall, and happy hour had commenced for the vast majority of revelers. But he still had a lot of work to do…a lot of fences to mend. He walked over to the producer. "Anything more you want to add?"

Georgie held up his hand. "Only that, once this episode is in the can, you're losing me."

Nick stood there, stunned. "What did I do to deserve this?"

"It's not always about you, Nick. Vivian's gonna need me to help with the media side of her campaign."

Nick bit down hard on his bottom lip. He wanted to feel the pain. He wanted to draw blood. Then he breathed in slowly, knowing what he had to do. "Well, Georgie, you may be going off to become an ace-politico and, from the looks of it, a possible contender to replace Vivian's soon-to-be-ex, but for now you're still on company time."

This time, Nick was the one to hold up his hand. "Tonight, tomorrow, maybe the next day, I need you to get a rough cut put together ASAP of this episode."

"What, no 'please'? Don't you think you're being a little selfish? This from the man who just stood

up and preached the importance of love and self-
less dedication?"

"It may sound selfish, but trust me, I have two
other people in mind."

CHAPTER FORTY

The next Friday

NEAT ROWS OF FOLDING CHAIRS lined the triangle of grass in front of the school chapel. Family and friends filled every seat. Nick stood at the back. In his hand, he held an engraved graduation invitation.

Amara had sent it to him. It arrived after he'd sent by FedEx a DVD of the rough cut of the Reunions episode.

He looked like crap. He'd barely slept and just about forgotten about eating. He couldn't remember when he'd touched a drop of alcohol. Probably that was a good idea.

On the stage in front, three rows of young women sat in long white dresses. Their hair was shiny and healthy, their faces filled with excitement and their ankles neatly crossed. If they weren't so visibly happy, Nick would think it was the sacrifice of the vestal virgins, though undoubtedly there might be some technical disputes regarding the *virgin* part.

No matter. His daughter had invited him to her graduation despite his worst efforts. The rest of

this upstate New York town might be slowly de-
caying into the remnants of its nineteenth-century
manufacturing glory, but here inside the stone-and-
wrought-iron walls and gates, amid an impressive
array of Gothic buildings, forty of the fairest maid-
ens were graduating from the Edwina Worth School
for Girls.

Life was grand.

Nick spotted his ex seated in the audience. She
looked older. Who didn't? She sat next to a boring-
but-solid-looking guy wearing a blue blazer and exhibiting male-pattern baldness. Nick watched him
pass Jeannine a snowy-white handkerchief. She took
it with a grateful smile. He smiled back in acknowledgment.

Still, if his ex had aged, she'd aged well. She
clearly kept herself in shape, had a great haircut
and—Nick had to admit it—appeared to be happy.
He was glad. Jeannine deserved to be happy. The
two of them had made a hash of their marriage, but
they'd produced something wonderful—Amara.

And this was Amara's graduation. Right after
he'd opened the invitation in the morning, Nick had
hopped on an Amtrak train to Albany and rented a
car at the station. Even with GPS, he'd gotten lost
twice. But now he was here.

The headmistress, the one who had been so of-
ficious on the phone, was actually giving a halfway decent speech. *My jokes were better, though,* he

congratulated himself. He was trying to buck himself up even though things had looked pretty bleak these past few days.

And then they called the roll to hand out diplomas. It went alphabetically, and Nick cursed the fact that Amara's name came toward the end. Also, where was Larry when he needed him to take a picture of something that really mattered for a change?

"Amara Kristina Rheinhardt," the headmistress announced. "Degree awarded cum laude."

That's my girl, Nick thought. Amara was admitted to the honor society representing the top ten percent of her class. Why wasn't he surprised? After all, she'd been admitted to Grantham University, which had one of the most competitive acceptance rates in the country. He beamed.

Jeannine turned around, as if sensing his presence. For once, he didn't feel the instant tension that usually characterized their rare face-to-face encounters. Instead she nodded her head, as if to say *We did it.*

Nick pointed toward her. "No, you did it," he mouthed, giving full credit where credit was due. They'd never be a happy ex-couple. They'd spent too many years fighting to bury the hatchet. But at least today they could both act like adults and make it about Amara's achievement and happiness.

And when the student orchestra played the final notes of Vivaldi's *Four Seasons* as the graduates processed down the center aisle, Nick breathed a sigh of relief. But he still held back—held back as he watched Jeannine embrace Amara, then the new husband with a hug showing pride and awkwardness. Nick secretly enjoyed witnessing the awkwardness. He was competitive enough that it mattered.

Only then, when Nick saw Jeannine point him out to their daughter, and he saw Amara's reaction—a cautious smile—did he risk a step forward. *Take whatever you can get,* he lectured himself.

Amara navigated around the clumps of parents and graduates and moved toward him.

He met her halfway. "Congratulations, sweet pea. I'm so proud of you."

Amara hugged her diploma to her stomach. The ribbon circling the empire waist of her dress drifted over the blue leather case. "I see you got my invitation."

He jammed his hands in the pants pockets of his charcoal-gray suit. For her, he'd even worn a tie. "I figured it meant that you watched the rough cut I sent you."

Amara nodded. "You were really hard on yourself in it, Dad."

"As well I should have been. I nearly lost what was most important to me. It just took me longer than most to figure it out."

"But, you did it in the end," she reminded.

Her words were precious. Still, she didn't fling

her arms around him in abject joy, Nick noticed. *Take what you can get,* he repeated to himself.

Nick raised his head in the direction of his ex. She was chatting with some other parents. "Your mom seems to know a lot of people," he commented, searching for something neutral to say.

"She does work at the school," Amara pointed out.

Nick winced. "You're right." That was a stupid comment. "Is that your mom's new husband?" He nodded in their general direction. The guy stood dutifully by Jeannine's side, occasionally shaking hands and what looked to be accepting congratulations. "He's seems nice enough." It was the truth. *Think before you speak. Always speak the truth.*

Amara glanced over at her stepfather, then back at Nick. "Yeah, Glenn's a nice guy."

Glenn was also sunburned from the honeymoon, Nick noticed. His nose was peeling badly. "He looks like someone who'd never forget to call his daughter's school."

"Yeah, that's true. But he can't make an omelet."

Nick stared down at his daughter. He pressed his lips together and smiled. "You listened to the part with my speech, then?"

She nodded.

"It's just the first cut, you know. It will be better when it's all finished."

"Relax, Dad. Of course I watched it and listened

to every word—a bunch of times over. And don't worry. Glenn may be a great guy, but you'll always be my dad." She looked down at the diploma in her hand. "It meant a lot what you said, you know." Then she raised her eyes. "Thank you and I love you."

Nick felt a weight lift off his shoulders.

"I also sent an invitation to Penelope," Amara said.

Nick immediately searched the crowd for the telltale mass of red curls.

"She's not here, Dad," Amara said, quickly answering his question. "She sent her apologies, saying that the university lawyers and all the people involved had an important meeting today." Amara frowned. "I hope she's okay. Penelope is too nice to be unhappy."

Nick nodded a troubled smile. "Penelope is too nice for a lot of things, probably me included."

"She sent me a present, you know," Amara added. "A first edition of *Runaway Bunny,* signed by the author Margaret Wise Brown. It's this classic children's book."

"I'll have to read it one day."

"You should."

Nick hesitated. Then he reached into the inside pocket of his suit jacket. "Speaking of Penelope doing things—she sent me this envelope asking me to give it to you."

Amara held out her hand. "What is it?"

"I don't know. I didn't open it. It was addressed to you." He watched Amara tuck her diploma under her arm and rip open the heavy-paper envelope. A key dropped out.

Nick bent and picked it up. Amara blindly took it as she silently read the contents handwritten on several cream-colored pieces of paper. When she finished, she looked down and stared at the key in her hand.

"I don't believe it. It's the key—" then she pointed to the letter "—with directions to Penelope's house in Calabria. She says that it's a graduation gift—the use of her house in Capo Vaticano for two weeks— just you and me. She goes on... Hold it, I need to find the place."

She flipped through the pages and dropped her diploma.

Nick picked it up. That seemed to be his job at the moment. But then he supposed a parent frequently had to pick up after his child—at the right times, at least.

"She goes on to say that we have to visit the Riace bronzes in Reggio di Calabria and the Byzantine church in Stilo." Amara pronounced the words slowly. "I'm sorry. I know my accent's terrible."

"It's fine." For the first time in days, Nick's insides were starting to relax.

Amara's head moved back and forth as she read

on. "'Then you must dine on the sweet red onions of Tropea and of course have the local 'nduja on crusty bread. When you've accomplished all that, then you must celebrate with a dip in the pool at sunset and watch the sea turn blood-orange-red as it dips behind the island of Stromboli.'"

Amara raised her eyes. "She writes just like she speaks, doesn't she?"

He nodded, unable to form words. Was it premature to start to feel happy again? Maybe he should aim for partially happy?

Amara lowered the letter and studied him through narrow eyes. "You know, you're not completely redeemed just because Penelope gave us this present." She glanced down at the key in one hand and the letter in the other. When she looked up, a smile spread across her face. "But on the other hand, I'd be a fool to turn down a vacation like this."

"It would seem so," he mustered.

"So, can we go? I realize there's airfare involved."

"Forget the airfare." Then he stopped and did the right thing, the mature thing. "You'll have to ask permission from your mother first."

"Oh, right." Clearly she had forgotten that. "Is it okay if I ask her now?"

"Go, go." He pushed her encouragingly and watched her scamper over, display the letter and key to her mother and have what seemed to be an endless chat.

Finally—*finally*—Amara came skipping back, a huge smile on her face. Still, she got waylaid hugging several of her friends.

Nick itched to have his daughter put her arms around him, too. "So?" he ventured when she made her way back.

"She said I can go if I go now—before my lifeguard job starts at the lake and the tutoring and the language class at the community college. The whole commitment thing. You know, I'm not to back out of responsibility." Amara rolled her eyes.

Nick wanted to laugh. But he attempted to keep a straight face for Jeannine's benefit. "No, I think your mother's absolutely right. It's important to follow through on your promises."

"But are you free? I mean, to just take off like that?"

Nick could easily have said that he really needed to get this episode in the can, or that he needed to sit down with his story team to finalize the next episode after that and go over the shooting schedule— not to mention start scouting next season's shows.

But he didn't. "I'm all yours," he said simply.

"I don't believe it." She jammed the letter against her breast.

All that grief just last week, and now it's forgotten, Nick thought.

"Am I the luckiest person or what?" she asked, squeezing her eyes shut.

"No, I am," Nick corrected.

Then Amara opened her eyes and flung herself into her father's arms. The letter, the key and her diploma embedded their outlines into his chest. It felt so good. Nick didn't care if he was tattooed for life.

CHAPTER FORTY-ONE

THE CICADAS WERE BUZZING in the tall grass. Pale ocher-colored butterflies flitted around the mounds of rosemary that billowed over the pebbly way. She had parked the car under the arbor of wisteria halfway down the driveway and taken the rest of the journey on foot. Now, as she rounded the crest in the hill, she stopped, breathing in the smell of late spring in southern Italy.

The heat at the end of the day seeped into her bones. She welcomed it, especially after the night flight to Rome, followed by the daylong drive southward. In the near distance, she could hear the splashing of water from the pool and the sound of high-pitched chatter. Amara. Then a few lower-toned mumbles. Nick. Then more splashing, more laughter.

She gazed past the citron trees and the oleanders to the sea beyond. The sun, partway into its descent, rimmed the prominent peak of Stromboli across the stretch of salty water. She had read online that the volcano was manifesting minor activity. But on this side of the water, peace appeared to reign.

She removed her flats and stepped carefully up the stone steps to the pool. Twin blue-glazed pots of happy succulents stood sentry on either side.

And then she saw them. Amara was doing the breaststroke, her head above water. She swam toward the deep end of the pool where her father rested with his elbows propped up against the white mosaic tiles of the gunnels.

She stepped up on the surrounding patio and stopped. That's when Nick saw her. Amara was talking away. But she stopped midstroke when she noticed her father's focus turn elsewhere. She twirled around, water splashing.

"Penelope," Amara shouted. "You came."

AMARA IMMEDIATELY SWAM over to the side of the pool closest to Penelope. "We've done everything you told us to do in your letter."

"You did?" she asked.

"We drove on these tiny winding roads over the mountains to the little church, La Cattolica, at the town at Stilo. It took us forever to go over the mountains with all those tiny villages half falling down and with people who looked like they had never seen strangers before."

"They probably hadn't," Nick said quietly, swimming up behind her.

"But we made it," Amara said triumphantly, bobbing up and down in the water. "And today we went to Reggio—I'm still not sure how we survived the crazy streets and drivers. I mean, at one point we even drove right through a gas station like it was a perfectly normal thing to do."

"I was just following the car in front of us," Nick spoke softly again.

Amara continued speaking at a rapid pace. "Anyway, we got there after I asked directions from this one old man—in Italian, no less."

"He wasn't that old," Nick qualified.

Penelope smiled. "I'm so glad you're able to use your Italian."

"You bet. So we saw the Riace bronzes. Oh, my God. I couldn't believe how amazing they were," she gushed, barely stopping for air. "And now after going to the *trattoria* up the road and having pasta with sweet onions, we're having a sunset swim in the pool—just like you said to do in your letter." As if to prove her point, Amara did a lazy backstroke toward the deep end.

Penelope lifted her chin and stared at Nick. "What? No, 'nduja?"

"I was waiting—hoping, really—for you." Who was he kidding? He hadn't thought he'd had a chance in hell of seeing her here or elsewhere.

"That sounds like a line," Penelope answered, apparently unconvinced.

He pulled himself up out of the water. "You

always did know me too well." He paused. "So you got the DVD? Of Reunions weekend?" *Was it too much to hope for total happiness?* "What did you think?"

Penelope seemed to consider her reply. "In my opinion, you did enough self-flagellation that they'll no longer keep referring to you as the person who suffered from that gruesome massage."

Nick cocked his head. "That's a joke?"

"It's a joke. And it's not a joke."

A sign of hope, he told himself. But he wouldn't rush it. He wouldn't get down on one knee and dramatically profess his undying love for her, telling her that unless she reciprocated he was prepared to throw himself off the cliff.

No, he wouldn't do all that—even though he meant it… Well, maybe not the cliff part. Instead, he'd do the right thing, not the selfish thing like he once would have done. Penelope had taught him the importance of thinking of others—that that was real love. And she deserved as much.

"I hope the crisis is over back in Grantham, with work and your father," he inquired softly. His concern was genuine.

"Thank you for asking. Yes, the situation at work seems to have been resolved—the matter of the Grantham Galen manuscript and my father and me. It's not totally final—the lawyers still need to dot all the i's and cross all the t's, but at least we have the bones of an amicable agreement."

"So he's not going to jail, your father, that is?" Nick cut to the chase.

"We've all decided to give him the benefit of the doubt, especially after he acted so contritely when he met Daniel Himmelfarb. Luckily Mr. Himmelfarb was not interested in pressing criminal charges, merely establishing that the manuscript was once his father's. The university agreed, and in something of a publicity coup, the heirs have asked for the manuscript to be part of an exhibit on recovered treasures—a way of documenting the ongoing process of restoring artwork, rare books and other antiquities to their rightful owners. As a companion to that exhibit, I was asked to write a book, showcasing the Grantham Galen, now to be called the Himmelfarb Galen."

"Quite a mouthful," Nick quipped.

"Indeed." Her grim demeanor faltered slightly. Then she went on. "Naturally I plan to dedicate the study to Jacob Himmelfarb and his family, but I'm also considering dedicating it to my father. We're still not speaking, but I think it will serve as something of a peacemaker. His role in recovering the manuscript will never be clear, but he did, after all, guarantee that it wasn't lost forever and indirectly returned it to the rightful owners."

"And you? What about you?" Nick asked.

"If you mean about my curatorial position? I offered my resignation in light of my failing to recognize the correct provenance of the work, but the administration refused to accept it. Apparently, since I was the one who helped Mr. Himmelfarb reclaim what was rightfully his, I am somehow considered something of a hero. I argued that I should have been more diligent, but the editor in chief of the University Press said that I would have come to the proper conclusion when I began work on the book. It was overwhelming, really—the faith they all seemed to have in me, even Mr. Himmelfarb, who really is very dear."

"As well they should," Nick agreed.

Penelope blinked rapidly. "The president even suggested that I take a vacation to recuperate from all the stress. Remarkable."

Nick walked slowly across the stone patio, his footprints leaving tracks along the way. He wanted to swoop her up in his arms, but he told himself to go slowly, deliberately, just like Penelope would when she was making a decision. "So, all's well that ends well?" he asked.

Penelope frowned. "You don't have to recite Shakespeare to try to impress me, you know."

"How about the bard of Hoboken, New Jersey, then? Frank Sinatra." Nick took two steps closer, his suit dripping on the concrete. "'I have got a crush, my baby, on you.'"

"I never questioned the scope of your erudition. You can just use your own words," Penelope suggested.

"I'm more an action kind of guy."

"Which means?"

Oh, screw slowness and deliberation. He brought his head to hers and kissed her deeply, letting his lips and tongue and soul speak all the words for him.

In the background, he was vaguely aware of hearing whoops and hollers of joy from Amara. Then silence. He stopped in midkiss. "Are you thinking what I'm thinking?" he mumbled a millimeter from Penelope's lips.

"If you mean that despite the improbabilities, we are a superbly matched couple and hopelessly in love? I would think that statement would be obvious." She narrowed her eyes meaningfully. "But at the same time, I am compelled to voice my disagreement with the wisdom you recently proffered in a certain commencement speech. Specifically, I think there are moments when one *shouldn't* think. Not only shouldn't one think, one shouldn't even think before speaking—"

"You really did listen to the DVD," he said, overjoyed.

"Every word."

"It was for you, you know."

"I know. Now stop thinking, stop speaking and get back to kissing me."

And that's when Amara drenched them with a bucket of water.

* * * * *